F.

LARGE PRINT

Central Support Unit
Catherine Street Dumfries   DG1 1JB
tel: 01387 253820   fax: 01387 260294
e-mail: libs&i@dumgal.gov.uk

Dumfries and Galloway
LIBRARIES
Information and Archives

CUSTOMER
SERVICE
EXCELLENCE

The Government Standard

24 HOUR LOAN RENEWAL ON OUR WEBSITE - WWW.DUMGAL.GOV.UK/LIA

THE UNDERSIDE OF JOY

Up until now, Ella has counted herself as one of the luckiest women alive: she has a wonderful husband, two animated kids and an extended family who regard her as one of their own. Then the unthinkable happens and her soul mate, Joe, is killed in a tragic accident. She now clings to her children more than ever. But when Joe's ex-wife Paige, 'natural' mother to Annie and Zach, arrives at the funeral, Ella fears the worst. Pushed to the limits of love, Ella must decide who is, after all, the best mother for *her* children.

SERÉ PRINCE HALVERSON

◆

THE UNDERSIDE OF JOY

Complete and Unabridged

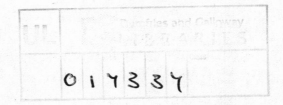

CHARNWOOD
Leicester

First published in Great Britain in 2012 by
Harper
An imprint of
HarperCollins*Publishers*
London

First Charnwood Edition
published 2013
by arrangement with
HarperCollins*Publishers*
London

British Library CIP Data

Halverson, Seré Prince.
  The underside of joy.
  1. Mother and child- -Fiction.
  2. Large type books.
  I. Title
  813.6–dc23

  ISBN 978–1–4448–1446–0

Published by
F. A. Thorpe (Publishing)
Anstey, Leicestershire

Set by Words & Graphics Ltd.
Anstey, Leicestershire
Printed and bound in Great Britain by
T. J. International Ltd., Padstow, Cornwall

This book is printed on acid-free paper

For Stan

1

I recently read a study that claimed happy people aren't made. They're born. Happiness, the report pointed out, is all about genetics — a cheerful gene passed merrily, merrily down from one smiling generation to the next. I know enough about life to understand the old adage that one person can't make you happy, or that money can't buy happiness. But I'm not buying this theory that your bliss can be only as deep as your gene pool.

For three years, I did backflips in the deep end of happiness.

The joy was palpable and often loud. Other times it softened — Zach's milky breath on my neck, or Annie's hair entwined in my fingers as I braided it, or Joe humming some old Crowded House song in the shower while I brushed my teeth. The steam on the mirror blurred my vision, misted my reflection, like a soft-focus photograph smoothing out my wrinkles, but even those didn't bother me. You can't have crow's-feet if you don't smile, and I smiled a lot.

I also know now, years later, something else: The most genuine happiness cannot be so pure, so deep, or so blind.

★ ★ ★

On that first dawn of the summer of '99, Joe pulled the comforter down and kissed my forehead. I opened one eye. He wore his grey sweatshirt, his camera bag slung over his shoulder, his toothpaste and coffee breath whispering something about heading out to Bodega before he opened the store. He traced the freckles on my arm where he always said they spelled his name. He'd say I had so many freckles that he could see the letters not just for Joe, but for Joseph Anthony Capozzi, Jr — all on my arm. That morning he added, 'Wow, *junior*'s even spelled *out*.' He tucked the blanket back over me. 'You're amazing.'

'You're a smart-ass,' I said, already falling back to sleep. But I was smiling. We'd had a good night. He whispered that he'd left me a note, and I heard him walk out the door, down the porch steps, the truck door yawning open, the engine crowing louder and louder, then fading, until he was gone.

Later that morning, the kids climbed into bed with me, giggling. Zach lifted the sun-dappled sheet and held it over his head for a sail. Annie, as always, elected herself captain. Even before breakfast, we set out across an uncharted expanse, a smooth surface hiding the tangled, slippery underneath of things, destination unknown.

We clung to each other on the old rumpled Sealy Posturepedic, but we hadn't yet heard the news that would change everything. We were playing Ship.

By their pronouncements, we faced a hairy morning at sea, and I needed coffee. Badly. I sat up and peeked over the sail at them, both their spun-gold heads still matted from sleep. 'I'm

2

rowing out to Kitchen Island for supplies.'

'Not when such danger lurks,' Annie said. *Lurks?* I thought. When I was six, had I even heard of that word? She bolted up, hands on hips while she balanced on the shifting mattress. 'We might lose you.'

I stood, glad that I'd thought to slip my underwear and Joe's T-shirt back on before I'd fallen asleep the night before. 'But how, dear one, will we fight off the pirates without cookies?'

They looked at each other. Their eyes asked without words: Before *breakfast*? Has she lost her *mind*?

Cookies before breakfast . . . Oh, why the hell not? I felt a bit celebratory. It was the first fogless morning in weeks. The whole house glowed with the return of the prodigal sun, and the worry that had been pressing itself down on me had lifted. I picked up my water glass and the note Joe had left underneath it, the words blurred slightly by the water ring: *Ella Bella, Gone to capture it all out at the coast before I open. Loved last night. Kisses to A&Z. Come by later if . . .* but his last words were puddled ink streaks.

I'd loved the previous night too. After we'd tucked the kids in, we talked in the kitchen until dark, leaning back against the counters, him with his hands deep in his pockets, the way he always stood. We stuck to safe topics: Annie and Zach, a picnic we'd planned for Sunday, crazy town gossip he'd heard at the store — anything but the store itself. He threw his head back, laughing at something I said. What was it? I couldn't remember.

We had fought the day before. After fifty-nine years in business, Capozzi's Market was struggling. I wanted Joe to tell his dad. Joe wanted to keep pretending business was fine. Joe could barely tell *himself* the truth, let alone his father. Then he'd have a moment of clarity, tell me something about an overdue bill or how slow the inventory was moving, and I would freak out, which would immediately shut him back down. Call it a bad pattern we'd been following the past several months. Joe pushed off from the counter, came to me, held my shoulders, said, 'We need to find a way to talk about the hard stuff.' I nodded. We agreed that, until recently, there hadn't been that much hard stuff to talk about.

I counted us lucky. 'Annie, Zach. Us . . . ' Instead of tackling difficult topics right then, I'd kissed him and led him to our bedroom.

★   ★   ★

I feigned rowing down the narrow hall, stepping over Zach's brontosaurus and a half-built Lego castle, until I was out of view, then stood in the kitchen braiding my hair in an effort to restrain it into single-file order down the back of my neck. Our house was a bit like my red hair — a mass of colour and disarray. We'd torn out the wall between the kitchen and living room, so, from where I stood, I could see the shelves crammed to the ceiling with books and plants and various art projects — a Popsicle-stick boat painted yellow and purple, a lopsided clay vase with *Happy Mother's Day* spelled out in macaroni

4

letters, the *M* long gone but leaving an indent in its place. Large patchworks of Joe's black-and-white photographs hung in the few spaces that didn't have built-ins or windows. One giant French window opened out to the front porch and our property beyond. The old glass made a feeble insulator, but we couldn't bring ourselves to part with it. We loved its wavy effect on the view, as if we looked through water at the hydrangeas that lapped at the porch, the lavender field waiting to be harvested, the chicken coop and brambles of blackberries, the old tilted barn, built long before Grandpa Sergio bought the land in the thirties, and finally, growing across the meadow from the redwoods and oaks, the vegetable garden, our pride and glory. We had about an acre — mostly in the sun, all above the flood line, with a glimpse of the river if you stood in just the right spot.

Joe and I enjoyed tending the land, and it showed. But none of us, including the kids, were gifted at orderliness when it came to inside our home. I didn't worry about it. My previous house — and life — had been extremely tidy, yet severe and empty, so I shrugged off the mess as a necessary side effect of a full life.

I took out the milk, then stuck Joe's note on the fridge with a magnet. I'm not sure why I didn't throw it out; it was probably the sweetness of the previous night's reconciliation that I wanted to hang on to, the *Ella Bella* . . .

My name is Ella Beene, and as one might imagine, I've had my share of nicknames. Of all of them, Joe's was one I downright cherished.

5

I'm not a physical beauty — not ugly, but nothing near what I'd look like if I'd had a say in the matter. Yes, the red hair intrigues. But after that, things are pretty basic. I'm fair and freckled, too tall and skinny for some, with decent features — brown eyes, nice enough lips — that look better when I remember to wear makeup. But here's the thing: I knew Joe liked the whole package. The inside, the outside, the in-between places, the whole five foot ten of me. And since all my nicknames fit me at their appointed times, I let myself bask in that one: Bella. So there I was. Thirty-five years old, beautiful in Italian, on a Saturday morning, making strong coffee, preparing a breakfast appetizer of cookies and milk for our children.

'Cookies. Me want cookies.' The sailors had jumped ship and were trying to make their eyes bulge, taking the glasses of milk from the kitchen counter and a couple of oatmeal squares. Our dog, Callie, a yellow Lab and husky mix who knew how to work her most forlorn expression, sat thumping her tail until I gave her a biscuit and let her out. I sipped my coffee and watched Annie and Zach shove cookies in their mouths, grunting, letting crumbs fly. This was the one thing *Sesame Street* taught them that I could have done without.

The sun beckoned us outside, so I asked them to hurry and get dressed, then went to pull on a pair of shorts and finally stick a load of darks into the washer. As I added the last pair of jeans, Zach ran in buck naked and held up his footed pyjamas. 'I do it myself,' he said. I was impressed he hadn't left them in the usual heap on the floor, and I picked him up so he could drop in his contribution. His butt was cool against my arm. We watched until the agitator sucked the swirl of fire trucks and blue fleece below into the sudsy water. I set him down and he careened out, his feet slapping down the wood hall. Except for shoe-lace tying, which Zach was still a few years from, both kids had become alarmingly self-sufficient. Annie was more than ready for first grade, and now Zach for preschool, even if I wasn't quite ready for them to go.

This would be a milestone year: Joe would save the sinking grocery store that had been in his family for three generations. I would go back to work, starting a new job in the fall as a guide for Fish and Wildlife. And Annie and Zach would zoom out the door each morning on their ever-growing limbs, each taking giant leaps along that ever-shortening path of their childhood.

★ ★ ★

When I first met them, Annie was three and Zach was six months. I had been on my way from San Diego to a new life, though I wasn't sure where or what it would be. I'd stopped in the small, funky town of Elbow along the Redwoods River in Northern California. The town was named for its location on the forty-five-degree bend in the river, but locals joked that it was named for elbow macaroni because so many Italians lived there. I planned to get a sandwich and an iced tea, then maybe

7

stretch my legs and walk down the path I'd read about to the sandy beach along the river, but a dark-haired man was locking up the market. A little girl squirmed out of his grasp while he tried to get the key in the lock and balance a baby in his other arm. She pulled loose and raced out towards me, into my legs. Her blonde head grazed my knees, and she laughed and reached her arms to me. 'Up.'

'Annie!' the man called. He was lean, a bit dishevelled and anxious, but significantly easy on the eyes.

I asked him, 'Is it okay?'

He grinned relief. 'If you don't mind?' *Mind?* I scooped her into my arms and she started playing with my braid. He said, 'The kid doesn't have a shy bone in her body.' I could feel her chubby legs secured around my hips, could smell Johnson's baby shampoo, cut grass, wood smoke, a hint of mud. A whisper of grape juice-stained breath brushed my cheek. She'd held my braid tight in her fist but she hadn't pulled.

★　★　★

Callie barked and, from the kitchen, I saw Frank Civiletti's police cruiser. That was odd. Frank knew Joe wouldn't be home. They'd been best friends since grade school, and they always talked over morning coffee at the store. I hadn't heard Frank coming, but there he was, slowly heading up the drive, his tires popping gravel. Also odd. Frank never drove slowly. And Frank always turned his siren on when he made our turn from the main road. His ritual for the kids. I looked at the microwave clock: 8:53. Already? I picked up the phone, then set it down. Joe hadn't called when he got to the store. Joe *always* called. 'Here.' I grabbed the egg baskets and handed them to the kids. 'Check on the Ladies and bring us back some breakfast.' I opened the kitchen door and watched them run down to the coop, waving and calling out, 'Uncle Frank! Turn on your siren.'

But he didn't; he parked the car. I stood in the kitchen. I stared at the compost bucket on the counter. Coffee grounds Joe had used that morning, the banana peel from his breakfast. The far edges of my happiness began to brown, then curl.

I heard Frank's door open and shut, his footsteps on the gravel, on the porch. His tap on the front door's window. Annie and Zach were busy collecting eggs at the coop. Zach let out a string of laughter, and I wanted to stop right there and wrap it around our life so we could keep it intact and whole. I forced myself out of the kitchen, down the hall, stepping over the toys still on the floor, seeing Frank through the paned watery glass stare down at a button on his uniform. *Look up and give me your Jim Carrey grin. Just walk in, like you usually do, you bastard. Raid the fridge before you say hello.* Now we stood with the door between us. He looked up with red-rimmed eyes. I turned, headed back down the hallway, heard him open the door.

9

'Ella,' he said, behind me. 'Let's sit down.'

'No.' His footsteps followed me. I waved him away without turning to see him. 'No.'

'Ella. It was a sleeper wave, out at Bodega Head,' he said to my back. 'It rose out of nowhere.'

He told me Joe was shooting the cliff out on First Rock. Witnesses said they shouted a warning, but he couldn't hear them over the wind, the ocean. It knocked him over and took him clean. He was gone before anyone could move.

'Where is he?' I turned when Frank didn't answer. I grabbed his collar. 'Where?'

He glanced down again, then forced his eyes back on me. 'We don't know. He hasn't shown up yet.'

I felt a small hope look up, start to rise. 'He's still alive. He is! I need to get out there. We need to go. I'll call Marcella. Where's the phone? Where are my shoes?'

'Lizzie's already on her way over to pick up the kids.'

I ran towards our bedroom, stepped on the brontosaurus, fell hard on my knee, pushed myself back up before Frank could help me.

'Listen, El. I would not be saying any of this to you if I thought there was a chance he was alive. Someone even said they saw a spray of blood. We think he hit his head. He never came up for air.' Frank said something about this happening every year, as if I were some out-of-towner. As if Joe were.

'*This* doesn't happen to Joe.'

Joe could swim for miles. He had two kids that needed him. He had me. I dug in the closet for my hiking boots. Joe was alive and I had to find him. 'A little blood? He probably scraped his arm.' I found the boots, pulled the comforter off the bed. He would be freezing. I grabbed the binoculars from the hall tree. I opened the screen door and stepped out on the porch, tripping on the dragging blanket. I called back, 'Am I driving myself? Or are you coming?'

Frank's wife, Lizzie, loaded Zach into their Radio Flyer wagon with their daughter, Molly, while Annie stuck her arm through the handle and shouted through her cupped hands, 'We're taking the rowboat to shore. Watch for pirates.'

I waved and tried to sound cheerful. 'Got it. Thanks, Lizzie.' She nodded, solemn. Lizzie Civiletti was not my friend; she'd told me that, soon after I came to town. And yet neither was she unkind. She would protect the kids from any telltale signs of panic. As much as I wanted to go to them, to gather them up to me, I smiled, I waved again, I blew kisses.

2

Frank drove the winding road with his lights spinning circles. I closed my eyes, didn't look at the rolling hills I knew would be shimmering, dotted with what Joe called the 'Extremely Happy California Cows.' *He's fine. He's fine! He's disoriented. He hit his head. He's not sure where he is. A concussion, maybe. He's wandering the beach at Salmon Creek. That's it! The wave pulled him out and dashed him down the coast a ways, but there he is. He's talking to some high school boys. They have surfboards. Dude. Did you ride that gnarly wave? They've built a fire even though the signs prohibit it. They offer him beer and hot dogs. They forgot the buns, but here's mustard. He's famished. He has a flash of memory. It all comes back to him.*

Us. Making up. Just the night before. Standing in the kitchen, easing our way back together, then falling into bed, relieved. We were lousy fighters, but we could win medals for making up. He had kissed my stomach in a southbound line until I moaned, kissed my thighs until I whimpered, until we both gave in. Later, as I drifted off, he propped himself up on his elbow and looked down at me. 'I have something I need to tell you.'

I tried to fight the pull of sleep. 'You want to *talk? Now?*' It was a noble effort to be more open, but, Jesus, right after sex? Wasn't that

12

womankind's most annoying tactic? So I was a man about it and said, 'You can't go and get me this blissed out and then tell me we have to talk.' I figured it was more bad news about the store.

'Fair enough,' he said. 'Tomorrow, then. We'll make it a date. I'll see if Mom will take the kids.'

'Ooooh. A date.' Maybe it wasn't about the store. Hell, I thought. Maybe it's *good* news.

He smiled and touched my nose. I hadn't said, *No, we have to talk now*. I hadn't fretted. I had immediately fallen asleep.

So, no. Joe could not be dead. He was eating hot dogs and drinking beer and talking surfing. He still needed to talk to me about something. I opened my eyes.

Frank sped through Bodega Bay — with its seafood restaurants and souvenir shops, the pink-and-white-striped saltwater taffy store the kids could never get past without insisting we stop — along the curved bayside road and its hand-painted sandwich signs advertising the latest catch, the air a mingle of smoked salmon and sea and wildflowers, up the curved ridge to Bodega Head, Joe's favourite place on the planet.

There was the trailhead to the hike we'd taken so many times, along the cliff. On one side the sea down below, on the other a prairie of shore wildflowers — with the yarrow, or *Achillea borealis*, the sand verbena, or *Abronia umbellate* — down to the grassy dunes. Joe was always impressed with my ability to not only identify the birds and wildflowers, but rattle off their Latin names too, a gift I'd inherited from my father.

The parking lot was full, including several sheriff's cars, a fire truck, paramedics, and there at the end by the trail, Joe's old truck. He called it the Green Hornet. I grabbed the binoculars, got out of Frank's cruiser, and slammed the door. A helicopter headed north, following the shoreline, its blades thumping, a thunderous, too-rapid heartbeat fading away.

I had no jacket, and the wind whipped against my bare arms, burned my eyes. Frank draped the comforter around me. I said, 'Please don't make me talk to anyone.'

'You got it.'

'I need to go alone.' He pulled me into his side, then released me. I walked to Joe's truck. Unlocked, of course. His blue down jacket, stained and worn in, just the way he liked it. I slipped it on. Warm from the sun. I left the blanket in the car so it would be warm for him too. His thermos lay on the floor. I shook it: empty. I lifted the rubber mat and saw his keys, as I knew I would, and stuck them in my pocket.

Through the binoculars the water flashed a multitude of lights, as if taking pictures of its own crime scene.

In March and April, we'd packed a picnic and brought the kids out to watch for whales. We'd searched the horizon with the same binoculars, marvelled at the grey whales' graceful sky hopping and breaching. We told the kids the story of Jonah and the whale, how one minute Jonah was tossed overboard into the sea, and the next minute swallowed by the whale, along for the ride. Annie rolled her eyes and said 'Yeah.

14

Riiiiight.' I'd laughed, confessed to them that even when I was a little kid in Sunday school, I'd found the story hard to swallow.

But now I was willing to believe anything, to pray anything, to promise anything. 'Please, please, please, *please* . . . '

I headed down the lower trail, seeing Joe taking each step, strong, alive. An easy climb up First Rock, the white water swirling far below, unthreatening. *But you broke your own rule, Joe, didn't you? The one you always told me and Annie and Zach: Never turn your back on the ocean.* The Coast Guard boat moved steadily, not stopping. I glanced over my shoulder at the cliff. It looked like the clenched fist of God, the clinging reddish sea figs its scraped and bleeding knuckles. *Please, please. Tell me where he is.*

I climbed down the rock. The sun's reflection off the water made me wince. Farther down, I saw it wasn't the water, but metal wedged deep between two other rocks. I stepped over to investigate. Was it . . . ? I scrambled down closer. There, waiting for me to notice it, lay Joe's tripod. His camera was gone.

Wait. That's it. That's what he's doing. He's hunting for his camera. He's sick about it. He's in the dunes somewhere, lost. All those deer trails, confusing, every dune starts to look the same and it's hard to tell what you've covered and the wind is whipping and you're tired and you have to lie down. So cold. A doe watches tentatively but she senses your desperation and she approaches, lies down to warm you and she licks the salt off your nose.

15

You are fine! You're just trying to find your way back. 'Don't be angry,' you'll say, wiping my tears with your thumbs, holding my face to yours, your fingers locked in my hair. 'I'm so sorry,' you'll say. I'll shake my head to tell you all is forgiven, thank you for fighting that wave, thank you for coming back to us. I'll bury my nose in your neck, the salt will rub off on my cheek. You'll smell like dried blood and fish and kelp and deer and wood smoke and life.

I wandered the dunes past dark, long after they called off the search for the day. The half-moon disclosed nothing. Frank said even less. Usually he never shut up.

Joe's Green Hornet sat empty, the only vehicle in the parking lot other than Frank's cruiser. I wanted to leave the truck for Joe, so I unlocked it, replaced the keys under the mat. I slipped off his jacket and left that for him too, along with the blanket.

I climbed in with Frank, quiet, as the dispatcher gave an address for a domestic dispute. I wanted to be with the kids but I didn't want my face to let on, to drive a spike through their contented unknowing.

Frank offered to keep Joe's parents and extended family away at least until morning. I nodded. I couldn't hear his parents or brother or anyone else cry, couldn't hear anything that would acknowledge defeat. We needed to focus on finding him.

Once home, I called the kids. 'Are you having fun?' I asked Annie.

'Oh yes,' she said. 'Lizzie let us take off all the

cushions on all the furniture and build a house. *And* she said we can even sleep in it tonight.'

'Too cool. So you want to spend the night?'

'I think we better. Molly will only sleep out here if I'm with her. You know Molly.'

'Yeah, then you better.'

'Night, Mommy. Can I talk to Daddy?'

I leaned over, pulled the lace on my boot, swallowed, forced my voice to sound light. 'He's not here yet, Banannie.'

'Okay, well then, give him this.' I knew she was hugging the phone. 'And this one's for you . . . Bye.'

Zach got on the line just long enough to say, 'I muchly love you.' I hung up, kept sitting on the couch. Callie lay down at my feet and let out a long sigh. The hall light picked up objects in the dark room. I'd set up Joe's tripod in the corner to welcome him. Its three legs, its absent camera now seemed a terrible omen. I stared at the Capozzi family clock ticking on the end table. Yes. No. Yes. No. I opened the glass. The swinging pendulum: this way. That way. I stuck my finger in to stop it. Silence. My fingertip steered the hour hand backward, back to that morning, when this time I felt Joe stretching awake, kissed the soft hair on his chest, grabbed his warm shoulder, said, 'Stay. Don't go. Stay here with us.'

★   ★   ★

The next day a Swiss tourist found Joe's body, bloated and wrapped in kelp, as if the sea had

17

mummified him in some feeble attempt at apology. This time I opened the door for Frank and hugged him before he could speak. When he leaned back, he just shook his head. I opened my mouth to say No but the word sank, soundless.

★　★　★

I insisted on seeing him. Alone. Frank drove me to McCready's and stood beside me while a grey-haired woman with orange-tinted skin explained that Joe wasn't really ready to be viewed.

'Ready?' A strange, high-pitched laugh eked past the lump in my throat.

Frank tilted his head at me. 'Ella . . . '

'Well? Who the hell is ever *ready*?'

'Excuse me, young — ' But then she shook her head, reached out and took both my hands in hers, said, 'Come this way, dear.' She ushered me down a carpeted hallway, past the magnolia wallpaper and mahogany wainscoting, from the noble façade to the laboratorial back rooms, the hallway now flecked green linoleum, chipped in places, unworthy of its calling.

How could this be? That he lay on a table in a cooled room that resembled an oversize stainless-steel kitchen? Someone had parted his hair on the wrong side and combed it, perhaps to hide the wound on his head, and they covered him up to his neck with a sheet — that was it. I took off my jacket and tucked it over his shoulders and chest, saying his name over and over.

They had closed his eyes, but I could tell the way his lid sunk in that his right eye was missing.

I used to tell him his eyes were satellite pictures of Earth — ocean blue with light green flecks. I joked that he had global vision, that I saw the world in his eyes. They could go from sorrow to teasing mischief in three seconds flat. They could pull me from chores to bed in even less time. Their sarcastic roll could piss me off, too, in no time at all.

His amazing photographer's eye with its unique take on things — where had it gone? Would Joe's vision live on soaring in a gull or scampering sideways in a nearsighted rock crab?

His hair felt stiff from the salt, not soft and curly through my fingers. I pushed it over to the right side. 'There, honey,' I said, wiping my nose on my sleeve. 'There you go.' His stubbled face, so cold. Joe had a baby face that he needed to shave only every three or four days, his Friday shadow. He said he couldn't possibly be Italian; he must have been adopted. He'd rub his chin and say, 'Gotta shave every damn week.'

He was handsome and sexy in his imperfection. I ran my finger down his slightly crooked nose, along the ridge of his slightly big ears. When we first met, I'd guessed correctly that he'd been an awkward teenager, a late bloomer. He had an appealing humility that couldn't be faked by the men who'd managed to start breaking girls' hearts back in seventh grade. He was always surprised that women found him attractive.

I slipped my hand under the sheet and held

his arm, so cold, willed him to tense the thick ropes of muscles that ran their length, to laugh and say in his grandmother's accent: *You like, Bella?* Instead, I could almost hear him say, *Take care of Annie and Zach.* Almost, but not quite.

I nodded anyway. 'Don't worry, honey. I don't want you to worry, okay?'

I kissed his cold, cold face and laid my head on his collapsed chest, where his lungs had filled with water and left his heart an island. I lay there for a long time. The door opened, then didn't close. Someone waiting. Making sure I didn't fall apart. I would not fall apart. I had to help Annie and Zach through this. I whispered, 'Good-bye, sweet man. Good-bye.'

★   ★   ★

I don't even pretend to know what might happen to us after we die because the possibilities are endless. I have a degree in biology and feel most at home in nature, yet I'm confounded by *human* nature, by those things that cannot be observed and named and catalogued, a woman of science who slogs off the trail into mystery and ponders at the feet of folklore. So I often wonder if Joe had watched us that morning while we were playing Ship, in those bridging moments between before and after. Had he watched us from the massive redwoods he so revered, then from a cloud? Then from a star? The photographer in him would have delighted in the different perspectives, this after-a-lifetime chance to see that which is too deep and wide to be contained

20

by any frame. Or was that him, that male fuchsia-throated Anna's Hummingbird, *Calypte anna*, that hung around for days? He flittered inches from my nose when I sat on our porch, so close, I could feel his wings beating air on my cheek.

'Joe?' He took off suddenly, making giant swoops like handwriting in the sky. I know the swoops are part of their impressive mating ritual. And yet now I can't help wondering if it was Joe, panicked, attempting to write me a message, frantically trying to tell me his many secrets, to warn me of all that he'd left unsaid.

3

Frank drove me home from McCready's, then left to pick up the kids. I sat at our kitchen table, staring at the pepper grinder. A wedding gift from someone . . . a college friend of mine, I think. Joe had made a big deal about that gift, thought it was the perfect pepper grinder, and I'd made fun of him, said, 'Who knew? That there was a perfect pepper grinder out there and that we would be so lucky as to be its proud owners?'

Zach and Annie pranced onto the porch, in the front door. Their singsong *Mommymommy-mommy!* broke through to me, through my new watery, subdued world, and with them, a slicing clarity. I forced myself up, upright, steady. I said their names. 'Annie. Zach.' Joe told me once that they were his *A* to *Z*, his alpha and omega. 'Come here, guys.' Frank stood behind them. I knew what I had to say. I would not try to sugarcoat this, like my relatives had with me when I was eight and my own father died. I would not say that Joe had fallen asleep, or had gone to live with Jesus, or was now an angel, dressed in white with feathered wings. It would have helped if I'd had a belief system, but my beliefs were in a misshapen pile, constantly rearranging themselves, as unfixed as laundry.

Annie said, 'What happened to your knee?'

I touched it but couldn't feel the bruise from

22

the fall I'd taken in the hallway only a day ago.

'You better get a Band-Aid.' She gave me a long look.

I knelt down on my other knee. I pulled both of them to me and held on. 'Daddy got hurt.' They waited. Frozen. Silent. Waiting for me to reassure them, to say where he was, when they could kiss him. When they could make him a get-well-soon card and put it on the breakfast tray. *Say the words. They have to hear them from you. Say them:* 'And he . . . Daddy . . . he died.'

Their faces. My words were carving themselves into their sweet, flawless skin. Annie started to cry. Zach looked at her, then sounding somewhat amused, said, 'No, he didn't!'

I rubbed his small back. 'Yes, honey. He was at the ocean. He drowned.'

'No way, José. Daddy swims fast.' He laughed.

I looked up to Frank, and he knelt down with us. 'Yes,' I said, 'Daddy is a good swimmer . . . Daddy was. But listen to me, Zach, okay? A big wave surprised him and knocked him off the rock. Maybe he bumped his head; we don't know.'

Annie wrung her hands and cried, 'I want my daddy. I want my *daddy*!'

I whispered into her hair, 'I know, Banannie, I know you do.'

Zach turned to Frank. 'It's not true. He'll swim back, won't he, Uncle Frank?'

Frank ran his hand over his crew cut, covered his eyes for an instant, sat back on his heels, and took Zach onto his lap. He held him. He said,

23

'No, buddy. He's not coming back.' Zach whimpered against Frank's chest, then flung himself backward while Frank maintained his hold. Zach let out a howl that rang with the rawness of unfathomable loss.

★ ★ ★

I don't remember what happened next, or I should say, I don't remember the sequence of things. It seems that at once our long gravel driveway filled with cars, the house and yard with people, the fridge with chicken cacciatore, eggplant Parmesan, lasagna. Joe's family took up most of the house. My extended family was just my mom, and she was still on a plane from Seattle. In a strange, sad way, the day reminded me of our wedding two years before, the last time all these people had caravanned up our drive, gathered together, and brought food and drink.

Joe's family was loud — as they had been in the celebration of our marriage, and now in mourning, even in the early hours of disbelief. His great-aunty, already draped in black, was the only family member who still spoke Italian. She beat her shrivelled bosom and cried out, 'Caro Dio, non Giuseppe.'

And then periods of stunned silence washed into the room while each person sat, anchoring his or her eyes on a different object — a lamp, a coaster, a shoe — as if it held an answer to the question, Why Joe?

His uncle Rick poured stiff drinks. His father,

Joe Sr, drank many of those drinks and began cursing God. His mother, Marcella, held Annie and Zach in her large lap and said to her husband, 'Watch your language, Joseph. Your grandchildren are in the room and Father Mike will be walking in that door any goddamned second.'

I sat in Joe's favouurite chair, the old leather one handed down from Grandpa Sergio. Annie and Zach climbed up on me, curling themselves under my arms, the gravity of their small bodies like perfect paperweights, keeping me securely in place. Joe's brother, David, kept calling from his cell phone in tears, as he and Gil, his partner, inched along in traffic on the 101.

Later, while the kids napped, David found me in the bathroom. He said through the door, 'Sweetie, are you peeing or crying or both?' Neither. I had stolen away for a few minutes and was staring at myself in the mirror, wondering how everything on my face was still as it always had been. My eyes sat in their assigned places above my nose, my mouth below it. I unlocked the door. He came in, shut the door. His arms hung at his sides, palms towards me. His face was ravaged and unshaven, but he was, as always, utterly beautiful; his Roman features so perfectly chiselled and his body so carved that his friends referred to him as The David. We leaned into each other. He whispered, 'What are we going to do without him?' I shook my head and let my nose run onto his shoulder.

★　★　★

25

That night, in bed with each arm around a sleeping child, my tears slipping back into my ears, I wondered how we'd get through this. But I reminded myself that I'd survived another grief that had threatened to undo me.

★ ★ ★

I had come to think of my seven-year marriage to Henry as The Trying Years. Trying to push a boulder up a hill. Trying to push Henry's lackadaisical sperm up to my uterus. Trying to coax my stubborn eggs through my maze of fallopian tubes. The urgent phone calls to Henry to meet me at home for lunch. The awkwardness of sex on demand. And afterwards, lying on my back with my feet in the air, I'd will egg and sperm to *Meet! Mingle! Hook up!* (I was convinced by then that my eggs had shells, that I had tough eggs to crack.) I wanted children so badly that the want spread itself over me and took me hostage; it tied me up in it so that my days became as dark and knotted as I imagined my uterus to be: a scary, uninviting hovel.

Then I finally got pregnant.

And then I lost the baby.

I lay on the couch with old towels underneath me and listened to Henry make the phone calls in the kitchen, feeling as inadequate as the terminology implied. I *lost* the baby — like keys, or a mother-of-pearl earring. Or *spontaneous abortion*, which sounded like all of a sudden we didn't want the baby, like we had made a quick, casual choice. And then there was *miscarriage*.

The morphing of a mistake and a baby carriage.

More trying. Trying to get pregnant, trying to stay pregnant. Trying shots, gels, pills, hope, elation, bed rest, more bed rest. In the end, despair.

Again. And again and again and again. Five in all.

And then one Easter morning — while the neighbourhood kids ran up and down the dwarfed aprons of lawns, their voices pealing with sugared-up joy, wearing new pastel clothes and chocolate smears on their faces, filling their baskets with a plethora of eggs — Henry and I sat at our long, empty dining room table and decided to quit. We quit trying to have a baby and we quit trying to have a marriage. Henry was the one who was courageous enough to put it into words: There was no us left apart from our obsession, and perhaps that's why we'd kept at it with such tenacity.

At that time, it seemed I would always be sad. Little did I know that the universe was about to shift just six months later, when I drove through Sonoma County and took the winding road someone had aptly named the Bohemian Highway. 'Good-bye, Bio-Tech Boulevard!' I shouted to the redwoods, which crowded up to the road like well-wishers greeting my arrival. At the bridge, I waited as a couple of young guys with dreadlocks, wearing guitars on their backs, crossed over to head down to the river's beach, and they waved like they'd been expecting me. I turned into Elbow and stopped at Capozzi's Market. Good-bye, Sadness in San Diego.

Joe and I were the same height; we saw things eye to eye. We slipped into each other's lives as easily as Annie's hand slipped into mine that evening in front of the store. We didn't sleep together on our first date. We didn't wait that long. I followed him home from the parking lot, helped him change diapers and feed baby Zach and tell Annie a story and kiss them good night, as if we'd been doing the same thing every night for years. Though neither of us was pitiful enough to whisper the cliché that we usually didn't do that sort of thing, we both admitted later that we usually didn't. But the deepest wounds have a tendency to seep recklessness. He helped me carry in my suitcase, found a vase for a bucket of cornflowers — my *Centaurea cyanus* that I'd set on the passenger-side floor, brought along for good luck. We talked until midnight, and I learned that the wife whose paisley robe still hung from the hook on the bathroom door had left him for good four months before, that her name was Paige, that she had called only once to check on Annie and Zach. She never called in the three years that followed. Not once. We made love in Paige and Joe's bed. Yes, it was needy sex. *Amazing* needy sex.

★ ★ ★

But now I lay in bed thinking, *All I want to do is go back.* 'We want you back,' I whispered. I slipped my arms out from under Annie's and Zach's heavy heads and tiptoed into the bathroom. There was Joe's aftershave, Cedarwood Sage. I opened

28

it and inhaled it, dabbed it on my wrists, behind my ears, along the lump in my throat. His toothbrush. His razor. I ran my finger along the blade and watched the fine line of blood appear, mixing with tiny remnants of his whiskers.

I turned on the basin taps so the kids wouldn't hear me. 'Joe? You gotta come back. Listen to me. I can't fucking *do* this.' The sleeper wave had come out of nowhere, and now I felt that wave in the bathroom, the inability to breathe, fighting the thunderous slam that ripped away Joe . . . Annie and Zach's daddy. They'd already been abandoned by their birth mother. How much could they take? I had to pull it together for them. But at the same time I knew that their very existence would help hem me in, keep all my parts together.

I dried my face and took a few deep breaths and opened the door. Callie pressed her cold black nose into my hand, turned and thumped me with her tail, licked my face when I bent to pet her back. I wanted to be there for the kids when they woke, so I climbed back into bed and waited for the sun to rise, for their eyes to open.

★ ★ ★

Annie stood on a stool, cracking eggs. Joe's mom was going at my fridge with a spray bottle, the garbage can full of old food. I went over and hugged Annie from the back. The yolks floated in the bowl, four bright, perfect suns. She broke them with a stab of the whisk and stirred them with concentrated vigour.

29

She turned to me and said, 'Mommy? You're not going to die, are you?'

There it was. I touched my forehead to hers. 'Honey, someday I will. Everyone does. But first, I'm planning on being around for a long, long time.'

She nodded, kept nodding while our foreheads bobbed up and down. Then she turned back to her eggs and said, 'Are you, you know, planning on *leaving* anytime soon?'

I knew exactly what she was thinking. *Whom* she was thinking about. I turned her back around. 'Oh, Banannie. No. I will never leave you. I promise. Okay?'

'You promise? You pinkie promise?' She held out her pinkie and I looped mine in hers.

'I more than pinkie promise. I promise you with my pinkie and my whole big entire self.'

She wiped her eyes and nodded again. She went back to whisking.

People kept arriving and fixing things: the unhinged door on the chicken coop, the fence post that went down in a storm months before; someone was changing the oil in the truck. Who had driven it home from Bodega Bay? Who had put Joe's jacket back on the hook, and the blanket back on our bed, and when? The drill started going again. The house smelled like an Italian restaurant. How could anyone eat? David, the writer in the family, who was also one helluva cook, was working on the eulogy out on the garden bench he'd given us for our wedding, while some of his culinary masterpieces graced the table. Everyone seemed to be doing

30

something constructive except me. I kept telling myself that I had to be strong for the kids, but I didn't feel strong.

My mom, who'd arrived from Seattle, hadn't let Zach out of her sight and was digging in the dirt with him and his convoy of Tonka trucks and action figures. Joe's mom and Annie kept busy cleaning, stopping to wipe each other's tears, then going back to wiping any surface they could find. I found myself wandering back and forth between Annie and Zach, drawing them in for a hug, a sigh, until they would slip down off my lap and back into their activities.

While she cleaned, Marcella sang. She always sang; she was proud of her voice, and rightly so. But she never sang Sinatra or songs from her generation; she sang songs from her kids' generation. She loved Madonna, Prince, Michael Jackson, Cyndi Lauper — you name a song from the eighties and she could sing it. Joe and David had told me that when they were teenagers, blaring stereos from their bedrooms, Marcella would shout up from the kitchen, 'Kids! Turn that crap *up!*'

While she scoured the grimy tile grout in my kitchen with a toothbrush, she started singing in an aching soprano: '*Like a virgin . . . for the very first time.*' I let out a strange, sharp laugh and she looked at me, shocked. 'What, sweetie? You okay?' She hadn't intended to make a crack at my housekeeping, was so preoccupied with sadness that she didn't even realize what she was singing. But I knew Joe would have got a kick out of it, that on another day, in another layer of

31

time, we both would have pointed out the lyrics, laughed, and teased her. She would have responded by swaying her big bottom back and forth, adding, 'Oh yeah? Take this: *The kid is not my son* . . . ' But instead she searched me for further signs of grief-stricken insanity to accompany my shriek of laughter. I shook my head and waved to say, *Never mind*. She took my face in her thick hands. 'Thank God my grandchildren have you for their mother. I thank God every day for you, Ella Beene.' I reached my arms around the massive trunk of her.

'Why don't you sit down?' I said, then started to take the spray bottle from her hand. 'Rest. Let me pour you a cup of coffee.'

She pulled it back. 'No. This is what I do. This is all I can do. Resting, it makes it worse for me.'

I nodded, hugged her again. 'Of course.' Marcella always believed in the clarity of Windex.

★   ★   ★

The next morning, I slid my black dress from its dry-cleaning bag and lifted my arms and felt the cool lining slip over my head. I considered slipping into the plastic instead, letting it tighten against my nostrils and mouth, and letting them lay me in the same dark hole with Joe. It was the thought of the kids that helped me push my feet into the black slings my best friend, Lucy, bought me — 'You cannot wear Birkenstocks to a funeral, my dear, even in Northern California' — and find both of the silver and aquamarine

32

drop earrings Joe gave me our first Christmas together.

At the church, thirty-six people spoke. We cried, but we laughed too. Most of the stories went back to the time before I knew Joe. It seemed odd that almost everyone in the church had known him much longer than I had. I was the newcomer among them, but I found a certain comfort in telling myself that they didn't know Joe the way I did.

Afterwards, I remembered having conversations I couldn't quite hear and receiving hugs I couldn't quite feel — as if I'd wrapped myself in plastic after all. The only thing I could feel was Annie's and Zach's hands slipping into mine, the solidity of their palms, the pressings of their small fingers, as we walked out of the church, as we stood at the grave site on the hill, as we walked down towards the car. And then Annie's hand pulled out of mine. She walked up to a striking blonde woman I didn't know, standing at the edge of the cemetery. *Perhaps one of Joe's old classmates*, I thought. The woman bent down and Annie reached out, lightly touched her shoulder.

'Annie?' I called. I smiled at the woman. 'She doesn't have a shy bone in her body.'

The woman took Annie's other hand in both of hers, whispered in her ear, and then spoke to me over her shoulder. 'Believe me, I know that. But Annie knows who I am, don't you, sweet pea?'

Annie nodded without pulling her hand away or looking up. She said, '*Mama?*'

4

Annie had called her *Mama*. She and Zach called me *Mom* and *Mommy*. But not *Mama*. Never *Mama*. I'd never questioned it, or really even thought of it, but the distinction rang out in that cemetery: *Mama* is the first-word-ever-uttered variety of *mother*. The murmur of a satisfied baby at the breast.

I recognized Paige then. I'd once found a picture of her, gloriously pregnant, that had been stuck in a book on photography entitled *Capturing the Light* — it was the one photo Joe had forgotten, or maybe had intended to keep, when he purged the house of her. I was astounded at her beauty and said so. He'd shrugged and said, 'It's a good picture.'

Now I could see that Joe liked his wives tall. She was taller than I, maybe five-eleven, and I wasn't used to being shorter than other women. I had what some people referred to as great hair, those who happened to like wild, red and unmanageable. But Paige had universally great hair. Long, blonde, straight, silky, shampoo-commercial hair. Computer-enhanced hair. Women comfort themselves when they look at magazines, saying, 'That photo's been all touched up. No one really has hair like that, or skin like that, or a body like that.' Paige had *all that*, along with Jackie O sunglasses, the single accessory our culture associates with style, mystery and a strong, grieving widow and mother . . . or in her case, mama.

Annie called her *Mama*.

These thoughts bungee jumped through my mind in the eight seconds it took her to rise gracefully on her heels, holding Annie in her arms, and walk towards me, extending her hand. 'Hi. I'm Paige Capozzi. Zach and Annie's mother.'

Mother? Define *mother*. And her name was still Capozzi. *Capozzi?* Joe Capozzi. Annie Capozzi. Zach Capozzi. Paige Capozzi. And Ella Beene. *One of these things is not like the others; one of these things doesn't belong.*

Zach hid behind me, still holding on to my hand.

'Hey, Zach. You've grown so big.'

I heard Marcella mutter next to me, 'Yeah. Children grow quite a bit in three years, lady.'

Joe Sr said, 'What's she — Oh, for Christ's sake.' He reached his arm over Marcella's shoulders as they turned and walked away.

I thought about telling Paige my name. *Hi, I'm Ella, Zach and Annie's mother.* Like we were contestants on *What's My Line?* I said nothing. People gathered. Joe's relatives, excluding his parents, all took their turns saying reserved, polite hellos to her, but you'd think it was a family of Brits, not Italians. David stood next to me and said, 'Why, nice to finally see you, Paige. You're looking quite radiant . . . ,' and then under his breath, he whispered to me, 'for a *funeral*.'

Aunt Kat, who always acted like an entire welcoming committee bound up in one tiny woman, did manage to say, 'Come to the house. We're all going to the house.' Everyone turned to me.

David said, 'How hospitable of you, Aunt Kat, to invite Paige to Ella's home for her.'

I felt my mouth turn up in a smile; I heard myself say to Paige, 'Yes, of course, please do.' By then she'd set down Annie, who stood between us looking back and forth, like a net judge in a tennis match. My heels sank into the grass.

Paige said, 'That would be lovely. My flight doesn't leave until tomorrow. Thank you.'

I didn't want to know anything about Paige — not where her flight was returning her to, not what she did for a living, not if she had more children, and if so, not if she would hang around this time to help raise them. But okay. She was leaving. She would stop by the house for an hour at most to pay her respects to a man she had clearly not respected while he was *alive*, and then she would drive off, and by tomorrow she would fly far, far away, back to the Land of Mothers Who Left.

Gil and David drove the kids and me home. David turned around to say something, then looked at Annie and Zach leaning into my sides and evidently decided to shut up and face front. I stared at the oval scar on the back of Gil's domed head, wondering how long it had been hiding under his hair before he'd shaved it all off. Was the scar from a childhood wound, from a bike accident in his teens, or had it happened more recently? A quarrel with a crazy lover, before he'd found David?

Annie sighed and said, 'She's pretty!'

Annie was three when Paige left. How much could she possibly remember? I asked her, 'Do you remember her, Banannie?'

Annie nodded. 'She still smells good too.'

She remembered her scent. Of course. I'd inhaled every one of Joe's recently worn T-shirts, grateful now for my tendency to let laundry pile up. I sunk my face into his robe every time I walked by where it hung in the bathroom, dabbed his aftershave on my wrists. Of course Annie remembered.

At the house I kept my distance from Paige. It was easy to tell where she went, because the floor seemed to tilt in her direction, as if we were on a raft and I was made of feathers and she was made of gold. Annie came up and leaned against me, and I smoothed back her hair, ran my fingers through her ponytail. Then she was off, taking Paige by the hand, leading her into the kids' room. My fiercest ally, Lucy, whispered in my ear, 'That woman's got nerve,' but no one else broached the subject. At funerals, it seems most people leave old grudges at home.

And yet. I certainly didn't want to chat it up with Joe's ex-wife on the day of his funeral, or any other day. What did she want? Why was she here? Annie kept dividing her time between the two of us, as if she felt some sort of obligation when she should have been thinking of no one other than her six-year-old self and her daddy. Zach wore his path between Marcella, my mom, and me.

Once I walked around a corner to find Paige

and Frank's wife, Lizzie, embracing, crying. My face went hot, and I whirled back around to the crowd in the kitchen. Even though Frank had been Joe's best friend since eighth grade, I had been in Frank and Lizzie's house only a handful of times. She and Paige had been close friends. And so, she'd explained to me the first time I met her, she and I would not be. When I'd reached out to shake her hand, she held mine in both of hers and said, 'You seem like a nice person. But Paige is my best bud. I hope you understand.' And then she'd turned and walked away, joining in another conversation. Since then, we'd greeted each other, made a few stabs at small talk about the kids, but never once had a real conversation. Joe and I had never so much as had dinner with Frank and Lizzie, always just Frank. Everyone else in Elbow had welcomed me, but Lizzie's rejection reared at times, chaffing, a sharp pebble in a perfectly fitting shoe.

I fixed Annie and Zach paper plates of food, but it wasn't long before they started showing signs of utter fatigue; Zach lay across my lap, sucking his thumb, holding his Bubby, his name for his beloved turquoise bunny that had long lost all its stuffing, and Annie was amped up, running in circles, which she frequently did right before she passed out. 'Come on, you two. Tell everyone good night and I'll tuck you in.'

'No!' Annie whined. 'I'm not tired.'

'Honey, you're exhausted.'

'Excuse me? Are you me or am *I* me?' She had her hand on her jutted hip, and the other finger

38

pointed to her chest. Paige peeked around the corner.

I took a deep breath. Annie could sometimes act like a six-year-old adolescent. The truth was, we were all exhausted. 'You are you. And I am me. And me is Mommy. As in Mom.' And I pointed to my own chest. 'Me.' I stood up. 'And what Mom-*me* says, *you* do.'

She laughed. I sighed relief. 'Good one!' she said, delighted. '*You* got *me* on that one.' I looked over to see Paige turning away. The kids made their good-night rounds, Paige hugging each of them and crouching down, talking to them. God, it was weird to see her there, in our house, chatting with our people, holding our children.

In the old rocker in their room, the kids climbed onto my lap and I read to them and stayed until they fell asleep, which was only about five minutes. I noticed a crate of old books that I'd stuck in the back of the closet, now sitting by the rocker. Had the kids dragged that out, looking for something? Most of them were books they'd outgrown or just got bored with, but maybe they seemed new to them again. Or maybe Annie had shown them to Paige.

I slipped out, quietly closing the door. David handed me a shot of Jack Daniel's and whispered, 'She left. She's outta here.'

I wasn't much of a Jack Daniel's drinker, but I raised the shot and gulped it, then grabbed Joe's down jacket and went outside. The fog had unfurled, chilling the air and sending home everyone but the closest friends and family, who had crowded inside, looking at photo albums and getting drunk. Through the picture window I watched them, a portrait of a family enduring; the warm lamplight surrounded them like soft, old worn-in love.

I pulled on Joe's jacket and headed for the garden. I wanted the company of tomatoes, of scallions, of kale. I craved lying down between their rows, burying my face in their fragrant, damp dirt. Maybe later I'd go down to the redwood circle and lie there, in the middle of that dark arboreal cathedral, Our Lady of *Sequoia sempervirens*. Joe had told me that the Porno Indians believed that on a day in October, the forests could talk, that they would give answers to the people's wishes. But October was still a long way off.

Lucy came running up behind me. 'No wandering off alone.'

'Pray tell, why not?'

'You need a friend. And a good bottle of wine. Even better, a friend with her own vineyard.' She held up a bottle of wine without a label; the designer was still working on it.

'Okay, but let me bum a cigarette.'

She shook her head. 'Don't have any.'

'Liar. You're PMSing.' I'd kicked a vicious habit fifteen years before in Advanced Biology at Boston U when they showed us a smoker's lung. I'd transformed into a typical ex-smoker: a zealot who self-righteously preached about seeing the light of not lighting up. But that night a cigarette sounded like salvation. And Lucy was one of those rare breeds who could smoke a few cigarettes a few times a month when she was stressed, usually right before her period. I knew her cycle because it was the same as mine. Moon sisters. We'd met only when I'd moved to Elbow, but we immediately fell into an easy alignment that went way beyond our cycles. She had long black hair, but she said she should have been the redhead because her name was Lucy. Sometimes she called me Ella Mertz. She and David had become my closest friends. Besides Joe.

We ended up sitting on the bench by the garden, smoking without talking. The cigarette hurt my throat, made me light-headed. She handed me the bottle.

'What, no glasses? Is this the latest craze in Sonoma wine tasting?'

'Yeah, but usually we wrap it in a brown paper bag too.'

'*Distinguished*.' I tipped the bottle back and took a swig of pinot noir.

A voice came from behind us: 'I just wanted to say good-bye.' I jerked around to see Paige, who reached out her hand to me. I couldn't extend my own because I was holding the bottle of wine in one hand and a Marlboro Light in the other. Class act if there ever was one.

'Oh, sorry, here . . . ' I stamped out the cigarette and shoved the bottle back at Lucy. 'I thought you left.'

'I realized I hadn't said a word to you since we got here, so I wanted to thank you for letting me come over. I know this must be a difficult time for you.'

I studied her, saw the origins of Annie's eyes,

Annie's wilful chin, Zach's noble forehead. 'Thanks.'

'You've done a good job with the children,' she said, her voice cracking the slightest bit, a hairline fracture in the marble goddess. 'I should be going.'

I stood. She raised her chin. I did not want a hug from her and figured she probably did not want a hug from me. But we had been hugging people all day — it was what you did at times like this — and so we gave each other stiff pats on the back, a stiff not-quite hug. She did smell good, much better than I did. Better than cigarette smoke and booze.

★   ★   ★

When I finally made it to bed, both kids had already left theirs and climbed into ours — mine — and were asleep. I was glad for their company. About two in the morning, Annie sprang up in bed and cried out, 'Hi, Daddy!' I jolted awake, expecting to see him standing over us, telling us it was time to get dressed and head out for a picnic.

Annie smiled in the foggy moonlight, her eyes still closed. I wanted to crawl inside her dream and stay there with her. Callie sighed and laid her head back down over my feet. Zach sucked noisily on his thumb while I tried to let the rhythm lull me back to sleep. Exhaustion had settled into my muscles, bones, and every organ — except my brain, which zigzagged incessantly through moments of my life with Joe. Now I tried to guide it to the few conversations we'd had about Paige, digging up the same information I'd once tossed into the No Need to Dwell pile. Back then, I didn't want to live in the past, not his or mine. I didn't ask the questions because I didn't want to know the answers.

But I had wanted to make sure their ending was final, that there was no chance they could get back together. The last thing I wanted to be was a home wrecker.

At the house that first night I met Joe, the only evidence of Paige that I'd noticed was her bathrobe, and when I returned the next evening after a day of job hunting, the bathrobe was gone. Joe must have emptied the house of everything Paige, because I never found another indication that she existed, except for the one photograph of her pregnant.

'Four months ago,' Joe had said in his one offer of explanation soon after we met, 'while the kids and I were at my mom's for Sunday brunch, she packed up all her things.' We had been lying in bed, a candle flame still creating moving shadows on the wall, long after our own shadows had stilled. 'She took all her clothes except her bathrobe, which she'd practically been living in.'

He said Paige had been depressed. She got to the point that she'd forget to change clothes and take a shower. She went to live with her aunt in a trailer park outside of Las Vegas, so at least he knew someone was taking care of her. It was hard for me to imagine someone choosing a trailer park in the desert, leaving behind all the natural beauty of Elbow, the cosy home, let alone

43

Joe and Annie and Zach. But she wouldn't see him, wouldn't talk to him. She'd left him a Dear Joe letter.

'She said she was sorry but that she wasn't meant to be a mother. That the kids would be better off without her. She said she loved them but she wasn't good for them. She told me she knew I could do this, that I was a natural father in all the ways she wasn't a natural mother, that my family would help me . . . blah, blah, fucking blah.'

'It's ironic,' I told him. I thought about keeping my own failures, well, my *own*, but I'd already blown every dating rule, so there was no point in stopping then. 'I've wanted to have children, but I haven't been able to. I was depressed and lethargic, too . . . My ex-husband could tell you similar stories about me wearing the same clothes for three days and forgetting to bathe.'

I told him about the five babies that didn't make it. We held each other tighter, as if our embrace could serve as a perfectly fitted cast that could help heal all the broken parts of us.

★   ★   ★

My mom had slept on the couch, had a fire going in the woodstove, and was already making coffee and oatmeal, toast and eggs, when I got up. My mother stood in my kitchen in her robe and moccasins, looking like an older version of me — tall, slim, a bit of a hippie — except her braid was salt-and-pepper. I got my red hair

44

from my dad. She held out her arms to me, her silver bracelets clinking, and I entered her hug. Because her husband — my dad — had died when I was eight, she'd been through this, she knew things, but some of them couldn't be spoken. I loved my mother, but we'd never had the kind of mother-daughter relationship my friends shared with their moms. I'd never screamed that I hated her; we didn't go through that necessary separation of selves where I declared my individuality, because, truth be told, the shadow cast by my father's death always loomed between us, keeping us polite and slightly distant. Still, I loved her. I admired her. And I wished, in a way, that I'd felt passionate and comfortable enough to dump my rage and teenage angst on her. Instead, I'd pecked her on the cheek and closed the door to my room and finished my biology homework.

I poured myself coffee and refilled my mom's cup. Outside, the fog hadn't budged since the previous night; the cold grey shroud wrapped itself through the trees, as if trying to comfort them from the very cold it was inflicting upon them. The house, though, literally sparkled. I'd inherited my lack of housekeeping skills from my mother, so she hadn't had much to do with the cleaning. The night before, Joe's mother had crouched on her arthritic knees, wiping the hardwood as she crawled out of the front door. She'd washed all the dishes, emptied the compost bucket, and thrown the bags of recyclables into the recycling bin. The only remnants of the funeral were the stuffed refrigerator, the stack of sympathy cards from old friends and new, and the proliferation of calla lilies, irises, lisianthus, and orchids that lined the counters and the old trunk we used as a coffee table.

While my mom and I drank coffee by the fire, I asked her in the most casual voice I could muster, 'So? What did you think of Paige?'

She shrugged, somewhat carefully. 'A bit . . . I don't know . . . *Barbie* comes to mind, I guess. Or maybe it's insecurity. She's awfully stiff. And her ankles are a bit on the thick side, don't you think? Anyway, she's nothing like *you*.' As only a mother could say.

'Insecure? She's so . . . composed.'

My mom made a dismissive wave of her hand, then said, 'It had to be difficult to show up like that . . . But people need to make themselves feel okay. So I can understand why she came. Lord knows all kinds of people came to your father's funeral.'

She rarely mentioned my dad. 'Really? Like who?'

'Oh, you know. I don't remember who, exactly. It was a long time ago, Jelly.'

Door closed. I knew better than to press further. 'But what does Paige want? I'm worried about the kids.'

'You've been their mother for three years. Everyone knows that. Including Paige. And with Joe gone, you're the one constant parent in their lives.'

'She could come back.'

She sipped her coffee, set down her cup, which

read: Photographers do it in the darkroom. A present Annie had innocently insisted on getting for Joe. 'I doubt Paige is going to step up now. After three years of doing nothing. And if she did? Like I said, anyone can see you're their real mom.' She reached over and grabbed my hand and gave it a long squeeze. She said, 'We've got to talk business. I know it's the last thing you feel like doing . . . '

'I don't feel like doing anything.'

'I know. But I can help you with the paper-work. And I've only got a few more days.' She said we needed to check into the life insurance policy, call Social Security, request the death certificate. She sat up straighter and smoothed her robe over her lap. 'Jelly, I can make the preliminary calls, but they're all going to want to talk to you . . . okay?'

No. It was not okay. But I nodded anyway.

She patted my knee and stood. 'It will get your mind off that Paige woman.'

5

Marcella came by to watch the kids while my mom and I drove into Santa Rosa to take care of the paperwork side of death. I stared out of the car window at people going about their business — crossing the street, emerging from buildings, from parked cars, putting change in parking meters, *laughing* — as my mom drove us back towards Elbow, towards the store. I hadn't told her that Joe had an old life insurance policy that we were in the middle of updating. As in the *beginning* of the middle. As in he'd talked to Frank's dad's insurance guy, but I hadn't heard anything else. I thought the old policy was around $50,000, which would buy me a little time to figure out what to do, but not a lot, and this would worry my mom.

Back in San Diego, I'd worked in a lab in what we used to call the 'cutting foreskin of biotechnology', but I hadn't kept up on it, hadn't wanted to, really, since I'd discovered almost my first day on the job that I hated working in a lab. When I was a kid I read *Harriet the Spy* and felt certain that I wanted to be a spy, or at the least, an investigator. I walked around with my dad's birding binoculars bouncing on my chest, a yellow spiral-bound notepad jammed in my back pocket. I spied on the mailman. I spied on the neighbours. I spied on our houseguests. I wrote down descriptions just like my dad did when we went bird-watching. But after my dad died, I lost my curiosity about people. They were too complex to capture in a few hastily scribbled notes, too unpredictable and perplexing in their behaviours. I turned my attention to the plants and animals he had started teaching me about just before he died, and later, I majored in biology. Somehow I'd taken a wrong turn and ended up staring at cells under a microscope in that biotech lab instead of tromping through field and lake and wood.

Now I had the guide job for Fish and Wildlife lined up, but it was part-time, not enough for the three of us to live on and keep the store running. The store was Grandpa Sergio's, Joe Sr's, and Joe's legacy.

Sergio had started it as a place where the Italian immigrants could find supplies and keep their heritage alive, fulfil their nostalgic longings for their mother country. But during World War II, some of the Italian men, including Sergio, had been sent to internment camps. When Joe had told me, I'd stupidly said, 'Sergio was Japanese?'

Joe laughed. 'Ah, that would be no.'

'I've never heard of any Italian internment. How can that be?'

But Joe explained that, yes, some Italians and Germans, too, had been sent away to camps, though in much smaller numbers than the Japanese Americans. And Italians living in coastal towns had to relocate. Many from Bodega came to Elbow. But there was a reason I'd never heard about Italian internment: No one ever talked about it. The Italian Americans didn't talk about it, and the U.S. government didn't talk about it.

'But it happened,' Joe said. 'Grandpa never liked to discuss it. Same with Pop. But that's why Sergio and Rosemary insisted we call them Grandpa and Grandma instead of Nonno and Nonna. There had been a big push during the war not to speak Italian. Another one of the fallouts was that Capozzi's Market lost its 'Everything Italia' motto and became an Americanized hybrid. The mozzarella made room for the Velveeta. I think the store — along with Grandpa Sergio — kind of lost its . . . passion.' He shrugged. He took a long pause before he added, 'Trying to be what it thought it was supposed to be. Playing it safe.' I wondered, the way Joe's voice trailed off, if he was talking about himself as much as he was Sergio. But I didn't ask. Part of me didn't want to know.

My mom turned into the parking lot where Joe and I had first met. The wooden screen door slammed behind us when we walked in; the floors creaked hello. Joe was everywhere. Every detail, no matter how mundane, now held significance. The store — hybrid as it was — had composition, like his photographs. Somehow, and I don't quite know how he did it, the way he arranged everything — from the oranges and lemons, the onions and leeks, the Brussels sprouts and artichokes and cabbage in the produce section, to the aisles of canned and boxed goods and even the meat and fish behind the glass case — every item complemented another, so that when you opened that ancient screen door, felt the fan whirring up above and smelled the mixture of old wood and fresh vegetables and hot coffee, saw his scrawl on the chalkboard with the day's specials, you felt as if you were walking into a photograph of a time when everything was whole and good.

But the store that had been Joe was already fading. His cousin Gina had tried, but her careful handwriting on the chalkboard reminded me of a classroom, not the deli. The produce looked tired. I smelled bleach, not soup. Down one of the aisles, I noticed something that couldn't have just appeared in the past few days: a layer of dust on the soup cans and boxes of pasta.

I hugged Gina, who was as limp as the lettuce, then went upstairs to Joe's office. I let my hands linger over his desk before I opened the right-side drawer, pushed back the other files, pulled out the one marked *Life Insurance*. There it was: $50,000. Marcella and Joe Sr had bought him the policy when he and Paige married, years before the kids were born. We had changed it, naming me as the beneficiary, but increasing the amount became a work in progress. I found the forms from Hank Halstrom Insurance that Joe had started to fill out, but that wave came out of nowhere, and the forms were still here, waiting to be finished, waiting to be sent, waiting for business to pick up, so we could afford the higher payment.

There, on the first page only, was the handwriting that should have been on the chalkboard, the boyish quality of it. I traced the letters with my fingertip. Not long before, he'd sat in the same place, hunched over the same forms, just in case . . . someday . . . Had he wondered about his death then? About how? Or when? Or how the three of us would have to find a way to get up the next day without him, and the next?

I pulled a tissue out of my pocket and blotted the tear that had fallen on the form. I was not going to start that again. I held the tissue against my eyes, as if I could push the tears back inside their ducts. In some ways it was harder to be in the store than at home. Had I even set foot in this office before without Joe? He was the last person to sit in this chair, to rest his rough elbows on this desk, to punch our phone number into this phone, to speak into the receiver, to say, 'Hey, I'm heading home. Got the milk and peanut butter. Anything else?'

My mom was waiting. I took the insurance file and a thick stack of unopened envelopes that had been shoved in the to-do file.

I hadn't got involved with the bills. Joe had his system in place when I moved in. Besides, I was a mess when it came to paperwork. My mother would tell me this was an opportunity for personal growth. Time to *embrace* paperwork. Time to stop blubbering and get home to Annie and Zach.

I walked down the stairs, waved, and thanked Gina. She nodded, her eyes still a bit puffy behind her wire-framed glasses. She'd recently returned to Elbow after leaving Our Sisters of Mercy. At age thirty-two, she'd realized she didn't want to be a nun and was still reeling from that decision. Joe and I had privately called her his ex-sister cousin.

As I held the door open for my mom, I realized not one customer had come into the store while we'd been there, and it was noon. I knew it had been slow, but not *that* slow.

'Find it?' my mom asked as she backed the Jeep out.

I nodded. Within a couple of minutes we were pulling up the gravel drive, Callie running to meet us. A Ford Fiesta sat parked in my spot. My mom and I looked at each other and both lifted our eyebrows. Neither of us felt up for company, but people were being kind.

The kids' shoes were set out in a neat line by the front door. *How efficient of them*, I thought, picking up one of Annie's pink high-tops. They weren't even muddy. Probably something they'd learned when they stayed at Lizzie's. I guessed she might be the type who would have a hand-painted sign that said, mahalo for taking off your shoes. I'd been there so few times and so long ago, I couldn't remember what their shoe policy was; besides, who was I to argue with a little less tracked-in dirt? But there on the other side of the umbrella stand was a pair of Kenneth Cole leather pumps. I'd never seen Marcella wear any heels higher than an inch. I opened the screen door and said in the cheeriest voice I could muster, 'Banannie, Zachosaurus, I'm ho-ome!' No one ran to greet me. No one shouted, *Hi, Mommy*.

I walked in and set the files on the desk and looked through the window to see if I'd missed them playing in the yard. Annie's giggle spilled from their room. I walked down the hallway and opened the door. There, in our rocker, were Annie and Zach, sitting on Paige's lap. Zach was brushing a whisk of her silky hair against his cheek. Paige's arms looped in a fence around both of them; her hands held out an open book, like a gate. The book was by Dr Seuss, one that had been in the crate from the closet. The cover screamed at me: *Are You My Mother?*

6

'I missed my plane,' she said, closing the book and holding it face down. 'Marcella should be back in a minute. She went to check on Auntie Sophia.'

I nodded, kept nodding. My body shook so hard that one of my knees buckled. A crow shrilled, *Caw-caw-caw*, through the still damp air, staking its claim on a favourite branch or fence post.

Annie grinned at me, but Zach had already slid off Paige's lap and grabbed my leg. I picked him up, inhaled his fresh, loamy scent, now mixed with the increasingly familiar scent of Paige's perfume — jasmine, I was pretty sure. And citrus. But it had echoes of Macy's, not a garden or an orange grove.

My mother, who'd walked in behind me, placed her hand firmly on my back. 'Hello,' she said to Paige. 'Will you be needing a taxi to the airport, then?'

Paige shook her head. 'I've got the rental car.' She looked at her watch. 'And it's just about time to go.'

That, I thought, is an understatement.

I said, 'It can take a couple hours if you run into traffic . . . Where are you flying to?' *Siberia? Antarctica? The* Moon?

'Las Vegas. I left my card on the coffee table . . . '

Why the hell would I want your card?

' . . . so the kids can call anytime.'

Why would they want to call you? They don't even know you. They know the plumber better than they know you and they don't call him.

She hugged Annie for an excruciatingly long minute. My mom raised her eyebrows again. The crows cawed again. The *Corvus brachyrhynchos*. Crows have a bad rap, but they're highly intelligent, extremely adaptable birds, and I'm always defending them when people complain. Their calls all have many different meanings. I was pretty sure this one was sounding out a warning of some type. Paige finally let go of Annie, got up, and reached for Zach, whom I held a bit too tight. His smile was shy, but he went to her. 'Bye, Zach.' Her voice cracked again. Tears magnified her blue eyes, those eyes that looked so much like Annie's. She kept them from spilling, intent, it seemed, on not making a scene. I gave her credit for that much.

'Good-bye, Lady,' Zach said.

She handed him back to me. Finally, finally, Paige stepped out the door, slipped into her high heels, and clicked down the porch stairs.

Her perfume stuck around. I followed Annie to the great room, which Joe had fondly dubbed the not-so-great room. She sat at the watery glass window and watched Paige drive away.

'Banannie? Are you okay?' I went to her and knelt beside her.

'I . . . want . . . my . . . daddy,' she said in a whisper.

'I know, honey. I know.' I held her, but she

56

turned her head so her gaze stayed on the empty gravel river of driveway and the dust clouds Paige left behind. I didn't know what to say about Paige. She'll be back? I didn't know what she was planning on doing . . . or being . . . for Annie and Zach.

Zach tore in the room. 'Hey, mister!' he said, pointing to my boots. 'Shoes go outside. Come on, I'll show ya.'

My mom raised her eyebrows once again. She could never have Botox; her chief mode of communication lay in her forehead. I said, 'Hey, mister? I'm no mister, mister!' He laughed. 'And these boots were made for walking, not for sitting out on some old porch.'

He stood for a minute with his head tilted, looking up, pondering my statement. 'Oh, for Christ's sake,' my little boy said, an expression he'd learned from his grandpa. Then he went outside and pulled on his Batman battery-powered tennies and stomped back into the house, flashing red lights with each step.

★ ★ ★

After we fed the kids reheated tuna casserole à la the Nardini family, according to the masking tape on the bottom of the glass pan, we set them up for their naps. The *Are You My Mother?* book lay in the rocking chair. I dropped it back in the crate, shoved the crate back into the closet, and read *Little Bear* instead. Neither of them said anything about the Dr Seuss book, and they were both asleep before I got six pages into *Little Bear*. They were as worn out by everything as I was. I tiptoed to the closet and plucked the other book out of the crate, took it outside, and threw it in the trash can.

Back in the house, I picked up Paige's business card.

PAIGE CAPOZZI
The Home Stager
executive real estate and rental properties
'When it's time to stage, call Paige.' 800-555-7531

'A home stager,' I said to my mom, who was doing the dishes.

'Ahh. An interior decorator type, who comes in and tells you to get rid of all your clutter.'

'A Grandma Beene.'

'Exactly. Shirley hired one when she put her house on the market. She had Shirl rent a few pieces of furniture and get rid of that old peach recliner, thank God. She put fresh flowers around and an apple pie in the oven. Had her take down all the family photographs.'

'Why? That sounds kind of cold.'

'She said it was so a family coming in can visualize themselves there without being distracted by all your personal stuff. Guess you want to make them feel like they can make it their own simply by stepping in, not having to block out the evidence of your life. She also did a lot of feng shui placement to create positive energy.'

'Did it work?'

'Her house never looked so good. She sold it in two days. For above the asking price. You know real estate these days. It just keeps going up. Shirl had to stop herself from buying it back.'

'I always pictured Paige as this crazy woman living in a trailer park, zoning out on soap operas.' I looked around the house, saw it through Paige's eyes. I saw her clearing the shelves, filling trash bags and boxes marked *Goodwill*. The few shoes she didn't pitch, she would place out on the porch, in obedient lines. 'What the hell does she want, Mom?'

My mom shook her head. 'I don't know. But most likely, nothing. Except, perhaps, to find a way to forgive herself.'

★ ★ ★

My mom said she wanted to lie down too. I told her to stretch out on my bed. I hadn't slept much but knew I was too ramped up to close my eyes. I had to at least look at those files.

A thick stack of bills, all stamped *Past Due*, filled the payables folder. What? Joe was not a past-due kind of guy. He was a fanatic about paying his bills on time. If there had been a religious cult called Pay for Your Sins on Time, he would have been appointed their pope, or at least a most honourable guru.

But there it was, right in front of me. Evidence of slack. I leafed through the invoices. He hadn't paid Ben Aston for three months? Ben Aston had been his main produce supplier for years. He was a friend. Ben had scrawled across the bottom of the most recent bill, *Hey, Joey, Can we take care of this?* The amount due was highlighted: $2,563.47. The bakery bill said *Last Notice before Termination of Service*. In two weeks, the electricity would be shut off if a payment of $1,269 wasn't made. We owed Teaberry's Ranch, Donaldson's Dairy, the beer and wine supplier, and the telephone company. I started sweating. I needed to get outside.

I walked down to the garden and started pulling weeds, but not the way I usually did. Not carefully digging up the root. No. I clawed at them, wildly tearing them, and threw them in a pile. *What in the hell? You die on me? You up and die on me? On Annie? On Zach? And you fail to tell me what a god-awful mess you've gotten yourself into?* 'You've gotten *us* into?' I stomped on the pile, releasing droves of dandelion and sour-grass seeds to spread in the wind and multiply all over our land. Let them take over. Why should I care? 'Oh! And Paige shows up? Really? Now? After three years of, uh, let's see . . . that would be *nothing*? 'Hi, I'm Annie and Zach's *mother*'. What in the hell is *that* about?'

A car door slammed. Over my hissy fit I hadn't heard Marcella's Acura pull into the drive. I took deep breaths to calm myself down while Callie cocked her head at me, held her ears back, and asked with her eyes if I'd gone raving mad. I wondered if Marcella had seen my tirade, as I watched her take careful steps down the path. Everything about Marcella was big: her meals, her zest for cleanliness and order, her body, her voice, her faith, her heart, her love for her family, and — everyone knew it — especially her love for her sons. So now it was sadness that was the biggest part of her, and it showed in her slower walk and, as she got closer, in her face. She'd tried putting on lipstick, but it looked as futile as a painted-on smile — too bright and artificial against the pale sorrow of her skin.

'Ella, honey . . . I'm sorry about Paige. I tried to call you. Did you get my message?'

I shook my head. Elbow was the Bermuda Triangle of cell phone reception.

She took a deep breath. 'Auntie Sophia had one of her episodes. I didn't know what to do. Paige offered and I — '

'It's okay.' I shrugged. 'It's okay.'

'She — Paige — seems so different now.'

'Different how?'

'So . . . capable. She was whiny. Spoiled. She drove me crazy. She was no mother at all — all she did was whine and complain and mope around. Certainly no wife to Joseph.'

His name came out like a squeak. She said, 'Oh no. I wasn't going to do this. I'm sorry, honey. You have your own tears.'

I put my arm around her. 'You,' I said, 'of all people, are entitled to cry. We're going to get through this. Come on. Let's eat.'

She patted my hand. 'You sound so Italian when you say that.'

★　★　★

Marcella had brought minestrone and I made a salad with the lettuce from our garden — one

61

thing I'd picked and managed not to trample into the ground. Joe's dad came over too, carrying a warm loaf of cheese bread from the bakery in Freestone. When the subject of the store came up, I got busy putting ice in Zach's soup.

'One thing about our son,' Joe said. 'We were proud of the way he carried on that store. In this day and age, it's not easy. Those big-box stores. Everybody's gotta have fifty rolls of toilet paper just because it's cheaper? Then they gotta build bigger houses to hold all that toilet paper? All those tree huggers living in these parts should know better. They put solar panels on their goddamn mansions.'

'Joseph. Your grandchildren.'

'It's craziness. But Capozzi's lives on.' He poured more wine. 'Not many years after my father opened, we almost lost his store.' He and Marcella shared a long look. I knew exactly what he was referring to. The unspoken internment camp. 'But we persevere. I was worried that Joey didn't have what it takes. When he was younger, always off snapping pictures, head in the clouds.' He thumped his chest. 'But he did the right thing. That boy loved my father. He honoured his grandfather's name. Joey made us proud.' Marcella dabbed her eyes with her napkin, and Joe Sr changed the subject, asking Annie what she'd done all day.

Annie looked at me before saying, 'I played with Mama.'

Joe Sr asked, 'In the garden?'

'No . . . not *Mommy*. *Mama*.'

'Mama, Mommy. What's the difference. *Mamma mia*, that's what I say.'

'No, Grandpa. *This* is Mommy.' She poked my shoulder. 'But the other lady is Mama. You know what I mean, silly.'

As much as I loved Marcella's soups, especially her minestrone, each bite sizzled in my stomach, threatening anarchy. And the bread would not go down. Fear had parked itself in the middle of my digestive system.

Marcella said, 'Paige came by today, Grandpa.'

'What the hell for? Oh, for Christ's sake, that woman, if you can even call her — '

'Joseph Capozzi. Stop.'

'Well? That's what he got for marrying a non-Italian.'

'Hey,' I said, 'I'm not Italian, either.'

'Honey, the way you cook and garden and heap love on your kids, you're an honorary Italian. Which is just as good. Almost.' He tore off his bread and chewed, his eyes on me. He reached out and put his rough, calloused hand gently over mine.

★　★　★

After Joe Sr and Marcella left, I put the kids to bed and told my mom I wanted to check on something at the store. The parking lot was still almost full from the two restaurants in town. I wanted to get into the store without seeing or talking to anyone, so I went around back and climbed the stairs before turning on any lights.

I opened and shut the desk drawers, ran my

63

finger over the carved words on the underside of what had then been his father's desk, when Joe and David were bored nine- and seven-year-olds, waiting for their father to quit talking to a customer and close the store for the evening. Joe had shown me the carvings with a penlight, laughing as he told the story. He had used his pocketknife — a recently received Christmas present from their parents that David coveted but had been denied due to his younger status. Joe had carved *Joey's Market*. Two days later, David had got hold of the knife, drawn a line through Joe's name, and carved *Davy's*. And so it went, back and forth numerous times, a lopsided column forming, until they got distracted and started fighting about something else. If tenacity had been the indicator of whose market Capozzi's would become — according to the carvings, at least — the store would have been David's, the last name without a line carved through it.

At first, going through the books was like trying to read Russian, but eventually the message was clear in any language: The store was in worse trouble than I'd thought. It wasn't just the *recently* unpaid bills I'd found in the files. How could I not know this? Joe had refinanced and pulled money out right before we got married. The store was in deep, deep trouble. The last few months had been the most brutal. No wonder he hadn't sent in the application for the new insurance policy.

I knew things had been tough. Joe had discussed some of it with me. But he hadn't told

64

me the whole story. The store was losing money every day and had been for who knew how long? His parents didn't know — I was sure of that. But maybe Joe had told his best friend.

I dialled Frank and Lizzie's number, hoping Lizzie wouldn't answer. Lizzie, of course, answered and, in the middle of my apology, handed the phone to Frank. Frank mumbled a hello.

'Did you know about this?'

'Ella? Do you know what time — '

'Did you? Know about the store?'

'Where are you?'

'Here. At the store.'

'I'll be there. Give me a few minutes.'

I made coffee. The coffeepot said three a.m., and I'd thought it was still only ten or eleven. I tried to think: Frank's face when I'd told him I planned to keep the store. Had he changed the subject? Yes. I remembered. I'd thought it was too difficult for him to picture the store going on without Joe. He'd looked away, asked if Annie was getting excited about starting school, said that Molly had already picked out her Pocahontas lunch box.

I unlocked the front door and let Frank in. He'd pulled on a Giants sweatshirt and his jeans and Uggs. I poured him a cup of coffee.

My teeth chattered, though I wasn't cold. 'Tell me,' I said. 'Did you know about this?'

'What *this* are we talking about?'

'How many *thises* are there?' My voice shook while I tried to keep it low, keep it from screeching.

65

'Look. Back up, Ella. I know you have everything in the world to be upset about. But which exact thing are you talking about?'

I took a breath. 'The store, Frank. The fact that it's going under, and has been. *Way* under.'

'He kept thinking it would turn around, that it was just a slump.'

'Why didn't he tell me how bad it was?'

'Look. Calm down.'

I leaned towards him. 'Do not,' I said, 'tell me to calm down.'

'Financially, you'll be — '

'It's not about the money!' I slumped into the chair. 'He was struggling all alone. I thought that *recently* the store had hit a slump — but he never told me *how* bad it was — unless I just had my head too far up my own ass to see it.' I got up and paced. There was that time he flipped out over Callie's vet bill. That hadn't seemed like him, but I'd shrugged it off. And it was true he'd recently let me in on concerns over the store, but it had been struggling for years. 'How could I have *not* seen this? I loved this man. I talked to him every day, Frank. And his whole business and livelihood is barrelling down the tubes?'

Frank set down his coffee and pulled me into a hug. His chin moved against my shoulder as he spoke, just like when he came to tell me they'd found Joe's body.

'Don't you see?' he said. 'He didn't want to bring that shit home. He felt optimistic that it would turn around. 'People will get tired of driving to Costco,' he said. I told him that was the beauty of Costco; you only had to drive there once a month and you could load up with every little thing you could ever want for at least a month, if not six. He thought business would turn around any day. He didn't want it to interfere with what you guys had at home. He wanted your marriage to be different . . . than, you know, what it was like for him and Paige. Look, don't be mad at Joe. There was a lot of pressure on him to keep that store going.'

Joe had told me that before Grandpa Sergio died, he willed the store to Joe. Sergio said the store would be Joe's to run, and eventually he would also inherit the land it was on when his parents were gone. Joe quit college and his dream of travelling the world as a photojournalist, and returned home to help his dad run the store. Several years later, he bought the cottage that had once been Sergio's and Rosemary's — at a family-discounted price — and married Paige.

'I'm mostly mad at me, for not seeing it. I mean, I have to admit, I got upset when he did try to talk to me about money. I just had no idea how much he wasn't saying.'

He shrugged. 'Everyone's different, I guess. Lizzie would have been on my ass about it every day.' That didn't help. I must have flinched, because then he said, 'But that's just Lizzie. Financially, you'll be fine. My dad's guy Hank fixed Joe up with a sweet life insurance policy. You need to go home and get some sleep.'

I nodded, pressed my lips together. I didn't tell him that sweet policy never quite happened. 'Frank? Thank you. I'm sorry I woke you up and then dumped this all on you.'

'No worries. Come on, I'll walk out with you.'

'You go ahead. I'm going to put stuff away upstairs, and then I'll head home.'

'Promise?'

'Yeah.'

But I went back upstairs and looked through every file again and again. Everything was exactly where it should be; it was just that there were numerous payables files. I drove back home in early morning light and finally felt like I could sleep. I would figure out something.

When I walked into the kitchen, Annie sat on the kitchen counter talking on the phone, clicking her feet together, pink fuzzy socks ricocheting off each other. She giggled. Callie sat alert at my feet, thumping her tail on the floor, hoping doggy treats were in the grocery bags I carried, but they held only the store's books. Joe had always remembered Callie's treats.

Annie said into the phone, 'Okay. I love you too. Bye.'

She hung up. I picked her up off the counter and held her. Her soft tangles of hair tickled my neck. She smelled like the peach girly powder she'd talked me into buying her at Target. My angel of mercy in SpongeBob SquarePants jammies. 'Morning, Glory.'

'Morning, Mommy.'

'Was that Nonna?'

'No.'

'Lucy?'

She shook her head.

'Is this a guessing game?'

She shook her head again.

'Then spill it, buster. Uncle David?'

'No, silly.' She reached up and ruffled the hair on the top of my head, like she was the grown-up. 'It was Mama.'

7

Annie quit ruffling my hair and said, 'What's wrong, Mommy?'

I shook my head and forced the smile that had been refusing to show up and do its job. 'Nothing.'

'You don't like Mama, do you?'

'Well . . . ' I chose my words, plucking a few out of my internal tirade so that *Damn right, I can't stand the sight of her, I don't want her to call you or touch you or know you* got edited down until I strung together 'I don't . . . know her.' *But how could I, when she never visited or even called once in three years? Nice mother. Seems like she couldn't care less* came out 'But . . . she . . . seems . . . nice.' The effect was less than genuine.

But Annie, sweetly, genuinely, held up an honestly hopeful conversation on her end. 'She is very nice. She likes you. I think you could be friends like you and Lucy.' She held both hands out and shrugged, as if to say, *Where's the hard part here?*

'Oh, you do, do you!' I tickled her until she squealed, then set her down. 'How about some breakfast?'

'Zachosaurus!' Annie said, all big sisterly, and ran, then skidded over to Zach, who had just appeared in the kitchen in his fleece-footed jammies, dragging his Bubby and brontosaurus, his hair sticking out like a confused compass. I picked him up and breathed him in. Zacho-saurus. No one ever called him that but Joe and Annie and me. I wondered if Paige would now too.

While the kids gathered eggs and my mom slept, I sat on the back porch drinking more coffee, my mind pinging from the kids to Paige to Joe to the store to our bank account. I looked to the trees. They always calmed me. The redwood grove stood like our own appointed guards; their trunks rose straight and solid from the land, their branches so large, we had seen wild turkeys perched in them. The birds huddled, as big as Labradors, barely able to scrabble up from one branch to the other, letting out shrill laughter that kept startling us, as if a bunch of old British ladies were up there, gossiping. We watched them for hours one winter afternoon, a giant's version of a partridge in a pear tree.

Our oaks were more like wise, arthritic grandparents. If you pulled up a chair and sat awhile and listened, you usually learned something useful. The fruit trees were like our cherished aunties, wearing frilly dresses and an overabundance of perfume in the spring, then by summer, indulging us with their generosity, dropping apples and pears and apricots by the bucketfuls, more than we could ever eat, as if they were saying, *Mangia! Mangia!*

By the time my mom woke up and joined me with her coffee, I felt somewhat better from my group-therapy session with the trees. I wasn't as

71

worried about starving, anyway.

'Wow,' she said. 'I conked out. I didn't even hear you come in last night.' She took a sip from her cup. 'Jelly Bean.' She leaned over and moved a strand of my hair off my face. 'We need to talk. I have to head back tomorrow, and we haven't really had a chance to talk about the insurance and your whole financial picture. I can help you figure it out, but they need me back at the centre the day after tomorrow.'

I didn't tell her that although she had slept, I hadn't, and I was in no shape to discuss what I'd discovered. I hadn't even begun to wrap my mind around the whole situation. And as stoic as she could be about some things, like the time Zach wiped the contents of his diaper all over the crib, systematically covering each wooden slat with baby poop, this little financial dilemma would positively and completely freak her out. My mom worked as a bookkeeper for a nonprofit. She didn't make a lot of money, but she lived simply and, with the help of my dad's life insurance, had managed to never go broke. And so I said, 'It's all fine. I just need to talk to an accountant in the next few weeks.'

She looked at me, sipped her coffee, kept assessing me. 'You're exhausted. Are you sleeping?'

I shrugged, teeter-tottered my hand.

'Why don't you try to rest today, then, and I'll take the kids and go do something. We'll go to Great America or someplace that will exhaust *them*, and then everyone will be in the same boat.'

I was tired. But the kids needed me and I needed them. Their birth mother had begun circling and I didn't know if she was looking for a place to land, or preying, ready to snatch up Annie and Zach, or at best, keeping a distant watch on the nest she'd abandoned years before.

'Let's all go. I want to hang out with you guys.'

'You're going to have plenty of time with Annie and Zach, honey. Puh-lenty. And I'll be back as soon as I can. You need to take care of yourself.'

'I need to be a mom. I can rally. Let me have another three cups of coffee and a shower and I'm there.'

When I came back out, my mom was looking through one of our photo albums, shaking her head. 'You guys really perfected the art of the picnic, didn't you?'

I sat on the arm of the sofa. The only time the kids ever went to theme parks was when grandparents were involved. Joe and I avoided them. But we went on picnics whenever we could. It was something all four of us loved equally, but for different reasons. Joe liked to pursue his photography and still spend time with his family. I was enthralled with all the redwood-lined hiking trails, the abundance of animal and plant life. The kids loved to catch bugs and see if I could name them. Annie kept a little bug, flower, and bird book in which she painstakingly printed each letter I spelled out to her.

And of course, we all loved to eat. These were not your basic PBJ types of picnics. We made salads and spreads using whatever we could from our garden's stash, and I discovered an untapped joy of cooking. We had two kids who would eat anything, so I kept trying new ideas and we'd lie back in the sun and groan at how good everything tasted.

'Honey, would you rather go on a picnic today? It might be easier. We have all that food.'

I shook my head. Going on a picnic without Joe right then would feel like taking a dull knife and cutting a hole through the centre of me . . . and it wouldn't feel any better for Annie and Zach. 'No. Great America it is! Land of the expensive! Home of the brave moms and grandmas! Let's do it.'

★   ★   ★

After that day, whenever my mother and I referred to Great America, we called it Ghastly America — and it wasn't a political statement. It had to do with my lack of sleep and my dead husband and the ninety-five-plus-degree weather and the kids amped up on too much cotton candy and ice cream sandwiches. It had to do with me getting my period, and my body using the occasion to purge my emotions — which suddenly included being extremely pissed off. The heat baked everything, so the only ride that sounded good was the roller coaster called Big Splash. We waited in line for one hour and thirty-five minutes before we realized that Zach was way too short. Annie and my mom went ahead while I stayed behind with Zach, who had

74

a screaming tantrum, not because he couldn't go on the ride so much as because he couldn't go with my mom, whom he'd become more and more attached to during the past week.

Zach had been such a laid-back kid, I had very little experience in how to handle a tantrum like that — he screamed and jumped up and down and then splayed himself on the ground, refusing to get up. A blur of people shook their heads and stared. I stood there, unmoving. What did the experts say? I tried to remember something, anything, from one of the parenting magazines I'd read in the doctor's office. Walk away? Yeah, right. In a crowd of hundreds. Don't give in. Don't reward. But I finally got down and yelled over his screams, 'Zach! Listen! Stop screaming and I'll buy you another cotton candy! Would you like that?' He kept wailing. 'Cotton candy, Zach! Do you hear me?'

He stopped suddenly. He swiped his nose along his arm. 'And a Slushee?'

'And a Slushee.'

He got up and took my hand. I heard one woman say, 'No wonder,' and a man said, 'Way to work the parents, buddy.'

I stood and stuck my face about three inches from the guy's bloated, sweaty one. I said through clenched teeth, 'He no longer has parents, plural, buddy. Because, you see, his father just *died*, buddy.'

We walked away and I didn't look back. I bought Zach another cotton candy and a cherry Slushee and watched his lips turn as red as the rims around his eyes.

While my mom took Zach to a table to finish his treats, I took Annie on the Ferris wheel. Why I thought it might be fun to sit sizzling in a metal basket escapes me now, but that's what we did, and when a disgruntled operator deserted her post, we sat for ten minutes and willed another operator to take over or at least for God to stir up a breeze, or rain. Where was the fog when you needed it? Someone yelled up in a megaphone that a replacement operator would be there shortly. Great. I'd worked in a doctor's office in college, and they trained us to say the doctor will be with you *shortly*, never *in a minute*. *Shortly* was subjective. *Shortly* lacked any concrete commitment.

At first Annie was happy to point out the different rides, enjoying the view, but then she started whining. 'How much longer? I've gotta pee. I'm hungry. I'm hot. I wanna go home.'

I wanted to know: How could someone just walk away and abandon us, leaving us suspended in midair? I'd have to ask Paige about that one. How do you say to your babies and your husband, 'I'm done. Buh-bye,' and never look back? Leave them suspended, unable to move forward until a replacement operator by the name of Ella came up and pushed the right buttons. The replacement mother, the replacement wife. Is that how she saw me? Is that what I was? Is that *all* I was? But after sitting up there for ten minutes, I loved the replacement operator; when she let us off that ride, I wanted to hug her. I said, 'Thank you! We wouldn't have survived another minute without you.' She nodded, looking bored, directing us back into the hordes of people. Annie said, 'Mommy, aren't you being a little *dramatic?*'

Despite our being saved, the day kept on its downward spiral. I shuffled around, squinting. Too bright, too many primary colours, too many loud noises. And one of the loudest? Zach, who threw a tantrum whenever my mother let go of his hand. Her trip to the bathroom cost me a churro and another Slushee — this time grape.

On the way home we got stuck in five o'clock traffic, which, anywhere in the Bay Area or its ever-outstretching vicinities, begins at three o'clock. The kids fought over every toy like wild dogs over a porterhouse, and my mom, who always received compliments on her youthful appearance, looked every one of her sixty-two years and then some. The air-conditioning malfunctioned so that it felt like a person with a high fever was blowing at us through the vents, while in the rearview mirror I watched Annie rip Zach's Bubby from him until my mom screamed, 'Ella! *Stop!*' I slammed on the brakes just in time to stop us from smashing into a yellow Hummer. You know who would have survived that crash. Not us in the Jeep.

I calmly and quietly said to my mother, 'We almost got into an accident. Accidents happen randomly and with no warning. Joe was killed in a drowning accident, and now we could have been killed in a car accident. Just. Like. That.'

'Jelly? Are you okay?'

I shook from top to bottom, and the kids kept right on fighting. I hit the steering wheel with both hands and shouted, 'God*damn* it! I can't *drive*! Now, you two shut up! Shut *up*!'

And they did. No one said another word the entire drive home except the voice in my head, which told me over and over, *You, my dear, are the very worst mother on the planet.*

★ ★ ★

When we pulled up our driveway, Callie loped up to greet us, but the kids were out cold. Annie's cheeks were pink despite the sunscreen I'd covered them with. The side of Zach's face stuck to his car seat; drool ran down his T-shirt, which now held red and purple splotches that coordinated with his lips and chin. The Slushees had left what looked like bruises, but I felt I'd done far worse damage with my own temper tantrum. I could almost see their wings, so angelic were they in sleep, certainly incapable of causing an adult to scream at them at the top of her lungs. I carefully pried Zach from his seat; his arms and legs hung loose and heavy; his head lolled before resting on my shoulder. He let out a long, stuttered sigh. These were my angels who had just lost their dad. Whose birth mother had decided it was okay to poke and prod from a distance, enough to do little more than remind them that she'd left them. And now their evil stepmother had yelled at them for being kids.

We got them settled in their beds and tiptoed out to the kitchen. 'I'm sorry,' I said to my mom.

'For what?'

'You know. For losing it in the car.'

'Well, honey. It's understandable. They were acting up. You're exhausted. Give yourself a break.'

'But they're bound to act up right now.'

'That doesn't mean you let them scream and fight in the car. It was an intense situation. You didn't have time to remind them, 'Use your inside voices and nice words, children.''

'I didn't remind *myself* to use my nice words. I don't remember you ever yelling at me like that.'

'I didn't?' She knit her eyebrows. 'Didn't I? Well, after your dad died, you hardly made a peep. You'd been such a yacker, always into everything, disappearing for hours with that little notebook of yours. You know how the kids started saying 'Why? Why? Why?' when they turned three? You were still asking that all the time, even when you were eight.' She shook her head. 'Such a character, you were. And a handful! But then you got really quiet. All that happy hoopla just drained out of you.'

She stopped talking, pulled a bracelet back and forth over her hand.

We were a pair of skaters trying a new leap, a new twist, but it was time for one of us to pull back into our familiar routine, each of us depending on the other one to stay clear of obstacles or warm spots. 'You'll all get through this.' She smiled. 'I've been where you are. And you've been where they are. And we got through.'

Now she made it sound like it had been easy. Out the window I saw a squirrel stop on our

79

porch railing to inspect some land of pod, turning it in its paws. 'I still think about Dad all the time. All those camping trips on the Olympic Peninsula, how much he taught me in eight short years.' She reached out and squeezed my hand. 'So, Mom, how did you make it through that?'

She opened the refrigerator and took out a bottle of pinot blanc.

'Oh, *that's* how.'

She smiled. 'Tempting, I admit, but no.' She poured us each a glass.

'Actually, at first I did check out, as you probably remember . . . But then I kept thinking about my grandmother. Your great-grandma Just. She waited in Austria while her husband went to America. He said he'd find work and send for her. She waited a year and never heard from him. So she sold every single thing she had and took her two children and got on a boat bound for America. She didn't speak English. She didn't know a soul. I can see her as if I were there: a tiny woman with a braid past her waist, an arm around each child, freezing and miserable, holding on to them for dear life. Can you imagine? Huddled on that ship, bound for the great unknown . . . ' She shook her head and looked at me. 'And when I felt bad about my situation, I drew strength from her.'

'What happened to her?'

'Well. She found him. She actually found him! He'd drunk away everything he'd earned. Penniless, sleeping around, and worse, *violent*. So she kicked him back out and, ironically, set up a moonshine business during Prohibition, and raised those two kids — my mom and Aunt Lily — with a trapdoor covered by a braided rug under the kitchen table. It's the same kitchen table I still have.'

I didn't say anything. I was trying to figure out what part of the story she and I could relate to. Not the secret trapdoor. Not the moonshine business. Not the tiny mother with the two kids on the ship. Not the sneaky drunk husband. Callie barked and I turned to see the squirrel dive for the trunk of an oak and disappear.

'Ella.' My mother held my shoulders. 'We come from a line of strong women. I see that strength in you.'

'Thanks,' I said, our faces only inches away, almost too close to each other, too close to all the unspoken. I could have asked more right then, but I knew better; I'd learned my lesson long ago. I stepped back and picked up my wine, and she did the same. 'Hey, does that mean I get the old pine table? I love that table.'

She raised her glass. 'Not while I'm still breathing you don't.' We clinked our glasses. A wordless toast to another success: once again, we'd talked about my dad without talking about my dad.

8

The next morning I dropped my mom off at the airport shuttle bus, but not before she offered to postpone leaving and get someone else to cover for her at work.

I didn't want her to go. But I knew postponing her departure wasn't going to help us all get to the other side, or wherever the hell we were headed.

And so we drove her to the DoubleTree Inn, where she stepped onto the shuttle bus to the San Francisco airport and I pulled out cookies and juice to distract Zach, who otherwise would have definitely run up and grabbed her. We all waved, and I felt inspired by the fact that Zach's tantrums from the previous day had vanished. I buckled the kids into their car seats and headed home. At a stoplight, I turned to them and said, 'I'm sorry I yelled in the car yesterday. That wasn't a nice way to tell you to stop fighting. I'm sorry. Will you forgive me?'

Zach nodded big exaggerated nods and said, 'Uh-huh, uh-huh, uh-huh.' I'd never heard him do *that* before.

Annie said, 'Of course we forgive you, silly. But if you need a break, now might be a good time for us to visit Mama in Lost Vegas.'

The person in the car behind us honked, and I just made the light as it turned yellow again. Need a break? *That was an odd thing for Annie to say*, I thought, but the kids started singing 'I've Got Sixpence' and seemed almost happy. I didn't want to ruin the moment by drilling her. I just said, 'Annie, believe me, I don't need a break. Being around you and Zach is what I love most in this world.' But the thought niggled at me. Either Paige was asking Annie to visit, or perhaps Annie had come up with the idea all on her own. I wondered what Paige wanted, but I wondered more what Annie wanted. It made sense that she might want to spend time with Paige. But what if Paige built up something with the kids and then pulled her disappearing act again?

We drove up the driveway, past Joe's truck parked in its spot; the empty, hollow house waited, hungry, ready to swallow us whole.

Callie trotted up wagging her tail, but I felt as if we walked on a movie set, and everything was an illusion, and once I got closer and looked and prodded a bit, I'd have to face the truth. Maybe the cute, cosy house was just a cardboard facade. The vibrant garden, plastic and dusty silk. Word had got out that the director had abandoned the film and the studio was pulling out of the financing and there the three of us were, standing outside the pretend door without a script. I unlocked the door anyway, and we went inside.

The screen door slammed behind us. 'Well,' I said. Annie and Zach stood in the not-so-great room and looked at me, expectantly. 'Are you hungry?' I asked. They shook their heads. It was only nine thirty a.m. and my mom had fed us breakfast before she left. The house still smelled of toast and coffee. 'You want to go out and play?' They shook their heads again. Outside, the sun made everything sparkly and phony. The birds sang praises. The birds needed to give it a rest.

'Well,' I said again. I went to the armoire and pulled open the drawer and picked out three movies. *The Sound of Music, Toy Story*, and *Beauty and the Beast*. I walked to my room and closed the blinds and popped in *The Sound of Music* DVD. I took off my jeans and pulled on my sweats. The kids stood as if they were in a stranger's house. Movies were for night; they knew the rules. In the kitchen I made popcorn, then climbed into bed with the bowls. After a few minutes, I patted both sides of the bed. 'Come on.' And then I sang, '*Let's start at the very beginning* . . . ' and they climbed up onto the bed, giggling, plugging their ears. Another family joke Joe had started. Apparently, I didn't have the world's best singing voice.

Zach held Bubby with one hand and took his bowl of popcorn with the other. Callie jumped up and stuck her nose in Annie's bowl, then lay across the foot of the bed, chomping. We didn't get up to answer the phone. We didn't get up to answer the door. 'Shhhh,' I said when we heard a knock, and they stifled their giggles in the pillows. Even Callie agreed not to bark. She just whined and thumped her tail against the mattress and cocked her head at us as if to say, *You know, it could be* him . . .

With Joe's picture gazing at us from the

nightstand, we watched movies and we slept and we watched more movies. For dinner, I ordered a pizza delivered from Pascal's and stuck in *The Little Mermaid*. I almost got up to change it as soon as I remembered that Ariel saved Prince Eric from drowning. But I left it in. It might upset them, but better that it happened when they were with me than somewhere else, like at a friend's house. Or with Paige.

The storm came up. I wrapped my arms around each of them as Prince Eric fell to the bottom of the sea. I wondered again what it had been like for Joe. Had it been like Frank had thought, that he'd hit his head right as he was pulled under, that he didn't even know he would never see us again? I hoped so. I hoped his last frame of reference was the frame through his lens of the rusty ragged sea cliff against deep blue sky, not thoughts of Annie and Zach crying in my arms. When Ariel lifted Prince Eric up, up, up to the surface, and brought him back to life with her beautiful voice, all three of us had tears streaming down our faces. Annie planted her wet cheek into my neck and said, 'I wish mermaids were real.'

I said, 'Yeah, Banannie, me too.'

Zach said, 'If I were King Triton, I would have *ROARED* so that all the fishes and mermaids would lift Daddy back up to the *AIR*! I muchly would.' He laid his head in my lap and I smoothed his hair back. But then Zach started to sob, 'I want my *DADDY*! I want my *DADDY*!' and Annie broke down too, yelling even louder than Zach, the same words, over and over.

I held on tight. I thought of Great-Grandma Just and her two children on that big ship, headed for the great unknown. Eventually Annie's and Zach's yells and tears dissipated, their stuttered breaths evened out, and they finally slept, their small faces streaked with trails of dried salt.

9

The people of Elbow hung up their black clothes one day, and by the next week they were donning red, white, and blue. It was not out of disrespect for Joe, but in many ways in honour of him. In fact, Joe Sr and Marcella upheld their civic duty by being the first to swaddle their porch columns in Fourth of July banners, while the rest of the town soon followed their lead. Elbow does the Fourth of July like New York City does New Year's Eve. And if we keep that exaggerated analogy going, Joe was our own Dick Clark, and the front porch at Capozzi's Market was our own little Times Square. The Beach and Boom Barbeque was a forty-three-year tradition begun by Grandpa Sergio after the war, and it wasn't going to stop now. Yes, the man who had been sent to an internment camp apparently celebrated the Fourth with a vengeance. Joe had told me that it was such a part of their family's and town's tradition, he'd never questioned it.

Lucy found us in the garden. Zach's superheroes were taking over some long-lost planet from their spaceship *Tomato Basket*, and Annie had converted Callie into a horse.

I stretched my back and gave Lucy a hug. 'Your hair's warm,' she said. 'I thought you guys would be in your costumes by now.'

I shrugged. 'It's too weird. I can't even picture it without him.'

'I know. You're going, though, right?'

I nodded.

Annie said, 'I think we should wear our costumes, Mommy.'

'I thought you didn't want to, Banannie.'

'I didn't. But now I do. And I bet Zach does too.'

Zach nodded and did his *uh-huh* thing while he threw Batman into the cucumbers. Since Joe had been the town crier who led the songs and read from the Declaration of Independence, the four of us had dressed up in period costumes every Fourth. Annie and I wore long dresses and bonnets; Zach and Joe had pantaloons and vests and black hats.

David was going to take over the emceeing, so he had already picked up Joe's costume.

'Okay, then,' I said.

'Okay, then.' Annie hopped off Callie. 'Let's get this show on the road, people.' And she led us up to the house to get changed.

* * *

A year ago, I had swayed in the front row, holding Zach on my hip, blowing a plastic kazoo, while my husband stood on the front porch of Capozzi's Market and led the crowd in 'You're a Grand Old Flag' and 'America the Beautiful' and 'Yankee Doodle Dandy'. When he got to the line 'I've got a Yankee Doodle sweetheart, she's my Yankee Doodle joy,' he'd pulled Annie and me and Zach all up onto the porch and twirled us around and around while the crowd cheered and the patched-together band played on. The whole day was one ultra-corny, amateur ode to nostalgia, and I'd loved every minute of it. Can you see me? I was the one leading the march to the beach barbeque as if I were leading a top-university marching band, my happiness twirling up in the treetops and landing obediently in the solid grip of my hand.

None of us could have imagined then that the jovial man who'd sung out, holding his hat to his heart in front of his grandpa Sergio's store, would soon be a part of the history we celebrated. Or that he'd been dancing on the front porch of his hidden failure. Now I languished towards the back, sweating in my long, heavy dress, nodding and smiling to those who offered hugs or squeezed my arm; there was nothing left for any of us to say. I got through the moment of silence held in Joe's honour, and 'Yankee Doodle', but it was when David started us in on 'This Land Is Your Land', and we got to the line, 'From the redwood forest to the river's waters' — those last lyrics Joe had changed to fit Elbow — that tears ran down my cheeks. Lucy handed me a tissue. The tears weren't all sadness, though. Joe was gone. But his land was my land, his town was my town, his kids were my kids. I really had found home when I'd found Joe, and it was my home still.

★   ★   ★

'I'm scared,' I told Lucy later, while we sat on a rock watching Annie and Zach build a sand

89

castle that looked more like a sand Quonset hut, the crowd dispersing to head upriver for the fireworks. Across the river, hungry cries echoed from the large osprey nest on top of a dead tree that Joe had photographed less than a month before. 'I suddenly feel constantly aware of how much I can lose.'

She put her arm around me. 'Most people in your circumstances can't even see anything past what they've already lost.'

'Yeah. But not everyone has them.' I jutted my chin towards the kids. 'I never let myself think like this before. It all feels ridiculously fragile.'

'You *were* kind of la-tee-da,' Lucy admitted. 'I mean, no one's life is quite *that* carefree.'

'What do you mean?'

Lucy blushed. 'I didn't mean . . . well, you know. Nothing. Too much wine and too much sun make me blabber nonsense.'

It stung. La-tee-da? But I didn't want to ask. Maybe Frank had told her about the store. Frank could be a blabbermouth, with or without wine and sun. While Annie and Zach scooped river water into their plastic pails, Callie and a border collie raced down the beach towards the water. 'No!' I called out. But it was too late. They landed smack-dab on top of the kids' sand creation and flattened it.

★　★　★

If Elbow was still my town, Capozzi's Market was now my store, and the bills were now my bills. Julie Langer, one of the school moms,

90

insisted on taking the kids for a play date that Saturday, and so I was left to worry about finances while I dug in my garden.

If only my garden were a true reflection of the workings of my inner soul. All that rich, fertile abundance in precise and ordered rows! No wasted space, no shrivelled stems. And that life-affirming fragrance of clean dirt. I loved the paradox and truth of those two words: *Clean. Dirt.*

I set down my hand weeder and picked up the compost bucket and headed over to the bins. Our compost was the secret to our garden. And the secret to our compost was keeping the moisture down, giving it enough nitrogen and just the right amount of stirring. This batch was heating up nicely and soon would be ready to spread on the garden. I stirred in the coffee grounds, the egg shells, and the rest of the kitchen waste, along with some magical chicken manure. I added dry leaves I'd saved from the fall. Leaves Joe had raked.

The store, the store. What to do about the store? I didn't want to just let it die too. It had been so clear to me on the Fourth that along with being the family's legacy, the store was the heart of our town. Albeit a heart with badly clogged arteries. The tiny town of Elbow could no longer support its own store, and Capozzi's wasn't snazzy enough to bring in the wine connoisseurs and the foodies. But the ever-expanding wine country surrounded us, and tourists flocked. Joe had been bugged that everyone in Sebastopol was chopping down their apple trees and putting in grapes, but after living down south, I'd told him, 'Hey, vineyards beat the heck out of strip malls.' Still it was a change he didn't welcome; he called wine country *whine* country.

I turned the compost, dark as coffee. What did I know about running a store? Absolutely nothing. I could go on with my plan to start working in the fall as a guide. I'd just have to see if they could hire me fulltime instead of part-time. Did they even hire full-time guides? And then I'd need to hire a babysitter for Annie and Zach, when they got home in the afternoons. But what would become of Capozzi's Market? A vacant, cobweb-infested eyesore, the retro sign hanging by its corner, the screen door banging off its hinges while children dared each other to run up to touch the front step, scared by tales of lurking ghosts? If we could somehow save it . . . with the family's help . . . maybe Gina could keep filling in . . . David and Marcella might be able to work some hours . . . then I'd have more flexibility. Annie and Zach could hang out sometimes in the afternoons, do their homework in the office and help when they got a little older, like Joe and David had. I added more leaves. But hello? The store was not making it. It was as withered as the oak leaves I stirred into the compost.

Joe's meal scraps were in there too, decomposing and reincarnating. The last bagel, the last banana peel. The scraps from our last picnic together. I turned the shovel, full of compost. God, he loved those picnics.

He used to say that he wanted to bring back the picnic, that this area was founded on the pleasure of picnics.

That wasn't how it happened, exactly, but I liked the sound of it, and there was some truth to it: Whites first came to the region not to lay out a blanket under the redwoods but to chop them down. And yet, a hundred or so years ago, San Franciscans started building summer cabins and houses by the river so they could come up to picnic and swim.

There was an old photograph at the Elbow Inn of a group, the women wearing high-necked dresses with long skirts, the men wearing hats and suspenders and trousers, everyone relaxing on a huge blanket — or looking like they were *trying* to relax as much as possible in those getups — with a spread of food out before them.

The store had once offered 'Everything Italia' . . . before the wartime paranoia set in. But now, all these decades later, everyone adored Italian everything — art, food, wine, lifestyle. Dining alfresco, outdoors. Using the freshest ingredients. Growing your own garden. Slow food as opposed to fast food. The whole slower food and farm-to-table way of eating that I believed in had even sprung from Italy, jumped an ocean and a continent, and landed in Sonoma County. I knew the rest of the country would eventually catch on, but so many people in Elbow, and the surrounding communities like Sebastopol, which people referred to as Berkeley North, already ate organic foods and supported local farmers.

And then I saw it. I saw the store, the same,

but different, and wholly formed. I could even hear the bell on the creaky door, ringing on and on, as a steady line of customers came and left with full arms, full baskets, the chiming becoming incessant, like blessed church bells, clamouring on about resurrection and new life.

'Holy shit!' I shouted. That might just be the answer. I dropped the lid on the bin, pulled off my gloves, and ran up to the house. It was a crazy idea. But it might just work. I needed to call David. I needed to call Lucy. I probably needed to call a psychiatrist.

10

' 'Life's a Picnic'? Isn't that a bit ironic, considering the circumstances?' Lucy stood at my kitchen counter, pouring a glass of wine each for David and me, a smooth pinot noir from her vineyard in Sebastopol. The label now had a black Scotty terrier catching a red Frisbee against a white background. I loved the label. Wineries were getting so creative all of a sudden. So why shouldn't grocery stores too?

David said, 'Another lemonade-out-of-lemons story?'

'Exactly,' I said. 'Only we've got sandwiches to go with that lemonade, and salads and spreads . . . all made from local organic vegetables, of course, and gorgeous picnic baskets and maps and blankets.' I sounded like an overly zealous radio announcer, but I needed both of them to think it could work. And I needed David to help me *make* it work.

Lucy and David were my closest friends. Long before I met them, they'd attempted to sleep together. They were in high school, back when David was still trying to convince himself he was straight. He told me all his doubts had been erased that night; if Lucy couldn't do it for him, with her long black lashes, alabaster skin, and downright amazing breasts, no woman could. Lucy, on the other hand, told me she planned to stay single until George Clooney proposed to her.

Lucy sat on the couch and said, 'Before I forget, you both have to come see the vineyard again. It's magical right now. Absolutely . . . Okay, Ella, you were saying? Lemons?'

David swirled the pinot noir in his glass and raised it to the light. 'A crisp, vibrant mouthfeel. Blackberries and rhubarb lingering in a long finish. Yes. The vanilla and spices add lovely complexity. Exceptional, really, Lucy.'

'Oh God,' I said. He could be such a lovable snob.

'I feel more comfortable if you just call me David.' He spread his fingers, examining his nails. 'I can almost see this . . . picnics in the orchards, the vineyards, the redwoods, by the river, along the coast, we have it all. We team up with other businesses, inviting weekenders to come up and stay at the Elbow Inn, have a family-style dinner at Pascal's or Scalini's, and have an incredible picnic in the natural setting of your choice. It's not just about going wine tasting anymore . . . But it's a long shot, El. And it sounds expensive.'

I had called them, spilling over with ideas to transform Capozzi's Market into a store that catered mostly to tourists, a place they could stop and get all the fixings for an incredible picnic. We'd carry things you couldn't get at the box stores. Local artisan organic everything. Heavy on the Italian, but not locked into it; I could also see California cuisine and Pacific Asian influences. We'd have an olive bar and some of Marcella's stuffed sandwiches and salads — from baby beet with orange zest and dandelion greens to old-fashioned potato — that were

96

perfect for picnicking. Bread from the bakery in Freestone, of course. A kick-ass wine selection, with a weekly featured winery hosting tastings on the store premises on Saturdays and Sundays. Lucy's would be the first. I hoped David might be interested in taking on the role of full-time chef. And we'd have detailed, beautifully illustrated maps to the best local picnic spots, by our local recluse artist, Clem Silver, which might take some doing, but I was willing to try.

Yes, the store would be called Life's a Picnic — perhaps a bit tongue in cheek, perhaps a sort of middle finger to fate. Widowhood be damned. Lacking life insurance policy be damned. Collection notices be damned. I was going to figure out a way to do this. Plus, I was afraid to go off to a job when Paige was lurking around every corner. I needed to be able to work and have the kids close. Saving the store felt necessary in so many ways, some of which I was afraid to articulate to myself, let alone to Lucy and David.

He stared at his empty wineglass. As I reached for the bottle to pour him more, he said, 'I get it. Earthy sophistication. What this area's known for. Fine wine. Hemp picnic blankets. Caviar and alfalfa sprouts. But I don't know . . . I'm not really big into starvation. Do you think it would actually make, you know, *money?*' he asked. 'Oops.'

I followed his gaze out of the window to see a mouse dashing across the porch railing. In broad daylight.

'You need a kitty cat.'

'David. I do not need a cat right now. It's one little mouse.'

97

'Honey, they multiply.' He stared at me, but I didn't respond. He sighed. 'The knowledge of which seems to do nothing beneficial for us today but provides the perfect segue: We'll need to talk numbers.' David and Lucy were both good with numbers. Lucy had just bought a vineyard with a boutique winery. David had been a media buyer for an ad agency in San Francisco. But Gil had sold his dot-com company, happily retired, and now volunteered at the animal shelter. They'd bought a beautiful house up the river. David quickly grew tired of the two-hour commute, quit his job, and was looking for something local, but it wasn't like the area was teeming with ad agencies.

Everyone knew he needed something to do. At Easter, Gil had pulled me aside and said, 'I've gained nine pounds this month. He's cooking three gourmet meals followed by dessert — yes, dessert even after breakfast — every fucking day. The man needs a job.' Now I had just the job for the man. If I could convince him it was a good idea.

I smiled, trying to exude confidence. 'Yes, we can make money. You've got connections. You could have us in every wine and foodie rag on the West Coast.'

He nodded. Swirled his glass. 'You know Joe. He was such a purist about that store. He hated anything touristy.'

'I know. But that attitude was making us pure broke.'

Lucy said, 'She's got a point.'

'And this would be classy, David, not tacky — but not uppity, either. The food would be local and from scratch. With a big nod to what Grandpa Sergio started. Joe would like that.'

Lucy stood. 'Unfortunately, I'm tapped out moneywise right now with the vineyard. But I think this idea is spot-on. And I want to help every other way I can.' She came over and hugged me.

David finished off his last sip of wine. 'I don't know.'

'Aw, come on, David,' I teased. 'Didn't you always want the store when you were kids? Wasn't there a bit of sibling rivalry going on there? You know, *Davy's Market?*'

David's face took on the colour of the pomegranates I'd set in a bowl on the counter. 'What, when I was, like, five? I outgrew that obsession around the same time I quit wearing my Winnie-the-Pooh undies because Joe called them my Poo Pants.' He stood up. 'I'll think about it. And I'll need to see the financial information in black-and-white.'

You mean red? I almost asked, but didn't.

★   ★   ★

The rest of the week, while I wrote fourteen measly checks accompanied by notes that promised I'd send more as soon as possible, I tried to think of ways to convince David that the picnic store was a good idea. Sure, it was a little touristy for Joe's taste, but he'd mentioned how he wished he could somehow regain the original charm of Grandpa Sergio's store. And Joe would appreciate the ode to our picnics.

I had to convince David that this was a way to pay homage to that history, keep the store running, and make it profitable too. I needed David. I could cook up a storm for my family, but he could take it to a whole other level, and I obviously had some things to learn about the money side of a business. I felt desperate, and I still hadn't mentioned the life insurance problem, not to anyone.

I would definitely need the family to get on board. And that meant disclosing to everyone just how bad things were financially. I knew I should have already come clean, but it seemed like a betrayal. I needed to talk to Joe.

One night I picked up the phone and dialled the number at the store. I had done it before, many times, just to hear his voice, to hear him say, 'Thanks for calling Capozzi's Market. We're tied up with customers right now. Leave a message and we'll get back to you.'

But this was different. This time, I actually called to *talk* to him. Some part of me, my arm and fingers at least, momentarily forgot that Joe was dead, and picked up the phone and dialled his number so I could say, *Honey, what should I do? Come home, have dinner — I made lentil soup — and we'll figure this mess out. Oh, and can you bring some coffee?*

When the answering machine picked up, his voice knocked me into the present. I hung up the phone, then checked it. The dial tone, flat and lifeless, droned through my ear, through my head, my throat, my heart. Changing the store would mean changing the answering-machine recording, something I hadn't been able to bring myself to do.

★　★　★

The next week David, Lucy and I were out touring her vineyard, walking up the hill between the rows, the vines like outstretched arms greeting us in the late afternoon sun. Lucy was in love with this spot of earth and excited to share it in all its phases. She wore work boots and a broad-brimmed hat, tenderly touching the grapes and vines as she talked.

'The pinot noir grapes are starting to change from green to purple. If you look closely enough, each grape displays a different intensity of colour. Aren't they gorgeous?' She told us the process was called verasion. This was also the time in the growing season for stripping away some of the leaves in order to control the canopy. 'The more sun these lovelies get, the drier and more flavourful they'll be. By fall they'll be perfectly plump and ready for crush.' She mentioned *terroir*, the big buzzword among vintners and winemakers that was constantly debated.

'Terroir is that sense of place that you experience when you drink a glass of wine. This hillside has a history.' Lucy held her hands out as if she were giving a blessing. 'There is the climate, even the certain way the sunlight slants against this hill. And the geology — the layers upon layers of rock and volcanic ash from millions of years ago. The parent materials break down to make the soil what it is today, its mineralogy, the chemical balance.'

'I have one of those,' David said. 'Oh, wait, mine is a chemical *im*balance. My mistake, go on.'

Lucy rolled her eyes. 'As I was saying . . . terroir is the expression of the land the grapes come from. Others say terroir is about viticulture, the influence on the grape. It's the way the vines are hand pruned, the type of barrels, the whole winemaking process as well. And some say it's everything — from what occurred here throughout the ages to the moment the bottle is uncorked.'

'I've always thought,' I said, 'this might sound strange — but Annie and Zach, this place, Elbow, permeates them. I always want to breathe them in. It must be their terroir.'

Lucy said, 'The terroir of people? I can hear all the debating they'll get out of this one. Do go on.'

'It's . . . I can smell the land, this place, in their hair, in the creases of their necks, and on their fingertips. This wonderful loamy scent mixed with wood smoke, the tanoak and redwoods, the rosemary, the lavender. And okay, a little garlic from being at Marcella's . . . I don't know. It sounds funny when I try to explain it.'

David patted my back. 'Nothing a little bathing wouldn't fix.'

'Ha-ha. Very funny.'

'No,' he said. 'I actually get what you're saying. And I could even take it a step further. I've been thinking about your idea for the store.'

'Yeah?'

'Grandpa Sergio died years ago, but that grocery store still smells like him when I walk in the door — it's faint, but it's always there. Especially up in the office. His cherry tobacco pipe smoke. And it's mixed with Pop's Old Spice.'

'Nothing opening a window wouldn't fix,' Lucy said.

'Touché.' He shook his head. 'But no, that wouldn't get rid of it. Nothing will. Even changing the store, even remodelling it and turning it into a slightly different kind of store — it will still be Capozzi's Market. You'll still be able to feel the family *history* when you walk in. Maybe even more so with the big nod to the mother country, as Grandpa used to call it. That's what's important. If we don't try Ella's idea, we're probably going to have to let the place go and lose everything my grandfather, my dad, and my brother worked for all these years.'

I was afraid to say anything. Some kind of spell seemed to be on us there on that symmetrically furrowed hillside, surrounded by old gnarled vines and young grapes.

'Change can be good. You know, I always told Joe to quit fighting the tourist thing. To *celebrate* it. But I was just the baby of the family, not anyone who'd ever run the store. Grandpa made that clear,' David finally said. 'I still want to talk numbers. But I think you might be onto something, Ella. Let's talk about what you would need from me. I think I want a place at this picnic.'

I grabbed the both of them and let out a

victory holler. We ambled arm in arm down the hill to the small stone winery to celebrate. Despite the fact that now we had to talk numbers.

Lucy poured wine. We toasted to terroir, to Life's a Picnic. I told them about my life insurance problem. I also explained just how bad I thought the store's financial situation was. I could see them both *not gasping* as if their lives depended on it. Lucy poured more wine. David drummed his fingers and made a ticking sound with his tongue — a habit of his whenever he was thinking something through. I usually only noticed it when we were on the phone, but at that point in the evening David's tongue ticking was the only sound in the room.

Finally he said, 'Let me break the news gently to the folks, about the store and about the insurance. I know why Joe didn't fess up to Dad.' He seemed far away. 'Because he was always trying to make him and Grandpa proud. We both were. Even me with my desperate lack of Italian machismo. My dad seems to still desperately need that . . . pride in the store, pride in his father, pride in us.' His eyes filled and he stood up. 'In his two sons.'

11

The next morning while I washed dishes, I felt a tug on the leg of my jeans and looked down to see Zach staring up at me, sucking his thumb and holding Bubby, rubbing the turquoise satin of the bunny ears on his cheek.

'What, honey?'

He started swatting Bubby against the kitchen drawers. I turned off the water and knelt down. 'What is it, Zachosaurus?'

He sighed. 'When is Daddy coming home?'

'Oh, honey.' I hugged him. 'Daddy died. Remember? Daddy's not coming home.'

'I know. But *when* is he coming *back*?'

'He's not coming back.'

'When I'm a big boy?'

I shook my head. 'No. Not when you're a big boy.'

'That mama lady came back.'

'She did. But she didn't die. She just lives somewhere else and came to visit. Do you understand the difference?'

He nodded and sighed again. 'Can I have a oatmeal bar? A whole one?'

'Sure. But do you understand about Daddy?'

He started flipping Bubby up and down and doing a silly dance, saying 'Uh-huh, uh-huh, uh-huh, uh-huh, uh-huh! And some milk. Pleeeeeeeze.'

The now familiar *uh-huh* song, which had

started shortly after Joe died, seemed to be Zach's way of saying that he was done talking for the time being. He was three and having trouble understanding. Hell, I was thirty-five and still didn't get it some days. But I wished I knew how to help him.

★ ★ ★

Later that afternoon, Paige called and said something that shocked me, her words like big flashing signs emerging from the fog, finally telling me where we were headed if we continued down that road. She would often call to speak to Annie. I'd wanted to question Paige, but I could never get out the words; I always felt a physical barrier, as if something lay lodged in my throat, blocking any questions that carried the possibility of ruining our world. But that day when she called, I took a deep breath and squeezed out some words, asking her what her intentions were. I sounded like some grumpy father questioning a teenage boy about dating his daughter, which hadn't been *my* intention, but my own anxiety clamouring out.

'My intentions?' Paige asked. 'I beg your pardon? I'm Annie's mother. And I would like to speak to my daughter.'

I took another deep breath. 'Yes, I understand that you gave birth to Annie. But you've been gone a long time, and Paige, I'm just worried about Annie getting hurt.'

'Really? If you're so worried about hurting Annie, perhaps you should be more careful when

106

you drive so you don't almost cause a car accident and then scream obscenities at my children.'

I opened my mouth. No words would come out, but my heart beat so loudly, she could probably hear it echoing up through my throat.

She continued. 'Please put Annie on the line. Or do I need a court order?'

A court order? Did she say a court order? 'Paige, I just — Okay, I'll get her.'

What did she want? What did she *want*? Part of me understood that a relationship with Paige could be good for Annie. But part of me was scared of what that might mean for Annie and me and Zach. And what if, once they'd got used to her, Paige vanished into thin air again?

Still, she was Annie and Zach's mother — their birth mother, at least — and if knowing her did make them feel more secure in this world, and if she was serious about not disappearing again, that was far more important than any jealous, territorial feelings of mine. That's what I kept telling myself, anyway, as it became difficult to take a deep enough breath, which had been happening more and more often. Especially around two in the morning. *Breathe in.*

Paige. The kids. The bills. The store. Tomorrow. The next day.

Breathe out.

'Mommy?' Annie said behind me. 'Why are you blowing so much noise and letting out such big long breaths?'

I turned to her. She was six, but she'd matured

107

so much in the last few months. She'd had to. I didn't want to ask her, but the words came out before I could clamp my mouth shut.

'Banannie? Did you tell your mama about our trip to Great America?'

She nodded, big nods so her ponytail flipped up and down.

'What did you say?'

'I told her about the rides and how fun it was except for the Ferris wheel and how we got stuck up there forever.' She laughed, but it was a nervous laugh. 'Remember that?'

'I do.'

She stuck her hands in her pockets.

'What, Mommy?'

'Did you mention, possibly, that we almost got in an accident?'

The big head nod again. 'That was scary! Remember how the tires screeched?'

'I do.'

'Why do you sound so funny?'

'Annie? Did you mention that I yelled at you and Zach?'

Annie started whimpering and nodding, barely now, her chin tucked into her chest.

'Honey, it's okay. You're not in trouble. I just need to know.'

'She was asking me and asking me! She kept asking me questions and you and Daddy told me *always* tell the truth, no matter what. So I did. You did say the G-D word Grandpa always says before Grandma gets mad at him. Remember?'

I couldn't help but smile. Even though fear pulsed through me. 'I do, though I'm trying like crazy to forget. I'd kinda hoped you'd forgotten.'

'Nope. I remember it perfectly. You know' — she tapped her forehead — 'elephant memory. You said, 'You kids shut up! I can't goddamn drive!' And you hit the steering wheel really hard. And then you held your hand and said, 'Ow.' Did I do something wrong, Mommy?'

'No, sweetie. You didn't do anything wrong, I did.' *And Paige*, I thought but didn't say. Grilling Annie to get information. Shame on her. But then, I'd done the same thing by asking Annie about it. Shame on me.

12

Despite the scare from Paige, I pressed on. We called a family meeting. David had already filled Joe Sr and Marcella in on both my idea for the store and the financial situation. Joe Sr cut to the chase: 'Ella, you listen to me. This family has been through hard times before. Shortly after my papa opened Capozzi's, he had to go away, due to circumstances beyond his control. But this town, it pulled together and helped my mama, and the store, and our family survived. This store is my papa's, our family's legacy. And it will go to Annie and Zach someday.' He grabbed both my shoulders and looked me straight in the eye. 'Mother and I will do whatever we can to help save the store. We've got some money socked away for a rainy day. We'll help you remodel it. It's for our grandchildren. What grandparent can say no to that?'

If only Joe had known that's how his dad would react.

One thing Joe and I had managed to get right was our wills. We'd written them up when we got married, and he willed the store to me, with the understanding that I would be taking care of Annie and Zach if anything should happen to him. Now I agreed to invest most of the insurance proceeds and to sell an interest in the store to Marcella, Joe Sr, and David. In return, they would kick in money, and we'd remodel and add a commercial kitchen. Things would be tight for a while, no one was going to be making big bucks, but we were all willing to think of it as an investment.

Besides, everyone agreed that we *all* needed a big project, that we would do it to honour Joe. David patted Marcella's arm and said, 'I'd be honoured to be the chef, but only with Ma's help.' Marcella beamed — the happiest I'd seen her since before we'd lost Joe.

★   ★   ★

I wanted Annie and Zach to be in on the plans, so a few days after we settled everything, I took them on a picnic.

When Joe was alive, he was always the planner, the one who'd come home and say, 'Let's go,' always an element of surprise along the way. He loved to surprise us, to surprise just me sometimes too. He arranged for the kids to stay with his parents and made reservations at a bed-and-breakfast up in Mendocino or had the truck packed for camping. I'd never see it coming. His surprises had a kaleidoscope quality to them, revealing something new at each turn. A drive turned into a stop at an inn, which turned into dinner, which turned into an overnight, which turned into a weekend away, with picnics and packed clothes and books and thermoses of hot tea. He didn't plan expensive trips — he knew the owners, or Joe Sr did, or they were related in some way that always meant big discounts and extra desserts. The few times I'd tried to surprise him, I'd accidentally leave some clue — a phone number lying on the counter, or a message on the machine from the camera store. But he always covered his tracks. Once I'd joked, 'You cover your tracks way too well. You better not ever have an affair.'

I unbuckled Zach from his car seat, still thinking about how carefully Joe planned his surprises, how much I'd loved that about him, and how at the time, I'd known that was one thing that made our romance possible, even though it grew in the midst of needy young children. Surprise dates. Time alone. Knowing he cared enough to plan. Me, distracted enough to surprise. Distracted enough to think everything was okay, even when it wasn't.

Now it was my job to plan the outings and fix the things I hadn't noticed. Callie led us down the path into Quilted Woods, a place sacred to Joe and me, and one I wouldn't include on the picnic map. It was private property, but the owners didn't mind if the locals used it. They'd even built a wooden platform for people to give performances or have weddings under the redwoods.

I loved the way redwoods grow in circular groves, reproducing through 'suckers' — shoots that root in the ground and form new trees — which draw nourishment from the mother tree, even from its roots after the tree is long gone . . . hundreds, even thousands of years. And yet, if you were to take the younger shoots away from the mother tree and attempt to replant them, they would most likely wither and die.

The kids ran up to the stage area while I

112

spread the blanket in a clearing. The redwoods canopied a forest of Douglas fir, western hemlock, tanbark oak. Moss carpeted the rocks and fallen trunks, and a rich array of plant life — ferns, bleeding hearts, oxalis, wild ginger, to name a few — spread between them. Once, when no one was around and we'd drunk a little wine, Joe and I had made love in these woods. I'd worn a long skirt, which I kept on, lowering myself onto him. He unbuttoned my shirt, and I remembered how warm and buttery the slant of sun and his hands felt on my nipples, how hard and full and slow he was inside me. Now I felt a pull I hadn't felt since he'd died.

A bird, a mama killdeer, white-breasted with dark rings like necklaces, had seen me and was pretending to have a broken wing. She'd take a few tiny steps, dragging her wing on the ground. Then take a few more steps. What an actress. Her babies must have been close by, and she was doing a great job distracting me. I wish it could be that simple with Paige. Just pretend I broke my arm and then she'd somehow completely forget about the kids.

The kids.

I jumped up. Annie and Zach were gone. I looked towards the bridge, where they liked to throw sticks and run to the other side to watch them rush by. They weren't there, either. And what about Callie? I called out, but no one answered. The creek wasn't deep enough for them to slip in and drown — was it? I started to run, to call their names. Callie didn't even bark a response.

I found them too far past the bridge. How long had I been thinking about making love with Joe? Watching the killdeer? They were throwing handfuls of blackberries up in the air, yelling, 'Here you go! Here you go!' and laughing wildly.

'What in the world are you doing?' My fear and ready reprimand dissolved. Besides, I didn't want Annie to realize I'd lost track of them and then tell Paige. But what were they doing? Even Callie sat watching them, cocking her head in wonderment.

They kept snatching more off the bush, oblivious to the thorns, the juice and blood from their scratches mixing in tiny rivulets down their arms. Annie laughed again. 'Don't you know? We're sending Daddy berries.'

'To heaven!' Zach yelled. 'And someday I'm going to go to heaven to visit him! On Thomas the Tank Engine!'

'Actually,' Annie said, stopping to aim her grin directly at me. 'We're sending him *Rubus fruticosus*.' It was one of the first Latin plant names my father had taught me. And I had taught Annie. And like me, she had a knack for remembering.

★ ★ ★

Later, as we ate lunch, I told them how we were going to make the store a place to get picnic baskets and good lunches and games. I reminded them how Daddy's grandpa had built the store, how it had been in the family, and told them how it was ours and Uncle David's and Nonna's and Nonno's. That we would always remember Daddy whenever we were at the store. That now they were going to be a big part of it too, because I would need their help, and that someday it would be theirs, if they wanted it when they grew up.

'Daddy loved picnics,' Annie said.

'Yes, he did.'

'Daddy was the picnic *CRUSADER*!' Zach said, bolting up, while I reached out to keep a couple of cups from spilling all over our lunch spread.

'Yes, he was.'

'Mommy?' he asked. 'I want to be a picnic crusader too. Can I use this picnic blanket for a cape?'

'No, bud. You can't.'

'Because our stuff is all over it?'

'That's exactly why. You are one smart crusader.'

'Even without my cape?'

'Even without your cape.'

★   ★   ★

The overhaul of Capozzi's Market began immediately. The whole family joined us — all the aunts and uncles and cousins. The next weekend, close to everyone in Elbow turned out. I hauled away boxes of canned goods and disassembled shelving until my arms and legs and back throbbed, and then woke up the next day and did it again. Frank helped a crew working on a greenhouse-type addition at the

115

back of the store for the winter months, when the rain would deter even the most diehard picnickers.

Frank told me he was looking forward to having his coffee by the fire in the mornings. We stared at each other for a long moment, his eyes saying how much he missed Joe. I hadn't seen him enough since Joe died; he'd come by a few times, but it had just felt awkward and sad, both of us lonely for the same person, neither of us able to be that person for the other. Lizzie even stopped by with a big cooler full of drinks and snacks. She nodded in my direction but talked to David, not me, then slipped back out, waving to and hugging one person after another. I wondered if she'd talked to Paige, if they'd mocked my *What are your intentions?* question.

But Paige had called Annie only a few times since our conversation, and I hoped that she might be pulling back a bit. At least I kept telling myself that she was.

★ ★ ★

At first, the fact that we were taking apart Joe's store lay thick and cold as the morning fog, and we moved hesitantly, quietly. Me wondering: Why didn't we do this a long time ago, together? Why did Joe have to die before we fixed this? But the mood lightened when I began to feel Joe cheering us on. I saw what it must have been like for him to feel it slipping away, that it had begun to represent failure and that perhaps from wherever he was now, he might be relieved.

116

Maybe even proud.

I was taking down the family photographs when Joe Sr came up and said, 'Where are you going to put those?'

'I'm not sure, but definitely in a prominent place. Where do you think they should go?'

He took one from me. It was an old black-and-white. Someone had written in black in the corner, *Capozzi's Market, 1942*. Grandma Rosemary stood with two boys in front of the store.

'Which one was you?' I asked.

He pointed to the youngest, a boy of about seven or eight wearing a tilted cap and a smudge on his face. The other boy looked like a teenager. 'I didn't know you had an older brother.'

He nodded. 'He died in the war. Fighting for this country.'

'I'm sorry. That must have been hard.' He nodded again, still staring at the photograph. 'Hey, where's Grandpa Sergio? Is he taking the picture?'

He shook his head. 'No. He gave his son to fight against Italy, but he wasn't a citizen yet, so . . .'

I held up another photo, also dated 1942. 'He's not in this one, either.'

'No, honey. My papa wasn't around when those pictures were taken . . . Like I've said, he had to go away for a while.' These photos were taken when he was in the camps. I knew but I didn't ask. And with that, Joe Sr handed back the photo and turned and walked out the door. I understood. I'd grown up in a family that didn't talk about certain things, and I felt most at home not asking the questions.

I shuffled through the frames until I came to one, taken later, on the same front porch, with Sergio, Joe Sr, and Joe, as a toddler. Joe's arms were up, as if he were about to call a touchdown. Both men smiled down at him.

★　★　★

I forced myself to get up in the morning to do not only the things I needed to do, but also some of the things I loved. I fulfilled my duties at the store and spent time with Annie and Zach. Sometimes, in moments that felt a bit like grace, I combined the two, having them help me with restocking, deciding what picnic spots would be featured on the Life's a Picnic map, which Clem Silver had agreed to draw; he'd even ventured down to the store for a meeting.

At the store, I kept pulling out craft projects for the kids, and in between sanding and painting and hammering, I'd sit down to join them. I found an odd satisfaction in making messes and cleaning them up. I tried to keep my mind clear of anything but the task at hand, whether it was mixing shrimp and mango curry salad or deciding on a pattern for a beaded necklace, then following it exactly: two blue wooden beads followed by three green glass beads followed by one silver. No surprises. As predictable as the minutes ticking by. Until the time I pulled too hard and the string broke, scattering beads under the refrigerator case so that I could retrieve only enough to make a bracelet. And I remembered that even time — especially time — was far from predictable.

We worked in the garden too — harvesting more vegetables than we could ever use. I took bags of artichokes, tomatoes, basil, and more to Marcella and David, who added them to our menu creations.

I made juice Popsicles for Annie and Zach like my mom had made for me, in her old Tupperware Popsicle mould. I even filled Dixie cups with a Milk-Bone and chicken bouillon and froze them for Callie. I was on top of things in a way I never had been. Certainly, I assured myself, in a way Paige had never been and never could be. I was the poster woman for the perfect widow/mother/store saver/dog lover.

But then something would remind me that I really wasn't all that.

*　★　★*

One day I opened the freezer to find Zach's action figure frozen in a plastic cup of solid ice. Batman lay cold, masked, unmoving, his right arm reaching out for me, urging me to set him free. Zach ran in, sweaty and smudged, asking for apple juice. I held out the human Popsicle, and he said, 'Mr Freeze zapped him.' For days, whenever I opened the freezer, I found another victim of Mr Freeze's in a pie plate or plastic container: Spider-Man, Superman, Robin; apparently even villains like the Joker and Catwoman could not dodge Mr Freeze's ice machine.

119

I left them, but soon there was no room in the freezer. 'Zach,' I said. 'Honey? What do you want to do with all these frozen guys? We don't have any room.'

He shrugged. '*I* can't do anything. Dr Solar has to rescue them.'

I asked him when he thought Dr Solar might show up.

He looked out at the fogless morning. 'Today probably.'

Later, as I hung up clothes on the line, admiring how Grandma Rosemary had held it all together with Sergio gone — part of me tempted to pretend Joe was unfairly locked behind a chain-link fence with barbed wire instead of under a headstone — I heard Zach let out a scream that gave me goose bumps, even in the warm sunshine. I ran up to the house. Zach stood on the back porch, face red, tears streaming.

'Look what you made me do!' he wailed.

On the porch, in the direct sun, were the seven plastic containers Zach had lined up that morning, action figures floating facedown in the melted ice.

'Now they've all *DROWNED*!'

'Oh, honey . . . ' Why hadn't I thought this through?

'And they're *DEAD*! And they're never, ever, ever coming back! Even when I'm a big boy.'

I wanted to save every one of the masked hard bodies, the Caped Crusader, the Boy Wonder. I dumped out the water, pointed out that they all had superhuman powers, anyway, and could defy their untimely deaths. Zach had spent hours

120

playing with them every day, and I wanted him to keep enjoying them. But he insisted on burying them. He wanted to have a funeral for them. And I didn't try to fix this for him, because I couldn't fix the rest.

So I held him while he sobbed, and I helped him bury the plastic bodies out behind the chicken coop. Zach never asked me again when Daddy was coming back.

He began to understand, bit by bit, then more and more, the difference between Joe's death and Paige's departure, and life's never-ending track of good-byes.

13

By mid-September, the kids had started school, and we were ready to reopen the store.

We kept the old CAPOZZI's MARKET sign and, just under it, hung the new sign, LIFE's A PICNIC. There was still plenty of picnic weather during the Indian summer, and then the mostly pleasant fall days before the rains set in. But even in the winter, there would be plenty of sunshine between storms that would be perfect for picnickers. The greenhouse addition would provide a backup spot for when the rainstorms came in the deep of winter, and we also set round cafe tables and chairs on the covered front porch and in one corner of the store, near the woodstove.

Most of the aisles were gone. The deli counter ran along one entire wall. We'd stocked it with an abundance of cold salads — everything from curry chicken to eggplant pasta, and of course Elbow's famous elbow macaroni salad, which was your basic macaroni salad with salami thrown in, but we called it famous because of the Elbow connection. We offered sandwiches of every kind imaginable, including our Stuffed Special, made from hollowed-out bread rounds and filled with layers of meats, cheeses, vegetables, and pesto. Everything was made from scratch with fresh ingredients, locally grown whenever possible, grass-fed beef, free-range chickens, no hormone additives, and a whole lot of organic. I knew enough about biology and growing vegetables that I had become a pesticide paranoid, and I wanted to make sure that I was nourishing our customers, not slowly poisoning them. Yes, it was more expensive to use top-quality ingredients, and yes, our prices reflected that, but my gut — which happened to be fairly healthy, as far as I knew — was telling me people were ready for Life's a Picnic.

* * *

In the centre of the store, Peruvian and Guatemalan picnic baskets of different shapes and sizes were on display. Blankets and tablecloths hung from hooks down the sides. Retro board games of all kinds — Sorry!, Scrabble, checkers, and more — were set out to play; new ones were available to buy. There were four half aisles between the eating area and the deli counter, stocked with wines, crackers, and speciality food items. Behind those were the glass-doored refrigerator cases, stocked with beer, soft drinks, juices, and twelve different kinds of water. Bottled Cokes cooled on ice in the newly restored old-fashioned Coke machine, which I'd unburied from a corner of Marcella and Joe Sr's barn. Joe had always intended to restore it and use it at the market but hadn't got around to it. With my new appreciation for not putting things off until 'someday', I'd called a place in Santa Rosa called Retro Refresh. We'd painted the walls a pale goldenrod that

123

took three tries to get right, but as I stood in the middle of the store the day before we opened, the sun-washed plaster was warm and cheerful and actually made me smile. I stood in the middle of it all, aware that the corners of my mouth both turned *up;* there I was, a smiling fool of a woman about to open a store called Life's a Picnic only a few months after her husband had died. Life's a *trip* was more like it.

We'd sent out press releases to every publication and radio and even TV station within California. Just in case, David had said, it was the slowest news day in history and someone wanted to do a story on us.

The only thing missing was the map of the picnic sites. Clem Silver, who was a nationally recognized illustrator and painter, had said he'd have it ready, but we were opening in less than twenty-four hours, and no one had heard from Clem. The problem was exacerbated by the fact that Clem never answered his phone. When I'd questioned him on that one, he'd said, 'What kind of town recluse answers his phone?' He had a point. Clem *was* known to keep to himself. He lived up in the forest, in the dark shade of the redwoods. He had long white hair he wore in a ponytail, he had long fingernails stained with paint, and he smoked long ladies' cigarettes — Virginia Slims menthol. Apparently, he also took a long time getting his work done.

The door chimed and David and Gil came in carrying boxes and bags with Annie and Zach dragging in metal buckets of kindling to set by the woodstove. Marcella followed with armfuls of hydrangeas. Lucy brought more wine.

I said, 'Lucy, I've got to track down Clem Silver. I know he lives up in the shadies, but I don't know where exactly.'

'Just follow Spiral Road all the way, past the sign that says beware of artist. It's the last house, about a quarter mile past what you'll *think* is the last house.' She pointed to the door. 'You're doing great. I've got the kids and everything here covered. Go.'

'Are you sure? You're dealing with harvest.'

'Crush will go on without me. And I needed a break from jeans and boots and purple stains. Go. And, El? Take your time. Take a break. Please.'

Lucy straightened her cream velvet hat, turned around with a swirl of her long paisley skirt, and called Annie and Zach to help with the tablecloths.

I ducked out the front door, glad to get away for a walk. I headed up the street, passed the tiny postage stamp-size post office and the two restaurants and the Elbow Inn, passed the Nardinis' house and the Longobardis' and the McCants', then crossed the busier road that divided the town of Elbow from the forest.

I walked the steep single-lane Spiral Road, which did, indeed, spiral the hill. The founders of this town had certainly been literal with some of their names. But it was the Southern Pomo Indians who had first referred to this area as the Shady Place. They would set up only temporary camps in the dark redwoods; they preferred to live in the sun-drenched oak-studded hills. The Kashaya Pomo even called themselves 'the

People from the Top of the Land', as if to boast, 'We live in the *nice, sunny* neighbourhood.'

Then the whites started moving in to lumber. After they built the railroad, San Franciscans began taking the train up to fish and play along the river. Some of them built summer homes in the forest, but few lived there yearlong, and that was still true. A lot of people who had houses in the shadies fled to places like Palm Springs for the winter.

I kept walking, taking the hairpin turns and pausing now and then to catch my breath. The houses sat farther and farther apart, the higher I went.

Finally, ahead, a sign that said, sure enough, beware of artist. Farther up I could see a house, but it was not the house I'd expected, not that of a man who rarely cut his hair or his fingernails.

This was a house that had been built with care and concern for every planed piece of wood, for every river rock fitted perfectly in the massive chimney and foundation. It was positioned so that it was never going anywhere. The hill could slide in an avalanche of mud and trunks, but the destruction would likely divide into two forks to go around this house, leaving it untouched. The front door held panes of stained glass and greened copper detailing and was flanked with pots of tiny white flowers trimmed in red, called lipstick salvia. A row of different sized and shaped chimes seemed to stir in their sleep, then settled back into the quiet. I knocked and set off waves of barking from somewhere deep inside.

A raspy voice said, 'Petunia! Pipe down, girl.

No need to get your britches in a bunch, Jerry.'
He opened the door and took a long look at
me. He had on an old Cal sweatshirt, covered in
paint stains, a pair of grey baggy sweats. His
ponytail was draped over his shoulder and lay
like a skinny mink stole down his chest. 'Oh! Ella
Beene! Come in, come in.' He turned and
scuffed down the hallway in lambskin slippers.
The dogs, who had stopped barking, took an
inventory of me too, then, seemingly unim-
pressed, turned to follow Clem. I stepped inside.

It was warm and golden with lamplight.
'Wow,' I said. 'I love your place.'

He turned, pleased. 'Why, thank you. I like it
too.'

'It's beautiful here in the forest.'

He nodded, kept nodding. 'Yes, yes! Makes
you understand how this was all under the sea
three hundred million years ago.' He smiled.
'Wait, I should offer you tea. Or coffee?'

I opted for tea, and while he fixed it, he talked.
'People think I live up here to get away from the
river, because of the flooding and what I went
through as a child.'

'What was that?' I asked.

'Oh . . . I forget you're not from around here
. . . It's an old story. Old, old story. But actually'
— he pulled down a box of tea bags — 'because
of what happened to Joe Jr . . . ' He looked at
me, nodding. 'Yes, I think you might like this
story.'

So Clem Silver told me about the flood of '37,
back when he was a toddler. His family had lived
on the river, three houses down from where

Marcella and Joe Sr lived, where the Palomarinos lived now. Clem wandered off and no one could find him. Everyone evacuated except for his mother and father, who were frantically looking for him. The river rose, and just as his mother picked him up from his study of a spiderweb behind the woodpile, a surge of water broke through and tore him from her arms, passed him downriver, out of her reach, then out of her sight.

'I remember hearing my mother's screams and being afraid, and then my ears and eyes and mouth filled with churning, followed by a beautiful quiet, like I'd never heard before. And up above me, this beautiful beam of light.

'Now, you hear people talk about their near-death experiences, about going towards 'the light' and all that. But in my case, being down in that dark river water, the light was all I saw, all I needed to see, and it led me to the surface, to air, to more years of life — not some heavenly encounter — which suits me just fine.

'But, Ella Beene? I've gotta tell you this: I almost drowned that day, and it was the most peaceful feeling I've ever had. I've been looking for that feeling ever since. And I think that in some peculiar way — and let's face it, I'm peculiar in every way — that's why I settled in this forest. It's the closest thing I can come to being at the bottom of that river.'

'You felt peaceful down there?'

'Yes.' He crossed his arms. 'I know it seems strange, but yes, I did.'

I stared at his grey whiskered chin, his pale

moist eyes. 'Thank you for telling me that story,' I said, looking away, glancing around the room, trying to keep from blubbering. 'And *this* definitely feels peaceful here.'

He said his ex-wife couldn't take the darkness. ' 'You're an artist,' she kept after me. 'Don't you need a light-filled studio?' I guess I was just as stubborn about staying put, a barnacle on a rock. But I appreciate the light that has to push its way through. The contrasts are what interest me the most. I notice the light more here, how it pours down like an elixir. Darkness forces our focus on the relevant, while the irrelevant fades away. How's that for artsy-fartsy talk? Here, Ella Beene, let me show you your map. I imagine this is what you came all this way for.'

I followed him, Petunia and Jerry out to his studio, which was more of the dishevelled shack I'd pictured him living in. There, on his table scattered with paints, old Orange Crush cans, and stuffed ashtrays, was the map.

I held it out before me: a fairy-tale-style treasure map to magical places, in colours and textures that were both natural and luxuriant. 'This is *it*. *This* is going to make the whole concept of Life's a Picnic *work*.'

'So you like it, then?' He chuckled. 'I can go ahead and make the copies?'

'I love it.' I hugged him, this old wizard who smelled of stale cigarettes and turpentine and knew enough alchemy to get inside my head and put on paper what I had blindly been working towards, who'd told me a story that had somehow made me feel better.

⋆ ⋆ ⋆

I left the golden warmth of Clem's house, and my mind slowed to absorb the cool, still quiet, to feel and see it fully, as I hadn't on the hasty walk up. Rusty pine needles carpeted the narrow road, muting my steps. The sloped land was a tangle of thick ivy, sword ferns, elk clover, redwood sorrel, blackberries, and poison oak. Bay trees and Douglas fir and tanbark oak looked more like bushes than trees next to the redwoods, which grew so high, I had to crane my neck back just to see the blue patch of sky floating at the top of this shadow world. Some of the houses were hobbit-like, clinging to the hill, glowing light from tiny windows in the noon darkness. Two shacks had slid with part of the hill, probably years ago; they had ivy growing through the siding, staking its claim. One house was recently burned hollow, charred black inside like the burned-out stumps of redwoods that still stood from fires long ago. Some of the places were lovely — older summer homes built at the turn of the century that had been kept up, while others were more modern, with lots of windows and skylights to let in the few shafts of filtered light.

Vines of ivy climbed and hung from the trees, almost like seaweed. It was dark and so quiet.

Like being underwater.

It had been almost three months. Three months! How was it possible? That I would never see him again, wiping his forehead with the back of his hand in the garden, grinning — or pointing his camera, his body curved like a comma as if to say *Pause here and see this moment?* Or juggling oranges at the market? Did we have oranges at the new store? Did I forget the oranges? Joe would have remembered the oranges.

There was the way he'd pick up Annie and Zach in one fell swoop, one in each arm, their laughter, their delighted *Daddy Daddy Daddys*. The way he'd swing them around the room and trot them on his knees, saying Grandpa Sergio's old ditty: *Giddy-up, pony, We're on our way to Leonis, To pick up some macaroni, So don't give me any baloney, Just giddy-up, pony . . . giddy-up!* and right at that point, launch them into the air.

Was he somewhere, watching? Did he know about the store? Did he approve? Was he happy, relieved, pissed off? Had I freed him to go on to be reincarnated or reach nirvana or become an angel or whatever it was he was supposed to go do?

There in those woods, I understood why *enchanted* so often preceded *forest*. There is a sense of the mystical, of the otherworldly, when you're surrounded by ancient living grandeur. When one beam of particled light looks celestial and another looks like it might be the product of a sorcerer's experiment. The air smelled of bay leaves, of loam, of wood fires and pine needles and mist — even though it was a warm, sunny day *out there* . . . and *way, way* up *there*. I remembered reading that in the redwood canopy, scientists had discovered copepods

131

— crustaceans that were part of the diet of grazing baleen whales. No one knew exactly how they got there, but anyone could imagine. The sparrows that flew by could have been a school of minnows. It was that kind of dreamy place; I could be walking on a sea-floor; Joe could come swimming by.

How long had it been since I'd passed a house? Where was I? I was fantasizing about my dead husband swimming through the forest, and I had a store full of food and relatives depending on my return, not to mention my sound mental health. I didn't want to be the woman who got lost on her way back from picking up a *map*. But what was all this about, really? I'd spent months remodelling the store, a new beginning that was also trying to save some part of Joe. It had felt good to have a project, to be so busy, so distracted. To act the part of a redwood, towering above, reaching for the sun.

But some part of me wanted to hide here under the fern fronds. To sleep with the slugs.

A twig snapped and my head jerked up. Above the road, a black-tailed doe stared me down with her huge ink-puddle eyes. Another snap, and I saw her two fawns below me, their spots fading in the early autumn, their legs still as fragile as wineglass stems. I stayed very still while the mama deer held my gaze. *I know how you feel*, I wanted to tell her. *We are one, you and I*. But I realized she saw me as the intruder, the one in between her and her babes. I didn't move. She must have finally signalled to them, because the fawns pranced across the road, right in front of me, so close I could have reached out to touch them, before the three of them bounded up the hill, disappearing into the forest.

I ran the rest of the way back to the store. Back to Annie and Zach.

14

The next morning, I lay in bed thinking about Clem's story, when I felt Zach climb under the covers and let out one of his long, meandering exhales until I opened my eyes. He rubbed his cheek with Bubby's ear and stared at the ceiling.

'I miss Batman. And Robin. I want them to come to the big, big party but they *CAN'T*. And Daddy *CAN'T*. And I'm all *ALONE*.'

'I'll be there, and Annie will be there.'

'I mean boys.'

'Uncle David? All your buddies?'

He sighed again. It seemed cruel that his favourite toys lay unnecessarily buried behind the coop when he needed them more than ever.

'Well?' I was winging it as I went. 'Daddy died for real, so he can't come. But Batman and Robin are pretend, so maybe, just maybe, they didn't really drown.'

He jumped up, eyes wide. 'Really?' I nodded. He said, 'But we sawed them. They were drowned for real.' He fell back on the bed and buried his head in Joe's pillow.

'Well? Yesterday? I heard an amazing story that a wise old man told me.'

'A true story? Or a pretending story?'

'True. Absolutely. When he was a little boy, even littler than you, he *almost* drowned.'

Zach gasped, and for a minute I was afraid the whole thing would backfire. 'Did he die like Daddy?'

'Well, no, he didn't. He almost died. He was under a lot of water. And he said he felt happy, even though he was almost drowned. But then he came to the top of the water and breathed in air and he lived.'

'Did a mermaid save him?'

'No. Remember? True story.'

'Oh.'

'So I was thinking . . . Maybe Batman and Robin only *almost* drowned.'

'And Catwoman? And the Joker too?'

'Every plastic being you can think of.'

Now he was jumping up and down on the bed, whooping and hollering. We raced outside, still in pyjamas, the dewy meadow grass licking our feet. I grabbed the shovel, with Callie joining in the digging once she saw what we were up to, and we had our own little action-figure Easter celebration, as we dug up one mud-caked plastic body after the other — the heroes and even the villains — redeemed now from their sins, born again the very morning that Capozzi's Market would experience its own joyous and miraculous rebirth.

★   ★   ★

Most of the town of Elbow turned out for the opening. They filled the store, spilling out onto the porch and the street, and even Clem Silver walked down to sign maps. The owners of the Elbow Inn brought their large historical photo of the picnickers on the river, framed and tied with a bow, to hang on the wall. I was glad and

135

appreciative to see everyone, but I also knew that Life's a Picnic was not going to survive on neighbourly goodwill alone. For one thing, each one of them could go home and pack their own picnics at a fraction of the cost. We needed hungry tourists. We needed wealthy out-of-towners.

We needed a boatload of publicity.

I grabbed David's arm. 'So where are the hordes of press?'

He patted my hand. 'Oh, don't worry. They'll trickle in over the next few weeks. But I'm expecting *someone* will show up today. Isn't it marvellous? Everyone loves it!'

'I heard Ray Longobardi talking about how he might need to take out another mortgage so he can go on a frickin' picnic.'

'Ray Longobardi is hardly our target market. Don't pay attention to *him*. His idea of a picnic is a Spam sandwich on Wonderbread with an Old Milwaukee. *I* heard Franny Palomarino raving about the luscious raspberry-painted porch furniture, and that this was the best chicken curry salad she'd ever tasted in her entire life. Do your lurking by Franny and maybe you'll calm down.'

Frank walked in carrying a basket of handmade soaps. Lizzie had her own very successful soap-making business she operated from their old barn. 'Lizzie couldn't make it,' he said. 'But she sent these.'

I took the basket. 'That's nice.' We both knew that she could easily have made it to the opening, but what she couldn't do was be my friend. 'Tell Lizzie I said thank you.' Frank hugged me and set off to overload his plate.

Annie wore an outfit similar to mine that she'd picked out, clogs with leggings, a long peasanty top. She'd asked me to pull all her hair back into a French braid, so her perfect pearl of a face glowed as she said to one of her friends from school, 'You would not *believe* how long it took to get these tablecloths arranged just right.'

I went over to her and said, 'You've done a great job with the place.' She beamed even brighter. Zach whizzed through with Batman and Robin and a trail of little boys following him. I opened the door. 'The fresh air is calling.' They ran out.

Lucy sat on the front porch. 'Don't worry, I'm still watching him. They just made a beeline before I could lay my body down in front of the door.'

'Thanks.' I looked around. 'Seen anyone jotting down notes, maybe carrying a microcassette recorder?'

She shook her head. 'Not yet.'

I shrugged, then started setting up glasses, filling them with champagne and apple cider, and passing them out. I gathered everyone outside, in front of the porch like they had been on every Fourth of July. I stood on the porch like Joe always had and raised my glass. 'To get this done? In just a couple of months? A downright miracle. You are people who not only show up, but work harder and longer than humanly possible. Who even bring food! Who babysit! I know I didn't grow up here in Elbow. But I hope

137

you consider me one of yours. Because I sure do. Here's to you, Elbow, California. Here's to Grandma Rosemary and Grandpa Sergio, who planted the seeds, Marcella and Joe Sr, who nourished with their blood, sweat, and tears. And finally, to Joe, who loved picnicking, loved this place, loved all of you. Thank you.' We hung his apron and the photo of Joe, his dad, and his grandfather, and toasted to the great success of Life's a Picnic.

★ ★ ★

Walking home, with the kids' hands in mine, I felt both giddy and bone tired. Everyone — with the exception of Ray Longobardi — had raved about the food, the store, the map, and how this was going to boost business for the restaurants, the canoe and kayak rentals, and the Elbow Inn. The only disappointment had been the lack of any press coverage, but I realized opening a picnic store wasn't page-one news. Just then a young, slightly overweight man bustled towards us. He wore slacks and skater shoes, a windbreaker. 'Ella? Ella Beene?' he asked.

He had reporter written all over him. Finally! 'Yes, that's me. And yes, I am the owner, or I should say, *one* of the owners. But the original idea came to me when I — '

'So you're Ella Beene? I need to give you these.' He unzipped his windbreaker and pulled out a manila envelope. 'Sorry. It's just my job,' he said, in an awkward attempt to sound friendly. He turned and jiggled back across the street, crouched into his Hyundai, and drove off.

I stared at the envelope. It had my name handwritten on it, with my address and the address of the store, nothing else. I knew what it was.

Annie tugged on my arm. 'Mommy? Was that the man with the news?'

15

I settled the kids into bed and fired up the woodstove. I plopped down on the couch, braced my feet on the trunk, told myself the envelope held something other than what I feared most.

Maybe just another loose end of Joe's, more financial bad news. *Let it be that. I can deal with that.* The tirade I had in the garden when I'd first realized how deep the money problems ran seemed silly now. I considered *not* opening the envelope, set it down, picked it back up. The fire popped and I jumped. Taking a deep breath, I pulled out the papers and began reading the petitioner's, Paige Capozzi's, declaration:

I am the mother of two children, Annie Capozzi, age six, and Zach Capozzi, age three. Their father, Joseph Capozzi, was recently killed in a drowning accident. I am asking that the children be allowed to live with me, their mother, and that full custody be granted to me.

And why in the hell do you think anyone would let that happen? Why you? The whole town of Elbow knows Annie and Zach better than you do.

I suffered severe postpartum depression after the births of both of my children.

140

When Zach was an infant, I became unable to function as a mother, and, although it was extremely painful for me, I felt it was in the best interest of my children to leave them in the care of their father in order for me to get the medical and psychological treatment I desperately needed.

My condition was temporary, but months later, when I attempted to resume contact with my children and their father, I was ignored. I wrote numerous letters, both to the children and to the father, but only the first few were answered.

Letters? Right, lady. You abandoned your children and your husband because you had a little case of the baby blues? And now you're so desperate, you're willing to lie?

I was recovering from illness and did not fully understand my rights with respect to custody, nor did I have the financial means or physical and mental stamina to fight the father for custody when he asked for a divorce. I concentrated on rebuilding my life with the intention of eventually reclaiming my right as the children's mother. I have become a successful home stager. My job is lucrative, my schedule flexible. I have an office set up in my home and so am in the position to provide financially and emotionally for Annie and Zach. Although their stepmother has done an adequate job as a caregiver, Annie and Zach are suffering the

141

loss of their father and need to be with their only living parent. I can give them the depth of love and support that only a real mother is capable of.

Oh, do not even get me started on what makes a real mother. Adequate? And let's talk about exactly what it was that you were capable of doing, what you did to Annie and Zach, the one thing that no mother in her right mind would do to her children.

I am asking that they be allowed to live with me in Las Vegas, where I own a beautiful home in a neighbourhood full of young children, and that full custody be granted to me.

I declare under penalty of perjury that the foregoing is true and correct.

A mediation date was set for October 1; an order to show cause hearing, whatever that was, was set for November 3. And a demand for some documents, including the fictitious letters.

Joe hadn't let on about just how much the store was struggling. I was shocked by that, but I could *almost* understand how it might happen; the store was Joe's business, literally. He'd thought he could turn it around and no one — even me — would have to know how bad things had become. I hadn't been involved in the day-to-day operations of the store. But the kids — that was different. When it came to Annie and Zach, Joe and I told each other every single thing. We went to their doctor's appointments together, took Annie to her first day of kindergarten together, shared each of Zach's new words — including the most colourful. Joe would have told me if Paige had tried to correspond with the kids. And I knew without question that Joe wasn't cruel.

I threw the packet as hard as I could, but it wiggled feebly three feet in the air before slumping to the ground.

*　*　*

I think I slept twenty minutes that night. The next morning, as soon as I got back from taking the kids to school, I called the troops — all of Joe's family, Lucy, my mom, Frank — and told them Paige had filed for custody. No one let on that they were worried. 'No judge in his right mind would give custody to that woman,' Marcella assured me.

Joe had handled the paperwork for his divorce without a lawyer, but I knew I needed one. Frank recommended someone, and I called her as soon as I hung up. She could squeeze me in during her lunch hour — could I make it? I left the kids with Marcella and made sure David and Gina could cover the store.

Driving in, I remembered the last time I'd gone to see a lawyer. It was when Henry and I decided to divorce. Henry, who had once, long ago, turned up as my cute lab partner in my Protists as Cells and Organisms class, said my name reminded him of L.L.Bean. He said he could picture me on a page from the catalogue, on the front porch of a cabin in Vermont, wearing a down vest and jeans and fishing boots, living a simple life. A couple of acres, a couple of kids. Sounded like a plan, and I was all for it.

But after Henry and I married, great jobs in the biotech industry lured us to San Diego and we moved into a peach stucco palace with easy freeway access amid hundreds of other peach stucco palaces. The joke around the Olympic-size pool in our gated community was that the houses stood so close together, when you wanted to borrow a cup of margarita salt, your neighbour could pass it to you through the bathroom windows.

'We can always *retire* in Montana,' Henry said. While I floundered, then withered as a research assistant, aching to be wearing that down vest in the woods instead of a white coat in the lab, Henry thrived. He loved his job as a biochemist, loved the vast array of beaches and the non-array of weather, loved the sparsely furnished peach palace and our virgin SUV that never once ventured off the pavement to climb a mountain. It never even hauled kids to soccer games.

Then came all the miscarriages, all the misery that left us staring at each other on opposite ends of an empty, long dining room table. At Henry's insistence, we each talked to lawyers. One said to me, 'At least you don't have children.' I stared at her. I watched her flick a pea of lint off the sleeve of her expensive-looking jacket and fold her arms on the desk. 'You'd be tied to him forever. You'd have to deal with him and then the stepmother, if he should remarry . . . which they always do. Immediately. Men want to be saved from single parenting and women want to save them.' She raised a perfectly plucked eyebrow, her own Arc de Triomphe. 'It's a nightmare. The most you could hope for is someone who tolerates the kids.' She shrugged. 'Few people can really love a child the way a natural parent does. Consider yourself lucky.'

Henry's meeting must have been just as dismal, because we both agreed to call off the lawyers and conquered the dividing on our own. I hadn't remembered that lawyer's words, how much they'd stung me then, and now they stung me again — for opposite reasons.

Gwen Alterman's offices took up most of the third floor of a brick building in downtown Santa Rosa. She was older than she sounded on the phone, maybe in her early fifties, and larger than I'd pictured her. Photos of her and her husband and their three kids caught my eye. I wanted to ask her if she was a stepmom or their natural mother, but I didn't. While she ate a Burger King chicken sandwich I told her my story. She handed me a box of Kleenex, which I gratefully took. I was on the clock, so I kept talking through the tears, apologizing, blowing my nose, telling her everything I could think of, even the fact that I was broke. She wrote notes and nodded, and once reached across her massive desk to pat my hand.

'So,' she said after I'd handed over the court documents and Joe's divorce papers. 'You've been hit. And hard. Let me ask you, were you ever appointed the children's legal guardian? In case something did happen to your husband?'

'No . . . no. We'd talked about it, but we never got around to it. Because it would require giving notice to Paige . . . and it didn't look like she was ever coming back, anyway.'

'I see. Well, that's too bad. But even so, if there's a God in this world, that woman shouldn't have a chance. Judges usually look harshly on abandonment cases.' She lifted her chained glasses from her matronly chest and set them on her face and began poring over the papers. I looked at the family photos and saw the unmistakable resemblance of both her and her husband to all three of their kids. No broken-blended family there.

Now Gwen Alterman looked at me over the top of her glasses and cleared her throat. 'She claims to have attempted contact numerous times? That puts a different slant on things.'

'Yes, but she's lying,' I said.

'Do you know for a fact that she didn't try to contact the children or their father? Because we've received a subpoena for those letters. If you have them, you have to turn them over.'

I shook my head. 'I've been there since shortly after she left. I've never seen a trace of her.' Except in Annie's and Zach's blue eyes and silky blonde hair, I thought. The one picture of her glowing and pregnant that I found in Joe's Capturing the Light book. The paisley robe that Joe got rid of after the first night we were together.

'What about your husband's family? Have they

146

had contact with her?'

'No. They're angry at her for leaving.'

'Why, exactly, did she leave? Depression? A little funk and she leaves her kids for three years?'

'That's all I really know,' I admitted. Gwen waited, peering at me over her glasses. 'You've gotta know Joe's family. No one really talks about this kind of thing. They're warm, loving people. But they, don't like to talk about . . . you know . . . difficulties.'

'Such as?'

I sighed. 'Well, for example, I know Joe's grandfather was sent to an internment camp during World War II, but no one talks about that. And our store was going under and Joe never told anyone how bad it was.'

'Was Joe's grandfather Japanese?'

I smiled. 'No. But that's what I thought when Joe mentioned it. Italians were sent too, just not nearly as many.'

She shook her head. 'I had no idea . . . Really?' Her phone buzzed once. She told her receptionist that she'd need another few minutes. 'Tell me, did it ever occur to you to ask Joe about the details concerning why she left?'

I stared at her. 'Um. No.' I didn't tell her how much I still, deep down, didn't want to know any of those details. 'Does she have a chance?'

'There's always a chance. But' — she glanced over one of the divorce papers — 'it looks like Joe's request for custody was completely uncontested. She signed off on everything without any fight. Do your children even know who she is?'

'Well, yeah — Annie remembers her. Zach doesn't, but he's certainly not afraid of her. He seems to like her. She's very . . . pretty . . . and she's okay with them, I guess.'

'Pretty is as pretty does, honey, and leaving your babies is never pretty. Or okay. The children know you first and foremost as their mother. You've fed them and diapered them and been there for them for the past three years while she's been God knows where? No. It is not in the best interest of the children for them to be taken away from their home, their loving stepmother, their relatives — I'll need letters from every one of them, by the way — in order to live in a strange place with a stranger. Especially since they're dealing with the trauma of losing their father. I think we have a strong case.'

I took a deep, shaky breath. 'You don't know how good that is to hear.'

She smiled again and took off her glasses. 'So. Tell me. Are you sleeping? Eating?'

I shrugged. 'Not much sleep. Some food.'

'Try yogurt. Milk shakes. Whatever you can, because, honey, you are going to need every ounce of your skinny self. And your kids are going to need you too.'

I nodded.

'I hate to lay this on you right now with everything else. But you're going to have to find a source of income. And fast. It looks like she's making bank — or at least she's painting that picture. From what I've heard, that's probably accurate if she's involved in any aspect of real estate in Vegas right now. If your financial picture is as dismal as you're saying it is, you might not appear *able* to support the children. If that new store of yours doesn't start making money right away, you might have to come up with another plan. But I will say it shows initiative and pluck, and you're preserving their family heritage, more than I can say for her.

'And one more ugly detail: My retainer fee is five thousand dollars. I'll need that to proceed. We should try to avoid a trial because that gets expensive. Then they'd do an investigation, get a social worker involved, interview teachers, doctors, family, friends — even the kids. But I really don't think we'll need to take this that far.'

I nodded again and tried not to look as hopeless as I felt. Why had I poured all my money into the store so soon? And my energy?

I could barely drag myself to the Jeep. I sat in the parking lot with my forehead on the steering wheel, my eyes burning with lack of sleep, and made myself turn the key in the ignition.

On the drive home the despair began rising. Not *now*. I needed a plan. I needed to eat. And sleep. I needed to take care of my kids. What were they feeling right now? I had a flash of memory: how confused and lost I felt after my own father died. That night after the Great America fiasco, my mom had reassured me, saying how she and I had made it through Dad's death, and we had. But I remembered those first months, how much I wanted my mom, and how blank her eyes went when I tried to talk to her. The sound of her TV through my wall all night, and when I came home from third grade, the drapes still closed, the porch light still on, the newspaper still on the front step, and my mother still in her nightgown. I could not do that; I needed to get the kids through this.

I needed to fight Paige. Make money. Stop sweating. Get my chest to stop hurting. Breathe. I wasn't even doing *that*. Why was I sweating? Did I have a fever? My chest hurt. My arm hurt. I still couldn't breathe.

And then it all became clear: What I needed most was to get to a hospital.

Memorial Hospital was just around two corners, but I was afraid to keep driving, afraid I might run my car off the road and hit a pedestrian. I parked and cut across the street, almost getting hit myself. The sweat continued pouring down my face, my chest crushed with pressure. I was a thirty-five-year-old skinny woman who ate a boatload of organic vegetables. I was also the daughter of a man who'd died at age forty of heart disease. I walked into the emergency room, up to the check-in desk.

'I think . . . I think I'm having a heart attack,' I whispered.

She took one look at me and picked up the phone and shouted into it. 'Possible cardiac arrest. Female. Thirty . . . ?' ,

'Five,' I said. Within seconds I was on a gurney, answering questions. What were my symptoms? When did they start? How severe was the pain? Who should they contact?

Who should they contact? *Joe*, I thought. *Contact Joe.* 'My husband,' I said. 'But he's dead.'

150

Who should they call? They asked again. Not Marcella — she was taking care of the kids. My mom was too far away. Who else was there? Lucy. They could call Lucy. I gave them her number along with my insurance card.

Four hours and five test results later, Dr Irving Boyle explained the fine intricacies of an anxiety attack, why I was the perfect candidate. He had a straggly grey beard that made him look more like a professor of philosophy than a doctor of medicine. He said, 'Your heart is fine.' He sat down on his stool and stuck his pen behind his ear and placed both hands on his knees. 'Except for the fact that it's broken. Sadness and depression can result in anxiety. Anxiety can result in the kind of attack you experienced today. Your husband's recent death is taking its toll on you, both physically and emotionally. I'm very sorry for your loss. I want to suggest you try an anxiety inhibitor and possibly an antidepressant to get you over this bump.'

This *bump*? But I knew by the gentle sympathy in his eyes that he wasn't minimizing anything. 'So what you're saying is, the good news is I'm not going to die of a heart attack, and the bad news is I'm not going to die of a heart attack?' The look on his face made me add, '*Kidding*.'

'We take suicidal references seriously around here. And especially in folks who've suffered losses like you have. I can understand why you might be feeling that way, but you have your children to think about. You have a lot of life — and wonderful times — ahead of you.' I

151

nodded. 'I know that. I do. There's no way I'm bailing on my kids.' I didn't tell him that someone was trying to take them away from me. That the grief was only part of what I was feeling. That I was also terrified of losing Annie and Zach. He asked me if I was tired and I asked him if it was possible to die from sleep deprivation.

He prescribed Xanax to help me sleep and help with the anxiety. I told him I wanted to wait on the antidepressant, that it seemed natural to let any grief I was feeling run its course. I wasn't depressed, I told him. Just tired and sad.

Lucy drove me home. Marcella had fed the kids and put their pyjamas on them, and the house smelled of eggplant Parmesan — Joe's favourite — and SpongeBob bubble bath. 'I'm sorry,' I told her, but she waved her hand.

'No worries. We had fun. How you doing? You doing okay?'

I squeezed her hand and nodded, but I felt so Not Okay. I'd spent most of the day in the hospital only to discover that I was a nervous wreck. A head case. Not completely unlike Paige.

Annie came running out of their room. 'Mommy! Mommy!' she sang. I hadn't seen her that happy since before Joe's death. I scooped her up in my arms. Her delight in seeing me worked like a salve for my soul. 'Can I tell her now? Can I?' she said to Marcella. Marcella shrugged, turned, untying her apron. 'Mommy? Guess what!'

'You cleaned your room?'

'No, silly.' She ruffled my hair again. She'd

been doing that a lot lately. I wasn't quite ready for parent-child role reversal. 'Mama invited us to Lost Vegas! She wants Zachosaurus and me to visit her next weekend!'

16

The next morning, at the store before it opened, while I made risotto cakes and brought the puttanesca sauce to a boil, I called Gwen Alterman and asked her what I should do about Paige's request. 'And I can't stand that she's manipulating Annie. That's got to stop.'

Gwen agreed. 'Making the request through the kids is fighting below the belt. I'll send her counsel a letter today to put an end to it. Now. You could say no about the visitation . . . and then they'd probably file a motion to compel. We'd need a psychological evaluation to show that she's not wacko, or that she won't steal the children. But you also don't want to look like you're antagonistic to a relationship between the children and their birth mother.' She paused, and I pictured her taking a multiple-choice test, weighing the answers, while I turned the burner down to let the sauce simmer. 'You don't want to come across as a jealous, overbearing type. You're loving. You're open to some visitation. But it's best for the kids to live with you. Period.'

I listened. I remembered to breathe. I held the phone with my shoulder, set down the copper mould for the risotto cakes, poured a glass of water, and opened the bottle of Xanax from my purse under the counter. Joe used to tease me about my reluctance to take medicine, even an aspirin. But after my afternoon in the emergency

154

room, the Xanax felt necessary. As I took one, it occurred to me for the first time that even if everything went my way in this case, Paige was still going to be a part of our lives. Forever. Unless she decided to disappear again. But visitation meant her and the kids . . . hanging out. On some kind of regular basis.

'Look,' Gwen said. 'I'll request a psych evaluation. They'll say no. I'll get a court order. At least it'll buy us some time.'

But that evening, as I chopped a bucketful of kale at home, she called me back. 'I don't believe this, but I've got a psych evaluation in my hand. Faxed over by Paige's attorney. She had one done a week ago, and she checks out. We're talking flying colours. Of course, we can order another psych eval from a doctor we choose, but then they'll want to have one done on you.'

I took another Xanax and wondered how I'd fare on a psych eval right then. 'Oh,' I said.

Gwen sighed. 'We can fight this and win.'

That sounded good — but for whom? Not for the kids, and I told her so.

Zach bellowed from the next room, 'I'm *telling*!' and I waited for him to bolt into the kitchen, but he didn't follow through.

'Zach is too young to go on the plane without me. How about this? She can come here and visit them in the area.'

'Say within a thirty-mile radius? What about overnight?'

I sighed. 'Okay . . . Yes.'

'Then we cross our fingers that this is a wake-up call and she'll realize being a mommy is way over her head.'

I went to check on the kids. Annie had pulled out the little pink suitcase Marcella had bought her for overnights and was filling it up with the dresses she rarely wore.

'I'm packing for Mama's house. It's not in the country like this one is,' she explained.

'Hence the dresses?' I asked.

She nodded. 'Hence the dresses.'

Zach said, 'I don't wanna wear dresses. They're barfy.'

'Banannie, I think your mama is going to come and visit you here — '

'What? No!' She stamped her foot. 'That is so boring! I want to go on the plane!'

'You will . . . someday. But for this first time, she's going to come here. Maybe you'll get to stay at a hotel.'

'A big hotel?'

'Hotels are barfy too.'

'Zach, what's with all the barf? Do you have a tummy ache?'

'No! I'm just packing my *BAR FY* jay-jays and my *BAR FY* clothes.'

'I see . . . Annie, I don't know if the hotel is big. You'll have to ask your mama.'

'At a big hotel, I could wear my dresses. I want to look *sophisticated*. Like Mama.' She added her black patent leather shoes that she'd worn to the funeral. She didn't pack her little Birkenstocks and clogs that matched mine. She stood with her hands on her hips, scanning the closet. 'I have nothing to wear,' she said, pushing a blonde strand of hair off her face. Zach stood up, carried over his brontosaurus and an armful of Matchbox cars, and dropped them in his Thomas the Tank Engine suitcase. I picked him up and kissed his ear, and he laid his head on my shoulder and let out a long, tired sigh.

'I know,' I said. 'Let's watch *The Sound of Music*.'

'Again?' Annie asked.

'Sure,' I said, shrugging. 'Why not?' I was hoping they'd fall asleep in my bed. I didn't want to sleep alone.

'Okay . . . I can finish this tomorrow, I guess.'

'Sure you can. Get your jays on. I'll make the popcorn and meet you in our room.'

Both kids did fall asleep early, by the time the storm hit the Von Trapp house and Maria sang 'My Favourite Things'. When the dog bites. When the bee stings. When I'm feeling sad . . . When the husband dies. When the ex-wife tries . . . to take away my kids . . . I simply remember my favourite things. Then her confrontation with gorgeous Captain Von Trapp, Maria plotting to make play clothes out of the curtains.

Lucy called to check in. I told her what I was watching.

'Again?'

'Maria. What a stepmom. What a role model. But then, she didn't ever have to worry about their mother coming back, because she was dead.'

'True story.'

'It *is* a true story,' I said. 'I could use a Mother Superior who could tell me, in a moving

157

rendition, what I should do. No, I need to *be* the mother superior. The superior mother, as judged by the court of the County of Sonoma.'

'You, my dear, are clearly the mother superior. Oh, I love that gazebo scene. God. Christopher Plummer. I've loved him since I was, like, six. Call me later.'

I hung up. Joe was gone, but I did still have some of my favourite things. Digging in the garden with my kids, collecting eggs with the kids, walking into town with the kids on their bikes, Play-Doh and finger paints and beads, ironing crayon shavings between sheets of wax paper — all the messy things that I loved to do with them. Many other things besides watching *The Sound of Music* . . . again, as Annie and even Lucy had pointed out.

Dr Irving Boyle was right. Because of Annie and Zach, I had a lot to live for. I was not only their mother; I was a good mother, a superior mother. We just needed to keep doing our favourite things. A weekend with Paige wasn't going to threaten what we'd taken three years to establish. Gwen Alterman was right too: It would only help our cause. Imagine Paige with her perfectly manicured nails covered in barfy finger paints. Ha!

★ ★ ★

Annie and Zach and I sat on the couch in the not-so-great room. Callie went from one to the other of us, pushing her head and her backside into us, thwacking us with her tail, panting.

158

The pink suitcase was packed to the gills, along with Zach's Thomas the Tank Engine suitcase; they waited by the door. At 10:15 a.m. — precisely when she said she'd arrive — Paige's rental car turned up our drive. Callie galloped down the hallway with Annie, while Zach, holding his Bubby, stood and watched me. I wiped my palms on my jeans and tried to smooth my hair down.

Zach jumped into my lap. 'Bella,' he said, planting a kiss on my cheek, 'you look *gorgeous*.'

I laughed and planted my own kisses all over his face. I knew he'd taken that line from Joe. My insecurity must have been bouncing off the walls for a three-year-old boy to be prompted to flatter me. He wriggled free, and I stood up, remembered to breathe a few abdominal breaths, then walked into the kitchen and picked up a dish towel so it looked like I was busy doing something. I'd been cleaning all morning, but the house still looked cluttered. She probably wouldn't even come in.

But she was already walking down the hallway and into the kitchen.

'Annie let me in.' She looked across to the great room. 'I've been meaning to tell you, I like how you tore down that wall. It looks much better. I knew it would. Do you mind if I use the bathroom?'

I had started to clean the bathroom but got distracted and then forgot about it entirely. I considered telling her no, she could use the bathroom at Ernie's Gas, but knew I couldn't get away with that. 'Oh? Oh, okay. It's through — Well, you know where it is.'

'I do,' she said. While she was in there, I was kicking myself for not cleaning the bathroom. Of *course* she'd have to use it. She'd driven all the way from the airport. I thought of my new prescription in the medicine cabinet and the hard-water ring around the toilet. Joe's after-shave that I kept on the counter for quick fixes. Would she open it, inhale it like I did, press some on her wrists? Or would she dump it down the toilet? Had I left my underwear on the floor? The old ones with the two rips around the elastic?

When she glided out, Zach ran over to me and grabbed my leg. I rubbed his back and handed her the kids' health insurance cards, their pediatrician's phone number, and some instructions including Annie's allergy to Ceclor and Zach's attachment to his Bubby. She didn't smell like Joe's aftershave, just her own jasmine citrus perfume, her signature scent that kept permeating my house. She took the insurance cards but handed me back Dr Magenelli's number and the instructions. 'Thanks. But I know Doc Magic and his number. Along with Annie's allergy. And as far as instructions, Annie's such a smart girl. I think she can help me with any questions that arise. But thanks, really. It was thoughtful.' She tucked the insurance cards in her streamlined wallet, snapped it shut, slipped it back into her streamlined shoulder bag. She wore white pants and a peach silky shirt that looked perfect against her skin. She must have never covered herself with baby oil and baked in the sun on one of those foil-coated space blankets when she was a teenager. She looked slightly different from the last time I'd seen her. She'd cut her fringe, wispy, framing her eyes, making them look even bigger.

'Let me get you their car seats,' I said.

'No need. The rental car has them built in. We're staying at the Hilton in Santa Rosa.' She turned to the kids. 'Did you two pack your suits?' They nodded.

Annie said, 'And quite a few dresses.'

'Excellent.' Paige looked at her watch.

I said, 'What a long day for you . . . '

'Oh, I don't mind. I'm thrilled to be able to see them. Okay, Annie, Zach, say good-bye to Ella.'

Ella? Nice try. And she didn't need to tell my kids to say good-bye to me.

Zach said, 'I wanna stay here.'

I bent down and smoothed his hair back. 'You can call me anytime. And Annie will be with you. And Bubby. And you'll be back tomorrow.' He started hitting the ground with Bubby. 'Okay, honey?'

He looked at Paige and slowly nodded. Annie took his other hand, and the three of us followed Paige down the porch steps. I knelt down and hugged them both maybe a little too long, and willed the tears to wait.

'Bye, Mommy!' they shouted from the car, waving as she drove them away. I watched until they disappeared around the bend, then watched the dust from the gravel dissipate in the morning air.

I slipped on Joe's jacket, and Callie and I went down to the chicken coop, Callie zigzagging in

161

front of me. We had four hens, Bernice, Gilda, Harriet and Mildred. When I reached under them, they'd each left me an egg, except for Mildred. She hadn't been laying as much. I wondered if she was in mourning too. I slipped the three warm eggs in the pockets of Joe's jacket and followed Callie back to the house.

I had a plan to keep occupied, to look for the documents Paige had requested. Gwen had said, 'You'll need to be able to tell the court that you've conducted a diligent search and you did not find the letters.' I would go through the boxes and files in Joe's office so I could sign off on that and be done with it.

I sat in his old office at Life's a Picnic and went through the files, flipped through the books, and pulled up tax records I'd once blindly signed without even reviewing. The signs of financial doom flashed from documents I'd never bothered to look at. Like some kind of fifties housewife, I'd stayed out of the finances and spent my days tending to the children. It naturally happened that way; it hadn't been a decision. It seemed to work for us then, but now I could see that it really wasn't working at all. Joe hadn't told me the truth, but some part of me clearly preferred it that way.

★ ★ ★

The door behind the file cabinet led to a storage area. The cabinet was too heavy to move, but I didn't want to ask David for help, so I emptied out the drawers and then pushed and shimmied the shell until I could open the door. I pulled the string to turn on the bare lightbulb that hung from the rafter. The air smelled of mould — and memories. Stacked boxes, a few pieces of old dusty furniture; a mirrored dresser and a secretary's desk that probably belonged to Joe's grandparents. If there were any letters, I'd find them there.

I started going through boxes. Not the marked ones that said things like *Joey's Baseball Trophies* or *Davy's Schoolwork*. But the unmarked boxes in the corner. In the first one I opened, I found the paisley robe.

I recognized it immediately, the swirls of teal, of honey and periwinkle, and now I could see how it would highlight Paige's eyes and complexion — even if she did wear it every day, all day, she still had looked amazing. Joe had saved it that evening after we met. He'd taken it from the hook on the back of the bathroom door, but he hadn't thrown it out or given it away or even sent it to Paige. He'd kept it. Because he missed her? Because he hoped for her return? Had he locked his office door as I had just done, and moved the file cabinet and opened the box to take out the robe and inhale her perfume the way I'd inhaled every one of his shirts?

Or maybe he had just stuck it back there with some of her other belongings, not wanting to deal with any of it. Maybe he'd forgotten about it all.

There were other things that I could bet he didn't care about. Old bottles of makeup. A box of tampons. A worn copy of *What to Expect When You're Expecting*. Some loose change and a brush still tangled with golden hair.

No, this was not a shrine. This was a box packed in haste, stuck away, forgotten.

I should have stopped then and closed up the closet, returned the cabinet to the wall, the drawers to the cabinet. But I didn't. I opened another box. And another. These held Annie's old baby clothes — almost everything tiny and pink or peach and white, little cotton mementos of an era I could never be part of. There was even a onesie with little ducks that I recognized. I'd bought the same one at GapKids during my first pregnancy. I'd left it hanging in the nursery closet when I left Henry. Where was it now? Had he packed it away in a box of other things I'd left behind? More likely, he had given it away.

Paige and I were both pregnant at the same time. When I'd first met them, I figured out that one of my babies would be the same age as Annie, almost exactly. I found Annie's baby book, which I had never seen, though that was one of the few things I'd asked Joe about. He'd shrugged and said he wasn't sure where it was. Did Paige stick it in this box, planning to retrieve it someday? It was homemade, covered in pink and white bunny fabric, with her name, Annie Rose Capozzi, and the date of her birth, November 7, 1992, cross-stitched in the centre. I thought about not opening it — for about two seconds. I knew nothing in it would make me feel better. But I looked anyway, at the photos of Paige, glowing even in labour, and Joe and Paige and Annie snuggled in a hospital bed, sur-rounded by pink bouquets and balloons, Joe's and Paige's smiles equally big, connecting them to their child like the two symmetrical sides of an anchor.

I flipped through more pages of Annie, and Annie with Marcella, with Joe Sr with Frank and Lizzie and David, but no pictures of Paige, not until Easter, five months later, where she resumed her place again, resurrected from oblivion. There weren't many pictures of Joe, since he was the one who'd taken most of them. Maybe that was worse, because these photos reflected what *he* saw, what *he* loved — his presence in them stronger than if he'd been standing in the middle of each one. The look on Paige's face, that type of secret smile shared with only one other person on the planet. And Annie in her arms.

★ ★ ★

Later that night, I sat in bed trying to pay too many of our household bills without enough bank balance. Mostly, I was waiting for Annie and Zach to call me. Callie lay at the end of the mattress, snoring, jerking her legs as she dug up dream gophers. I tried to sort all my mind's spinning into some sort of logical sequence, but to no avail. I pulled out the nightstand drawer and rummaged through it until I found my scratch pad and pen. In my handwriting were the words *chicken feed* and *rhubarb seeds*.

Yes, it was true. La-tee-da. My life had once

seemed that simple, like the title of a silly song, the kind you'd sing on road trips: '*Oh, I've got chicken feed, and rhubarb seeds, and a smile that's a mile long. I've got a boy and a girl and a husband that's a pearl, and a smile that's a mile long.*'

Joe took care of the groceries, filling bags of whatever we needed at the end of the day. The post office was next to the store, so he always picked up the mail. And when the store was slow, he did the books. Apparently, he'd had a lot of time to do the books.

I'd stepped into his life and had imposed little of my own onto his. I'd felt like a walking tomb that had been overly excavated, ready to collapse in on itself; there hadn't been any life left in me then. Stumbling into Joe and the kids — a ready-made family with a mommy-size gaping hole for me to fill. I hadn't questioned any of it. Why question what's so clearly destiny?

Joe and I went from not knowing each other's names one day to raising a family the next. We never went through the phases our friends did — the long, drawn-out exhales and rolled eyes, the 'I'll do it, then.' I eagerly jumped first when it came to the kids. And after months of going it alone, Joe usually let me.

We'd been together three years. But how well had we really known each other? Perhaps not as well as I'd assumed. Henry and I were married seven years, but even after all we'd gone through together, I never felt I was privy to a different Henry than the one others knew. The conversations he had with me could have easily been had with his colleagues at work, his baseball buddies, or his mother — depending on the topic. Nothing was reserved for only us, except when it came to trying to have a baby. But when we decided we were done trying, and I wanted to talk about adoption, Henry changed the subject. We were back to brief discussions concerning lab rats, the Padres, his father's hernia.

Joe and I loved to talk, our conversations twisting and turning from something incredible one of the kids had done to how great the eggplants looked to a poem about a blue heron he'd read in a journal. I thought he was one of the most interesting people I'd ever met. He was funny, creative, intuitive, artistic. After Sergio died, Joe quit college to help his dad, felt it his duty to honour his grandfather's wishes after all Sergio had been through. Joe gave up his dream of becoming a photojournalist, and photography became his hobby, where he chose to capture the best of what the world offered, always seeking out the most flattering angles and light. I'd loved that about him. But now I wondered at all he refused to look at, and the easy way his filtered perspective complemented my own.

I picked up Paige's business card. Callie stretched, lifted her head, then let it flop back on the mattress. She resumed snoring. I cleared my throat and practiced.

'Hello? Paige? This is Ella?' Too questioning. Too insecure.

'Hello, Paige. It's Ella. I'd like to speak to Annie now.'

No. Too insistent. I needed to sound light, as if

167

I really didn't have a care in the world.

'Hi, Paige. (It is *Paige*, isn't it?) Hey, it's Ella. Is Annie around?' I dialled and hung up twice before I let it ring.

'Hello. You've reached the cell phone voice mail of Paige Capozzi. Please leave a message, and remember, when it's time to stage, call Paige . . . ' and a beep.

I was going to hang up, but then I thought she probably had caller ID so I started talking. 'Um. Hi. It's Ella. Ella Beene? And you know . . . I was just thinking, um . . . about Annie and Zach. And I wanted to say good night. Gosh. I can't remember the last time I wasn't there to tuck them in. I . . . I think it was Joe and my three-year anniversary? When we drove up to Mendocino for the — ' *Beep*.

Wait. Didn't she have one of those press-pound-and-erase-your-message options? I pushed buttons. I shook the phone. I said, 'Hello? Hello?' Nothing. I hung up.

★ ★ ★

The phone rang, startling me because it was still in my lap.

'Hi, Mommy.' It was Zach, his voice like sweet relief filling my head, my body. I hadn't realized how tense I'd been, how scared, really, that something horrible had happened. My new fear of bad news.

'Hi, honey! Are you having fun?'

'No. I wanna come home. *NOW*.'

'Oh, Zach. What's wrong?'

168

'I want *YOU*.' I could see him as clearly as if he stood in front of me, the way he held the phone with both hands, Bubby lodged under his arm, his belly out, knees probably bent, heels together, toes apart and facing out, like some sort of ungracefully adorable plié.

'Honey? Listen . . . You'll be home tomorrow. You have Annie. And Bubby. And a cool hotel, right? And guess what else? There's a surprise in your suitcase. It's in the inside pocket. Want to go get it?'

'Okay!' He set the phone down. I'd packed a new stegosaurus for him and some pretty socks for Annie to wear with her patent leathers.

Paige said in the background, 'How nice of Ella. Tell her thank you, Zach.'

Ella? Again? Telling Zach to thank me? Shut up. Just shut up.

Zach picked up the phone. 'It's cool, Mommy!'

'Are you going to be okay now?'

'Uh-huh. Uh-huh, uh-huh, uh-huh. I'm going to go play. Annie wants to talk.'

Zach let out a ferocious-sounding growl, and then Annie came on the line.

I asked if she was having fun. 'Quite a lot.'

'Oh yeah?'

'Yeah . . . you should see my room!'

Oh God. Where were they? 'You mean at the hotel?'

'No. My room. Mama brought pictures. And it looks bigger than our not-so-great room.' She giggled.

'Wow.'

'Yeah. Wow.'

'Is it the guest room?'

'No. It's mine. It says Annie in big sparkly letters on the wall. And it's got lots of green.' How did Paige know Annie's favourite colour was green? And how did she get the room painted and set up so fast? 'And some other colours too. Like lavender and pink and cream. And this big, cool bed. That's a real castle!'

I was sweating again, feeling like I couldn't get a breath.

'Mommy?'

'Yes, honey?'

She whispered, pausing between each word, 'I . . . miss . . . you.' It was with utter shame that I realized how much I needed to hear those words, that for the first time ever, my children's emotional pain somehow eased my own.

17

Thin ribbons of sleep weaved in and out of my frenzied thoughts. When the Claytons' rooster crowed I sat up with a start. There *was* one letter. I'd forgotten. The letter Joe told me about. The Dear Joe letter, in which Paige had handed over the kids to him and said *arrivederci*. If I could find *that* letter . . .

I got up in the rosy-tinted darkness and pulled on my jeans and a sweatshirt over Joe's T-shirt. I picked up all my globs of Kleenex, scattered in the bed like jellyfish, then switched on the lamp, picked up the scratch pad, and jotted down all the things I needed to do. Life beyond rhubarb seeds and chicken feed.

After I cleaned the coop, I rushed down to open the store. I flipped on the lights and for a moment felt comforted. Even though all my money was sunk into it, even though we'd taken a risk and every day left us more tired and a little more broke, it still felt exactly right. I was looking forward to the day when I wouldn't be distracted by the custody worry and could focus on my mornings behind the counter, waiting on customers, planning menus with David while the kids were in school. David walked in just then, balancing a tower of boxes.

'Were your ears ringing?' He set down the boxes and started pulling out supplies. 'Because I was just talking to a reporter from the *Press*

Democrat. They want to talk to you too. And — you're gonna love this. *Sunset* might do a story on us. I'm working on *Real Simple* too. But those are months away.'

I nodded, kept nodding.

He reached for my shoulder. 'You okay? You look exhausted.'

'Why, thank you.' I straightened my back. 'I'm fine. It's just . . . I want to stay down here and play store with you, but I've got to go up and look through files for this discovery shit for the hearing.'

'Oooh. Sounds like too much fun.'

'Exactly.'

'This too shall pass. And soon your kids will be back home with you. You'll be walking them to school, then doing interviews for national magazines, giving them charming and clever quotes for their articles, stirring your homemade fresh-from-your-garden vegetable soup, and sashaying over to put another log on the fire.'

'Right now I'm going to sashay up to the office to bury myself in piles of financial papers.'

'Hey, did you roast the root vegetables?'

'Um. No.' I did not have time to roast root vegetables. 'Do you need me to chop them?'

'Oh. You didn't even chop them?'

'David. I'm sorry. I can do it now.'

'Are you *sure*?' No. I meant yes, I was sure that I couldn't. But I did. I chopped carrots and sweet potatoes and butternut squash and onions fast, the way he'd taught me, in big chunks, and I almost cut my finger off twice.

'Oh my God,' David said. 'Be careful. The

recipe calls for blood orange juice, not blood *and* orange juice.'

I filled a half hotel pan and tossed the vegetables with olive oil and thyme, salt and pepper, a touch of maple syrup and freshly squeezed blood-orange juice, managing to keep my own blood out of it, and stuck them in the oven so the whole store smelled of love and nurturing and wholesome goodness, and then I dashed up the stairs two at a time so I could quickly try to discover incriminating evidence regarding the woman who was trying to get custody of Annie and Zach.

★   ★   ★

I locked the office door, just in case David showed up bearing his lemon scones to ease my pain. I pulled out more of the unmarked boxes. I was going to find that letter and bring the true Paige to the surface.

I'd find the letter. I'd have Gwen Alterman shoot off a declaration so Paige would realize that she could visit with them but she couldn't push her way in now and take over, take Annie and Zach away from where they belonged. Here. With me. With us.

I found a box with Zach's empty baby book, not handmade like Annie's, but store-bought with blue bears. All the spaces — for first smile, first laugh, first word, first tooth — empty.

I found more photos too. Not family photos. Photos of Paige.

Undressing . . .

173

Nude.

As soon as it struck me what they were, I dropped them in the file and stood up. Dizzy again. I obviously needed a Xanax, so I took two out of my backpack and swallowed them. I kicked the box back into the closet, unlocked the office door, started walking down the stairs. I stopped. I turned around. I walked back, locked the door, pulled out the box, and I looked at every single photograph. I *studied* them. There was a series. In the first photos, she wore a long-sleeve blouse, a skirt. She looked young, maybe twenty. Many of the shots were of her face; for others she sat on a stool, stood, hand on hip. Different outfits. Nothing suggestive, really. But then she looked straight at the camera, her fingers working buttons. These shots didn't look posed as much as documenting someone undressing. There she was taking off her blouse. Stepping out of her skirt. Reaching back to unhook her bra. Slipping out of her underwear. And then standing — again, not suggestively. Face front. Perfect breasts front. Solemn face. No half-turned look over her shoulder. Nothing coy. She looked both unsure and defiant, woman and child, sexy and sad. What man wouldn't fall in love with her?

Again, Joe was in these photographs. Even though I couldn't see him, I could see his perspective. I would guess he hadn't slept with her yet. The legal discovery request meant something else, but *this* was a true moment of discovery, if there ever was one. Joe discovering Paige. Me, feeling as if I'd walked in on them.

174

Now . . . and maybe three years ago, when they'd hit a rough spot. I walked home, head throbbing, eyes burning, to the house Joe and Paige had set up for themselves and the kids that would soon follow. I fell into the bed where they'd made love, made Annie and Zach. I thought about calling someone, but I'd used everyone up. They needed a break from me. Hell, *I* needed a break from me. And besides, I didn't want anyone to know about this. All I needed was sleep. If I could just rest, I could think straight. I got up and took another Xanax.

Like I've said, I've never considered myself to be beautiful. Attractive, but never one to turn heads or inspire artists. Still, the way Joe had looked at me . . . I'd *felt* beautiful. But Joe never once asked me to pose nude. Of course, it wasn't like we had a lot of time between giving kids baths and changing diapers to set up a boudoir studio in our bedroom.

I climbed back into bed. Callie brought me her leash, but I just let her outside. She looked at me, disappointed, but she dropped her leash at my feet, trotted out to do her duty quickly, and came back inside, following me back into the bedroom. Utter exhaustion. I curled up under the covers. I pulled them over my head. 'I'm done,' I said aloud. Callie groaned and rested her chin on my legs, over the blankets.

It started raining. The kids were due home that night, but I could not get out of bed. I tried. I finally got up to pee and let Callie out again. *The good thing about Xanax*, I thought to myself as I tapped out two more, *is that it's not*

175

addictive. I slept. I woke to pounding rain, but only long enough to wonder how one single wave could take away all that was good and leave all this wreckage tossed up on the shore. And then I slept again.

Callie's yelp woke me. Car lights ran the length of my bedroom wall like a searchlight probing the deepest dark. Tires slapped through puddles. I heard car doors open, Paige's voice. I'd left the door unlocked, the lights out. I had to get up. Get. *Up*.

I pulled on my jeans. So dizzy. I stumbled out to the hall just as they burst in. Paige flipped on the light, and its brightness made me wince. The kids held big balloons freckled with raindrops. They wore bright trendy clothes. They'd had haircuts. *They both had bangs!* Like Paige. *Like battle lines drawn across their perfect foreheads*, I thought, *staking her claim on their minds*. And then I thought, *Oh man, does Xanax make you dramatic?*

Zach slept against Paige's shoulder, his mouth slightly open. Annie held on to her new lime green purse and matching balloon and looked at me.

'Are you sick, Mommy?' she asked.

'Um . . . Yes. The flu.'

Paige said, 'Oh! I wish you'd called. I could have kept them longer.'

'It's fine. I'm starting to feel better.'

'I hope they don't get it.'

I bent down and hugged Annie.

'The flu is really contagious,' Paige added.

Oh, bite me, Miss January. I took Zach from

her, his head heavy and bobbing between us. 'Good-bye,' I said.

She leaned over my shoulder and kissed Zach, and her hair swept against my face, leaving a trace of citrus jasmine in the air. He woke and wriggled out of my arms to pet Callie. Paige gave Annie a hug. 'Call me tomorrow, sweet pea, like we said.'

'Okay, Mama.'

'Be good for Ella.'

I closed the door before her foot hit the first step off the porch. I tried to shake it off, but instead I opened the door and stuck my head out. 'Ah, Paige?'

She turned.

'It's not *Ella*.'

'I beg your pardon? Do I have your name wrong?'

'The kids call me Mommy.'

'Really?'

'Yeah. *Really*. They have for three years. But you wouldn't know that because you weren't here.' I shut the door. Annie and Zach stood, holding their rain-spattered balloons, watching me. 'Anybody hungry?'

They shook their heads. 'All I want to do is sleep,' Annie said. 'That mama lady took us to a fancy-pants place.' Zach sighed and they climbed into their own beds before I had the chance to coax them into mine. It was for the best, I knew, to try to get back to some sense of normalcy, but still I had to bite my tongue to keep from asking if they'd get lonely in their own beds. They were too tired to talk much, and so I tucked them in and stayed with them, watching them fall asleep, their faces framed in their newly cut bangs, as the rain tapped out a lullaby on the roof. The balloons had risen and now hovered in opposite corners against the ceiling.

I felt so tense, I wondered if I'd be able to get back to sleep. I lay back down and listened as the rain picked up and began hammering, branches scraping against the house. Everything about Paige made me anxious. I hit the pillow, got up. How long had it been since I'd taken a Xanax? I couldn't remember, but I was sure it was time to take another. I took two more, just to be sure. I needed to be able to wake up refreshed so I could get Annie and Zach off to school.

But in the morning, their breathy whispers swept across my nose and cheeks. 'Why won't she open her eyes?' Zach asked Annie. I forced them open. Four wide blue eyes inches from my own asked me more questions, without words. I knew I should get up and make breakfast, but I got only as far as propping myself up on my elbows before I released them and fell back into the mattress.

'Mommy's just tired,' I said. 'Annie, will you pour cereal and milk?' She nodded. 'And . . . call . . . Uncle David.' Callie jumped off the bed and followed them out. Finally, after weeks of spotty rest, I was getting good sleep!

I dreamt — thick, long, dreams with twisted plots I couldn't quite remember after I woke. And then this: Joe and I scuba diving. Joe and I, holding hands, kicking our fins in long, smooth strides, gliding through the ocean with the grace and unity of choreographed dancers. He pointed out beds of sunset-coloured coral and a giant clam. I wanted to ask him a question, so I motioned 'up' and swam to the surface. I popped my head up to a grey sky and treaded water, waiting for Joe, but he never showed.

I dived back down to search for him, ploughing through tangled sea grasses, sound-lessly calling his name. Then I heard my own name, luring me from above. I struggled towards the surface, swimming with all my strength, kicking as hard as I could towards his voice.

I woke, flailing, in David's arms. 'Ella, sweetheart. It's me. It's David. You're dreaming.'

'I almost . . . ,' I whispered. 'Almost.' Almost talked with Joe, almost got some answers, but not quite.

'Girl, you've been sleeping all day.' David pushed my hair back from my face. 'And excuse me for being direct, but you could use a shower and a toothbrush.'

'Thanks,' I said, but only after I'd pulled the sheet up to cover my mouth. He got up to snap open the blinds, the wet leaves of the apple tree sparkling like chandelier drops in the afternoon sun. 'It must have been the Xanax.'

'This, from the woman who won't take an aspirin?'

'I've been anxious. The doctor prescribed Xanax.'

'Gil takes Xanax. But he doesn't sleep all day. Maybe you're sensitive to it. Or do you have your own Xanax *salt lick* hidden somewhere?'

I shook my head. 'No. But I took too many. Obviously.'

'Ella. You have every excuse in the world to batten down the hatch and wait this out, but you simply don't have that kind of time. You have two restless kids, a custody battle to win, and a persnickety brother-in-law who desperately needs your help.'

He pulled me up and out of bed, singing 'Good Morning Starshine' as he danced me across the floor, pushed me into the bathroom, closed the door. On the counter he'd placed a basket full of expensive-looking lavender and rosemary bath products, the softest washcloth I'd ever touched, and a loofah with a wooden handle. I peeled off Joe's stale, damp T-shirt and my underwear and turned the water on full blast, hot. I stood under it, trying to ignore the shame that ached in my gut, and slathered on soap and body wash and shampoo and conditioner, breathing in the scents until, eventually, the water turned cold, forcing me out.

David had inherited Marcella's energy and knack for cleaning. By the time I walked out in my robe, a towel on my head, he had the kids picking up strewn toys and piles of colouring books while he stood at the sink, yellow rubber gloves conveyoring dirty dishes into the dish-washer.

'Mommy? Are you better?' Zach asked. Annie just held an empty rice cake wrapper and watched me.

'Yes, honey. I'm so sorry I didn't take you to school.'

David said, 'I called earlier to check in, but the phone went to voice mail right away. I figured

180

you were talking to your lawyer, but I guess Annie was on the line.'

'Talking to Marcella?'

'Apparently not . . . ' David looked at Annie. 'Honey, who were you talking to?'

Annie shrugged. 'Um, just Mama.'

'Oh?'

'She was worried.'

I took a deep breath, tried to keep my voice steady. 'Worried?'

Annie stamped her foot. 'Because you *wouldn't* get up! You just *wouldn't*. She said *she* would take care of us.'

David said, 'Ella, don't worry, I've already spoken to Paige. I think I convinced her that we've got things under control.'

Annie said, 'Na-uh, Mama's coming. She told me she was coming. She told me she would fix us something to *eat.*'

David slipped off the gloves and went to Annie, as I should have, but my mind and muscles seemed to be experiencing a bad connection. He scooped her up. 'You want something to eat after all Nonna's cannelloni you devoured? I'll fix you anything you can fit in that over-stuffed tummy of yours.'

Annie would have usually laughed in glee, but she didn't. I went to them, smoothing my hand down her back, speaking over David's shoulder the way I had when Joe held her. 'Honey, I am so, so sorry. I didn't mean to sleep so long. I am so sorry you were alone to take care of Zach. You did a wonderful job, but you shouldn't have had to do that. Were you scared?'

She nodded, slightly at first, then big, heavy nods and a loud burst of tears. I took her from David and held her while she sobbed in my arms. Finally she said, 'You-you-you-you're mad at me! 'Cause I called Mama!'

'No, Annie. I'm not mad. You did the right thing.'

'But you don't like her!'

'Sweetie . . . It's just . . . it's just a hard time right now. For everyone. For you. For Zach. And for me too. I'm sorry. I am going to try a lot harder. I really am. I wasn't there for you today. And that won't happen again. Starting now, okay?'

She nodded, small nods again. Not-quite-believing-me nods.

How could I let this happen? Maybe I wasn't a better mother than Paige. Falling apart, unable to care for my kids or even myself. What if something had happened to them while I was in bed sound asleep on a Monday afternoon? I went into the bathroom and flushed the remaining Xanax down the toilet.

★ ★ ★

The rain stopped while the sunshine unfolded itself across our porch. We decided to go down to the river for a swim. They both loved going to the beach, and I was trying to make amends. Annie rode her two-wheeler, Zach his trike, and I walked alongside him on the pine-needle-covered path through the trees down to Elbow Beach, a wide triangle of perfect sand jutting out

182

to the water. Annie pointed to the osprey nest across the river, the huge crown of sticks on top of the tall dead tree. 'Let's watch the babies.' But the nest was quiet, empty, the osprey probably heading south by now. We had the whole place to ourselves. Most mothers had got up that morning and taken their kids to school.

While I spread out the blanket, Zach pulled his trike through the soft sand down to the river's edge, then hopped back on it and started to slowly push the pedals until the front tire was in the water.

'Zach, what are you doing? Honey, stop that.'

But he kept his feet on the pedals, his eyes on the water. I walked over to him and stuck my foot in front of the tire.

'You can't ride your trike into the river. Let's go for a swim instead.'

He shook his head, kept looking into the water.

'Zachosaurus? What is it?'

'I'm going somewhere.' He pushed harder on his pedals, so the tire spun a bit in the sand against my toe.

'Ouch! Zach, let's put your trike up by the blackberry bushes and I'll take you in the water. Now.'

He shook his head, still not looking at me. 'Is Daddy down there? I want to go see him on my trike.'

'Oh, honey. No, Daddy's not in the water.'

'Okay, GOOFBALL!' He jumped off and lay in the sand.

'Do you want to talk about Daddy?'

183

But he broke into the *uh-huh* song and scrambled back to his feet, pulled his trike up to the blackberry bushes, then raced back down and held on to my leg. When I asked him if all that meant that he was ready to go swimming, he nodded.

He'd always been too fearless about the water for someone who didn't quite know how to swim, but that day he stayed very close, crawling up into my arms. I understood, and welcomed his trust. It felt like an opportunity to do penance. My heart beat with sadness but without physical pain, without threatening to seize up and quit, beat steady as the words I whispered onto his slick, wet back, 'I'm here, honey. I'm here.'

As Zach clung to me, I checked for any sharp rocks or hidden objects in the water below so Annie could jump off the rope swing. She, too, looked to me for assurance. I nodded, and she leapt up, arms out, legs in an easy stance, a moment of pure freedom. Her face emerged from the water still smiling, and she came to me for a congratulatory hug. I lifted her up and held them both, weightless as they were, in the clear, cool water. Below the surface, I felt something slip past my ankle, a surge of water, a silky flick of a tail, and I flinched with the reminder that I was stepping through an entire world I couldn't see.

18

On the way home, we stopped at the store. David was filling an order of sandwiches for a group of eight. When he finished, he came out, gave me a high five, and sat down while I swept the porch. Annie said, 'Mama had a pool at the hotel, but Zach wouldn't go in it.'

'Oh?' I said, keeping my voice light, for Annie's sake as well as mine. I'd had such a good time swimming with the kids, I wasn't going to let my own problem with jealousy ruin it.

'He was scared, but not with you,' she said, obviously trying to make me feel good. That's how pathetic I'd been. 'Mama wears a T-shirt in the pool. Isn't that *different*?'

'She probably just doesn't want to get sunburned,' I said.

Annie took out the checkers and began attempting to teach Zach how to play. David said to me, 'Paige has always been that way. I thought it was overly zealous modesty, as if anyone gave a shit. Of course, *I* certainly didn't.' I smiled, almost told him I didn't think modesty was the problem, judging by certain photographic evidence. But I kept my mouth shut and steered our conversation back to the store, which was no longer sinking fast but certainly not sailing into the black, which was what I needed to happen. Soon. For so many reasons.

185

The next day, after I got out of bed and made sure my kids attended school instead of sitting in front of the TV, I dusted the store merchandise while I talked to Gwen Alterman about the upcoming mediation. She gave me the rundown, speaking fast, which I appreciated, since every minute of that call cost me about three bucks.

She reminded me not to attack, not to raise my voice, not to interrupt Paige. 'Stay calm. Don't forget to breathe. Start your counterargument with 'Nevertheless' . . . '

I set down a box of crackers and my dust rag and scribbled as much of this down as I could.

'I really believe she doesn't have much of a chance. Still, I've been shocked by mediators' recommendations before. I cannot stress how important the recommendation is. The judge makes the ultimate decision. But rarely does a judge go against a mediator's rec.'

* * *

Marcella kept the kids busy helping her make meatballs while I got dressed for the mediation. I should have bought something new, I thought, while I tried on baggy pants that used to fit a month before. I dug out my makeup bag and tried applying blush, a little lipstick, even mascara. I rarely wore mascara, but especially not since Joe died, and I never knew when the tears would show up, sending black rivers down my face. That day the mascara was a declaration,

186

a stand taken against the tears; I would not cry. I would remain calm yet warm, articulate yet loving, and my lashes would be long and voluminous, according to the label.

I looked in the mirror at my sorry attempt, my baggy clothes, my fake smile. Sad Sack o' Beenes. Buying something new to wear would have helped, but I couldn't justify spending money on myself when things were still so tight with the store. I slipped off the hair band holding my ponytail and tried fluffing my hair, trying to bring out my best asset, but it only looked unkempt. I tied it back into submission.

I kissed the kids, hugging them each as long as I could without cluing them in that something was up. I'd felt it was best not to tell them anything until we knew exactly what was going to happen.

'Where, exactly, are you going?' Annie asked, clearly sensing something was up.

'Oh, just a meeting,' I said. 'I'll be back in a few hours. You stay and help Nonna.'

'Mama said she has a meeting too . . . '

I tapped her nose. 'Oh yeah? Well, long, boring meetings are an unfortunate necessity of adult life.'

All the family members had offered, at different times, to go with me and sit in the waiting room. Even my mom said she'd hop on a plane. But this was something I needed to do on my own. The family was helping to save the store. I needed to save Annie and Zach — and myself.

Still, the terror gnawed away at my insides as I

walked down the linoleum corridors to Family Court Services Mediation. I found a seat in the front, towards the far wall. I scanned the room for Paige but didn't see her. Maybe she wouldn't show. Maybe there was a traffic accident holding her up, a delayed flight. The clerk at the window explained to a man in a cheap suit with two white stitches on the sleeve where the tag had been removed that since the restraining order was still in place, he would need a separate appointment with the mediator. He turned and walked out, not looking at anyone.

I peered down at my notes. Emotionally stable. Calm. Loving. Assuring. Understanding, even.

Maybe she wouldn't show.

'Capozzi versus Beene?' the clerk called. I went to the window. 'You're supposed to check in,' she said, handing me a paper.

I filled it out. Under 'relation to child' I checked 'stepmother.' I'd never done that before, always filled my name out under 'mother' for swim lessons, preschool registration, Annie's soccer. But there it was in writing for the mediator, and Paige would check 'mother' and the checks and balances would be in her favour from the get-go.

But not if she wasn't even there. I held on, hoping, until I heard the door open behind us and saw her glide up to the window to sign her name under 'mother'. Everyone watched her, probably wondering whose ex-wife she could possibly be, not seeing any suitable matches in the room. The men sat up a little straighter.

Actually, the women did too. And me. I sat up straighter.

She looked for a seat, then disappeared from my view. The more we waited, the more nervous I got. I studied my notes. It hit me somewhere between *Talk about close relationship with kids* and *What our days are like* that there was far too much at stake here. It couldn't possibly all come down to a quick meeting with a stranger.

The one mediator I'd had a good feeling about, who smiled warmly at the first couple she'd been assigned to, now came out and called our names. She had short grey hair and tanned skin, a flowing gauzy skirt and sandals. She looked up from her clipboard, took off her reading glasses, letting them hang by a silver and turquoise chain around her neck, and introduced herself.

After we all took a seat in Janice Conner's office, she said, 'I've reviewed your file, and I must say, this is an unusual case. I want you to know that I am both a mother and a stepmother, and I can understand where you're both coming from. I'd like you to each tell me what you think should happen, and why. Paige, you're the petitioner, so let's start with you.' She smiled at Paige. 'Why are we here?'

Paige smiled back. 'I want to start by apologizing to Ella.' She turned to me. 'You've been a good stepmother to my children, and I will always respect you for that. But many misunderstandings and missteps between Joe and I — '

'Joe being the children's deceased father?'

189

Janice Conner asked.

'Yes. You see, I don't think I ever intended to leave my children for good.'

'That,' I said, 'is simply not true. You told him you were never coming back.'

Paige ignored me and directed her speech to Janice Conner. 'I had a severe case of postpartum depression. I wasn't — Well, I thought it would be better for Annie and Zach to — for me not to be there with them. Joe didn't understand. I left. But I wrote letters. I did stop for a while, but when I resumed trying to contact him, he wouldn't take my calls at the store. When he filed for full custody, I was at my lowest point. I was, ah . . . ' She took a deep breath that escaped in a long sigh. 'I was in a psychiatric ward, and that's where I finally met the doctor who knew how to help me.

'So I kept writing letters to Joe and the kids. Even as I gave up custody, I knew it was only temporary. I planned to get myself together, get a job, let Joe come around. But he never did. Because he had met her.' She nodded to me. 'Ella.'

'Yes, Joe and I met four months after she left. After she told him she was never coming back and that he should move on.'

Janice Conner said, 'Okay. Let me interrupt here. It's unfortunate, Paige, that you and the children's father couldn't work things out. But here we are today. Three years later. The kids have an obviously loving stepmother to whom they've grown attached. They've just lost their father. Why now? Why should we upset their world

190

further and move them?'

Paige took another deep breath. 'Joe's death has hit Ella hard, and I don't think she's been there for the children. After the funeral, I found her drinking and smoking in the garden. Since then, Annie calls me frequently. She told me that Ella almost got in a car accident and screamed and swore at the kids.'

That again? Really? I shook my head.

'After I had them for the weekend, I dropped them off at her house, and Ella, she seemed drugged or under the influence of something. She said she had the flu, but I wonder about her drug use.'

Now I stared at Paige, but she kept her eyes on Janice Conner and continued.

'Meanwhile, the children and I have got reacquainted, and I'm so relieved to know that our bond was never broken. You know this: how strong the bond is between a mother and her child.' Paige smoothed her skirt. 'Whenever I talk to Annie, she asks when she can come visit. Plus, the store wasn't even making it three years ago and I wonder about Ella's financial stability.'

Janice Conner kept writing after Paige finally stopped talking, then glanced up at me, over her glasses. 'Ella, I'd like to hear from you now. What would you like me to know?'

My heart beat loudly in my ears. She knew the store was struggling three years ago? 'Basically?' I said. 'That she's not being truthful.'

Janice Conner smiled patiently. 'I know you have a different perspective, and now's your opportunity to tell your side of the story.'

191

'Nevertheless,' I remembered to say. 'There were no letters. She never sent one letter, except for the one she left at the house, telling Joe she wanted out and that he made a great parent, but she couldn't do it.' That's it. I didn't tell them that I'd looked through the boxes of Joe's things, just in case. But still, I'd found nothing.

Paige shook her head. 'I sent cards and letters. Many of them,' she whined. She looked at me. 'Where the hell *were* you?'

Janice Conner cleared her throat. 'I need to remind you both to keep your statements and questions directed at me. I do have a question for you, Paige. Did you ever send any of those cards and letters certified mail?' The room fell quiet for the first time. I looked over at Paige, who shook her head slowly, barely, looking at her hands in her lap. 'That's unfortunate. Because then we wouldn't be relying on a she-said' — she smiled — 'she-said scenario. Paige, do you think it's possible that the letters were never sent?'

Paige said no, but her face began to redden.

Janice continued. 'I've done that before, thought I sent something only to find it tucked in the bill drawer. You were on medications, going through a difficult time. Could you have given them to a nurse or orderly? Your psychiatrist? Or maybe stuck them in your suitcase to mail later? I'm not suggesting you didn't write them, only that — '

'No!' Paige almost shouted. Her face was flushed a vivid pink. Then, quieter, her eyes fixed on the ceiling, she said, 'You think they all tricked me?'

192

'Clearly, whether or not the letters were sent is not something we can resolve here today. So I'd like to steer the discussion back to Ella. Ella, what can you tell me about why Annie and Zach should remain in your care?'

I swallowed, thinking of Annie and Zach standing on stools making meatballs that morning with Marcella, apron strings doubled around their small frames. 'Because I'm the only mother they've known. Because we have a home, and a large, caring family around us. And a loving community, with lots of friends. It's great they might go to Paige's for a weekend and have a blast, but the truth is, they're sad. At my home, they're allowed to be sad, because I'm sad too. I don't see their father's death as some kind of sick *opportunity*.

'Yes, I've had a few bad days. But I'm grieving. I'm not going crazy. We're nothing alike. Nothing.'

I looked up at Janice, who was not writing as she had been when Paige talked. She flipped a page back. 'Can you explain the behaviour Paige described, her concern about drug use?'

I told her how the doctor prescribed Xanax, that I'd never taken anything like that before and took a few too many one day. 'But I haven't taken any since. I threw them away.' Though God knew I could have used one right that minute.

'Are you sure? Can you verify this with a letter from your doctor? Co-workers?'

'Yes, I'm sure. I've never been addicted to anything.' I explained, too, about the almost-car-accident, and why I'd yelled. 'These are things Paige has never experienced because she left.'

Paige uncrossed her legs, squared her shoulders. 'Fortunately,' she said, 'that was not the end of my story. It took a lot of hard work to pull myself up from that, and there was only one source for me to pull from: my love for my children. I am their mother. A mother who made mistakes, but also still thinks I made the right decision to leave when I did . . . Because I loved them then and I love them now. I can now give them a better financially and more emotionally stable environment than she can, and I am their *mother*. They should be with me.'

Janice was writing down everything Paige said.

'You're writing down everything she says, but it's not true.' My voice was on the rise. I took a breath, forced myself to speak calmly. 'Paige is someone new in the kids' lives. She buys them things. They have no strong emotional bond with her. Zach doesn't even know her! She's preying on Annie because Annie is extremely vulnerable. I'm worried what would happen to them if they were moved away from their home right now. Their mother left when they were very, very young. They've lost their dad. For good. And now, if they lose me too . . . and their grandparents, uncle, everyone. Annie and Zach will be devastated.'

She turned to Paige. 'What, exactly, does a home stager do?'

'Well, I interview — '

'She takes out all the personal memories and treasures that make a house a home and puts in a few pieces of carefully placed trendy furniture to make it look like someone else lives there,

194

possibly even the potential buyer. She fakes it. She fakes *home*. And she's good at it.'

'At least I don't expect the children to live in a tiny, cluttered shack.'

'Ha. A shack. *Right.* You make it sound like it's tar papered.' I looked at Janice and took another deep breath. 'It's actually a lovely, 1930s remodelled cottage the kids' great-grandpa built.' I went on about Elbow, their relatives, their friends, their pets — anything I could think of, rambling now.

Janice Conner held the clipboard up in the air, like a stop sign. 'Okay. Well. I can see that we're not going to come to any kind of agreement between you today. Now it's my turn: I want you to both listen to me. I want you, for the sake of those two children who have already been through so much, to stop this bickering. You cannot demean the other person in front of the kids. It will hurt them profoundly.' She looked at Paige, then at me. 'This is a tough one. Is there any chance either of you might be willing to move?'

'No,' we both said in unison. It was the one thing we could agree on.

19

I sat in the Jeep in the courthouse parking lot, talking to Gwen Alterman on my cell phone, blotting the black rivers on my face with balled-up tissue. Gwen assured me I was not the first person to insult the opposing party in mediation. 'Mediators are used to it. They hear it every day.'

'But you said — '

'That was the ideal. It would have been great if you could have stayed on course one hundred percent, but it sounds like you didn't do as badly as you're thinking.'

'No. I did. I was terrible. *I* wouldn't grant custody to me.'

'Look. Go home. Be with your kids. Make that store a success. We won't know anything for a week or two. Try not to think about it.'

But I thought about it, and thought about it. I thought about the fact that Joe had told Paige, or Paige had instinctively known the way wives *do*, that the store was struggling. I thought about how Paige had said she'd requested to see the kids. 'Where the hell *were* you?' she'd asked. I wondered about that, at least regarding the store. I was sure she was lying about the letters. I would have seen them, would have heard snippets of phone conversations, *something*. Joe wouldn't have been able to hide that too.

I hadn't been much of a praying woman, but I

196

prayed, and prayed, and prayed. Please, somehow, make Janice Conner see that the kids should be with me. Please, please don't take them away. And if Paige lost her marbles again? That wouldn't be entirely a bad thing . . . I knew that praying for someone to go crazy couldn't be winning me any heavenly points, or karmic points, or points on my own side of mental health, but I felt desperate. I cringed whenever I thought of the mediation, of my own stabs at Paige and my incompetent explanation of my 'bad days'. Of Paige's words, 'Instead, he met her.' Instead of what? Reconciliation? A different ending? A change from the direction that ultimately led to Joe's death?

★　★　★

If it wasn't for all the activity at the store, I would have been the one losing my marbles. Things were busy, and I needed to be there, helping David and Marcella. David managed to get more write-ups in the *Chronicle*, the *San Jose Mercury News*, and the *Bohemian*, which all raved about the food and the off-the-beaten-track picnic map (one reporter called it worthy of framing and hanging in your home — or the Metropolitan, which made Clem chuckle in delight). The reporters appreciated the whole concept of the store. 'They have even included a quaint glassed-in back porch amidst the trees, for those days when the weather doesn't cooperate.' Joe Sr read from one of the folded papers, then waved all the reviews at me. 'This idea of yours

. . . Hot damn! It might just work.'

It was the week before Halloween, which couldn't have been a better time for me to focus on other things besides mediation and the upcoming custody hearing and Paige. I loved Halloween. Elbow was the perfect place for it. No need to haul the kids to a mall for 'safe' trick-or-treating. Everyone in Elbow knew one another, we were short on traffic and long on kids, and Life's a Picnic stood right in the centre of it all. I had big plans.

I'd made the kids' costumes every year since I'd been there, and this year would be no different. Yes, there was the gentle tug at the corner of all those big plans, reminding me that next year might be starkly different. And all the years after that. But I tugged back hard and set to work.

'Mommy, what are you up to?' Annie asked. 'Besides five foot ten, that is.' She cracked herself up.

I burrowed in the back of our closet like one of the gophers Callie kept digging up. I still hadn't moved out Joe's clothes. It was one of those things I kept writing down on my lists but never crossing off. 'I'm looking for the . . . here it is.' I yanked and pulled out my heavy plastic Singer sewing machine case. 'Ta-da! It's that time of year.'

Annie looked at her foot, twisting her toe into the rug. 'I've been meaning to *talk* to you about that.'

'What about, Banannie?' Last year she'd been a tree. She wore brown cord pants and, on her torso, over a brown long-sleeve shirt, a big green pillowcase that I'd hot glue gunned with a ton of silk green leaves and stuffed with newspapers. We rigged up a little tree swing with rope and a small board, hung it from her arm, and stuck a stuffed bear on it. On her head, she wore a cap that we topped with a little bird's nest and a fake robin. Joe had even put a couple of little fake eggs in it. She'd won first prize at the Elbow Boo Fest. 'Have you thought about what you want to be?'

'Yes. I'd like to be Pocahontas.'

Not exactly original, but okay. 'Okay! So I'll need to find some suede. Oh, I know, we can make a bunch of beaded necklaces. Maybe we can rig up the canoe so we can pull you on the wagon . . . '

'Mommy? I was thinking . . . I think I'd prefer to, you know, *buy* a Pocahontas costume this year. You're busy, and they have them completely done, so I'll look perfectly, exactly like the *real* Pocahontas in the movie.'

'You mean the real *Disney* Pocahontas?'

'Exactly! I'll look fabulous. And Molly is going to dress up as Belle.' Frank and Lizzie's daughter was in Annie's class, and they'd grown even closer. Frank would be the one to take her trick-or-treating with us, definitely not Lizzie with her oath to Avoid Ella Whenever Possible.

'Fabulous . . . ,' I said. She had got taller. She looped her hair behind her ear and smiled. She'd always loved my homemade costumes, loved helping with the creation, the attention she always got. Certainly she didn't want to fade into the masses. Maybe she simply wanted to decide what she was going to wear, on her own. This was just the beginning of the beginning — I knew that. I wanted to be around for every one of the future mom-defying moments. Tummy-baring tops, piercings, tattoos. Gothic black from head to toenails. Or perhaps she'd target her defiance precisely at me, become a hairswinging cheerleader or a glittery mall rat. Or refuse to eat anything but McDonald's. But for now she just wanted a store-bought Halloween costume. One I couldn't afford right then. Those Disney Store costumes ran well over fifty bucks.

As if she could read my mind, she said, 'Mama said they have a Disney Store in Lost Vegas. She said she could pick up one and send it right away. But to ask you first.'

I nodded. Had the whole thing been Paige's suggestion? Or Annie's idea? Either way, it felt personal, even though the better part of me knew I needed to slough it off.

'Okay, Mommy?' She had her fingers woven together in a prayerful plea. Her eyebrows arched high on her forehead, her smile a bit forced, as if pretending I'd already said yes would help her cause. But how could I deny her this one request?

'Okay. *Fabulous*, even.'

She hugged me around my waist. 'I knew you'd say yes! I'm calling Mama right away! Thank you tons!'

The rejection hit me like a sucker punch, and after Annie skipped out I slumped down in the closet. Joe's old shirts and jackets hanging from the bottom rod seemed to part for me, then embrace me. I needed the real Joe, his real hug, but I sat there anyway, accepting what felt like some sort of understanding from his 49ers jacket, his periwinkle oxford that brought out the blue in his eyes.

Annie had been gracious, and I was glad I'd said yes. Couldn't I share with Paige the privilege of making Annie happy? I could try.

I got busy planning Zach's and my costumes. I knew exactly what I would be, but Zach was still deliberating between various types of insects. A praying mantis? A luna moth? A centipede? He pondered the possibilities.

★ ★ ★

Late October. The weather conducted its symphony of falling, twirling leaves — golds and reds and oranges against the huge evergreen backdrop — with skies that sustained a deep, clear blue. Many of the vineyards had turned to shimmering yellow, like lakes of captured sunlight pooling between the dark, forested hills. The bell on the store's screen door kept chiming, the phone kept ringing, the old cash register kept clanging, *Hallelujah!* Underneath all that, I listened and heard, when I'd hold them or sit in their room while they slept, the low, steady drumbeat of our hearts, Annie's, Zach's, mine, and the rhythm of the clock, counting days, hours, minutes.

I stood on a ladder, stringing cotton webbing from the store's rafters. The previous Christmas,

Joe had stood on the same ladder, in the same spot, while I'd handed him strings of white lights. When he stepped down I said we needed mistletoe. He grabbed me. 'We don't need no stinkin' mistletoe,' he whispered, then kissed me. The door chimed and he kept kissing me while Mrs Tagnoli said, 'Ooh la la.' In less than a year, I'd gone from glitter and twinkling lights and kissing to cobwebs and ghosts and regrets.

'*Buongiorno! Bellisima!*' Lucy, just back from a winery in Italy, called up to me.

'I'd come down to hug you, but I'm a little tied up at the moment,' I said.

'Oh, what tangled webs you weave.' She set down her basket. 'I brought wine. Italy! Italy is fantastic. I need to live in Italy.'

'You practically do. Sonoma County is Italy. Without the accent.'

'And the centuries-old buildings and the incredible art and cobbled streets and the melody of *Italiano* being spoken everywhere and all those lusty men.'

'But they're not George Clooney . . . '

'No, but this one guy, Stefano, could make me forget George' — she smiled — 'and I just *bumped* into *Stefano*. Again and again and again . . . '

'*Stefano*? Sex? I think I remember sex. Pray tell.'

'He's young. And gorgeous. And Oh. My. God.'

Marcella came out from the kitchen. Lucy mouthed, 'Later.'

Marcella put her hands on her hips, craned

her neck, and said, 'Oh my word. I guess I should have just left the real cobwebs up there.'

'She's Charlotte,' Lucy said. 'She's going to spell something if we give her enough spinning time.'

'I wish it were that easy. I could write something, like 'Ella. Some Mom'. Just like Charlotte wrote 'Some Pig'. And the press would come, declare a miracle, and we would be saved, just like Wilbur.'

'Ella,' Lucy said. 'No one needs a miracle to see that you're Some Mom. Now, come down from there and help me unload.'

Lucy filled my arms with wine, tablecloths, lovely Venetian blown-glass vases; she filled my ears with stories of long, hot afternoons with Stefano.

We could see the Bobbing for Coffins Parade committee heading towards the river to start setting up. This was an Elbow tradition, based on a big goof-up of the town's founding fathers. Back in the 1870s, lumber mills were cropping up much faster than the trees would ever be able to, and *thousand*-year-old redwoods were being sawed down in the prime of their lives — then came the trains, and then came the tourists, and Elbow was born. A prime location, a sandy beach — it was a town mostly built on the tourist trade rather than the logging industry, but the logs rolled by, just the same, on their way to Edwards' Mill a mile or so downriver. Most of the men of Elbow who weren't in the tourist business or summer homeowners worked in the lumber industry. Felling trees three hundred feet tall and as wide as twenty men standing side by side at the base is dangerous business, and many of them died doing it.

A cemetery was quickly established on a pretty, peaceful spot not too far from the edge of town, but not far enough from the edge of the river. The flood of 1879 revealed the error. The river overflowed, uprooting gardens, trees, carriages, a couple of horses, six cabins, and a dozen coffins. The coffins bobbed down the river, along with the logs, towards the mill. That which had been laid to rest for eternity had become restless.

The townspeople grabbed their rowboats, their fishing nets, their ropes, and set off to catch the coffins and pull them back to dry land, which they did. Though it was true that no one died in that flood, not even the horses, the newspaper reported that twelve bodies were found in the river, which was also true. The coffins that still remained in the ground were dug up, and the cemetery was immediately moved up to the sunny hill, where Joe was buried.

The burial blunder was celebrated every year with the Elbow Bobbing for Coffins Parade. People decorated their rowboats, canoes, and kayaks like floats. Life-size (or perhaps I should say death-size) plastic coffins were tied in between the 'row floats'. Tiki lamps lighted up each float and coffin. Tradition called for utter silence while the parade was in progress, and amazingly, everyone acquiesced, as the boats and coffins quietly moved downriver, the flames reflecting off the water, a silent dance.

★ ★ ★

I closed Lucy's trunk and said, 'Wow. Bobbing for Coffins. Why have I not seen how utterly morbid that is?'

Lucy smiled. 'Of course it's morbid. It's Halloween.'

'Do you think Annie and Zach will be okay with it? I mean . . . they did just see their drowned dad's coffin placed into the ground. I talked to them about it, and they both seem excited about the parade. But still . . . '

'I'm guessing they'll be okay. Besides, you'll be watching their every expression, and if it's suddenly not okay, you'll be there. El, it's Halloween. And they're kids. Amped up over candy. Who *love* the parade.'

That night, down at Life's a Picnic, we unveiled our costumes to hoots and applause from Lucy, David, Gil, Marcella, and Joe Sr.

'Hey, Boo-Boo?' David said to Gil. 'It looks like we might have ourselves a pic-i-nic basket . . . And a giant, ferocious . . . ant.'

'I'm a *formica*,' Zach said.

Gil said, 'You know the Latin? Your mom must be the famous entomologist, Ella Beene. Hey, where's Bubby?' Zach pulled Bubby out of his plastic jack-o'-lantern, like a rabbit from a hat. 'And look at our beautiful Miss Pocahontas.'

'Ella,' Lucy said, 'I think you've outdone yourself this time.'

I'd taken our wicker laundry basket and cut most of the bottom out of it and harnessed it over my shoulders with a couple of Joe's old

205

leather belts. I had covered my jeans with material from red-and-white-checked tablecloths. I wore a wild fruit-basket hat and had stuffed the laundry basket with newspapers, covered those with more tablecloths, and stuck in a bottle of wine, a hunk of cheese, a loaf of bread, a rubber chicken. I was, indeed, a picnic basket.

'No cracks about me being a basket case, please.'

'Oh, that would be too easy,' David said.

He had agreed to cover the store so I could take the kids to the parade and then meet Frank and Molly for trick-or-treating. I had to step out of the laundry basket in order to fit in the canoe, so I carefully did that, leaving the bulk of my costume at the store so we could run down to the river. I buckled their life jackets and we climbed into the canoe. Zach pointed to the plastic coffins. 'Those are pretend,' he reminded himself. A good reminder for all of us, really.

'Yes, Zach, those are pretend.'

There was a harvest moon, low and big and orange. 'A pumpkin moon,' he whispered. He was tucked in next to me, his red antennae poking me in the cheek, my head heavy with plastic fruit. Annie sat in front of us, dipping the oar in to guide the canoe. We were tied to the coffin in front of us and the coffin behind us, and the boats ahead pulled us along, but Annie sat at the helm, taking her role seriously. I watched them both; they were solemn but didn't seem scared. Zach watched the reflections of the moon and the tiki flames illuminated on the river, which slapped at the bottom of our canoe. Annie turned around. 'I'm tired,' she whispered. I scooted even closer to Zach and patted the seat.

'Careful.'

She climbed back to me, and I put my arms around both of them. We sat in the silence. Three peas in a pod.

No longer four.

The moment hung in the night like the moon. Peaceful, eerie, weighted. We reached the end just ahead of the last float and coffin, and then all mayhem broke loose. The music started. The kids went wild. Halloween officially began.

★ ★ ★

After I retrieved the rest of my costume from the store, Molly ran up to us, dressed up in her Disney Belle costume. Lizzie — not Frank — followed behind. 'Frank got called into work,' she explained without saying hello. 'Wow, look at you . . . ,' she said, looking me up and down. 'Cute.'

'I can take the kids if you want.'

'No, that's okay. I left the bowl of candy on the porch. When it's gone, it's gone.' She was only about five feet tall, but she walked with the grace of a gazelle. She'd grown up in Elbow, the high school home-coming queen, the valedictorian, and the class president. She'd gone to Stanford, had some high-level exec job for a while, but she'd grown disillusioned with the corporate world, came back, and married Frank, her high school sweetheart. Now she had Molly and ran her own business making the most incredible-smelling soaps on the planet. Lizzie's Lathers product line was so good, people were willing to drop $7 for a bar of soap, and the *Press Democrat* had run a full-page article with the headline: HOMEMADE SOAP COMPANY REALLY CLEANS UP. Everyone knew her and adored her, stopping to talk to her as we walked along — she so much more animated and warm with them than she'd ever been with me, me relieved when it was someone I knew, and they would direct the conversation to both of us. Usually it was to say that they liked my costume or to wish me good luck and tell me they were pulling for me with — and here is where they'd lower their voices — the ridiculous custody thing.

When we walked a stretch of road where we found our little group alone, the kids heading up to a front door, Lizzie said, 'Look, I know about the custody case. But I only know that there is one, nothing else.' Lizzie kept her eyes locked on the kids. 'Frank and I have an understanding when it comes to your family. It's a No Discussion Zone for us.' She shook her head. 'Sorry. It sounds cold. But when Joe and Paige broke up, it was hard on us. Too many things we could never agree on. I didn't want to lose my own marriage fighting over theirs. So.' She shrugged. The kids ran up to us, shouting about *a giant skeleton*, and Brenda Haley approached Lizzie with a question about the PTA cakewalk, and the moment was over.

When we dragged ourselves through our front doorway later that night, the message machine flashed. I didn't know whether to read it as a warning or a beacon of hope. I helped the kids out of their costumes, gently wiped the makeup off Annie's face, broke up a sugar-infused fight resulting in flying candy corn, read them some Maurice Sendak, kissed them good night. I built a fire, sat on the couch, rubbing Callie's belly, watching the red light go on and off. Staring at the flames, I pulled a loose thread on my tablecloth-covered jeans until I gathered enough courage to hoist myself up and walk across the floor and push the play button. It was Gwen Alterman, as I knew it would be.

'The mediator's recommendation just arrived.' She paused. 'Ella, it is in your favour. She recommends that full custody be granted to you. This is just as I expected. I doubt this will even go to a hearing.' I sank back into the couch. Joe's picture grinned at me from the book-shelf. Her message continued: 'She questioned why Paige didn't try harder to contact Joe. She wasn't convinced by Paige's claim that she sent letters. She does feel that Paige should have some visitation rights, but it's not extensive. Four to six weekends a year, with a couple of weeklong visits as the kids get older. And that's something we can negotiate. I'm expecting to hear from Paige's counsel tomorrow. He surely knows that they don't have a chance for custody now.'

She told me to celebrate. She'd stick a copy in the mail and let me know when Paige's lawyer called. 'You're probably out trick-or-treating with your kids, as you should be. Happy Halloween, Ella.'

I pressed my lips together, pressed my hand over my lips, pressed my other hand into my gut, shook with such relief and joy, such intense gratitude, and at the same time, an utter disbelief that this all was coming to a happy ending, which meant, of course, a beginning. A beginning without Joe, yes, but a new beginning with Annie, Zach, and me. I followed Callie outside. The moon that had been low and orange earlier that evening towered high above us, whiter and clearer than I'd ever remembered seeing it before or since. Perfect, round, whole.

I ran around with Callie, the light so bright, our shadows danced on the land. I leapt, I wriggled, I skipped, I held her paws and said, out of breath, my heart banging, 'Yes! Yes! Yes!' I scrambled back inside, into their rooms, and pried a sticky Sugar Daddy from Zach's hand. I watched them sleep, studied the flutter of their eyelashes and the up-and-down, up-and-down of their small chests.

I didn't think of Paige, not until later, when I climbed into my bed, the moonlight following me, like a spotlight on a star. The Ella Beene Show. I squinted. Or maybe it was an interrogator's moon. Paige was alone in that big hollow house in Las Vegas with the dinosaur bedroom, the princess bedroom, and I remembered how lonely those big new houses with their empty decorated kids' rooms could be. Henry and I had lived in such a house. I could have easily been in her position that night. Instead, we were here, in our warm, moonlight-drenched cottage, the kids tucked in their familiar beds, the days ahead tumbling towards us, seeming so full, open, promising.

20

I called everyone the next morning. Marcella spoke for all of us when she said, 'Oh, Ella! I can breathe again. I can breathe!' My mom said, 'Oh, Jelly,' and I could tell she was crying. Joe Sr brought me a huge bouquet of his garden roses, which he knew I loved. They were pale peach with coral edges and gave off a hint of cloves; he hugged me so long and so hard, I knew he was crying too. 'Let me take those kids to see their nonna,' he finally was able to say. 'She made panettone to celebrate.'

I walked down to the store to put some time in on the books. Our new books showed more promise than the old ones Joe had sweated over. We were almost making it. But things would slow down when the rainy season began. We kept hoping the glassed-in porch addition could pull us through the winter weather.

The whole place smelled like nutmeg and cinnamon. 'Pumpkin tarts,' David said when I closed my eyes and inhaled. He took off his apron and gave me a hug. He told me he and Gil wanted to bring over a surprise for Zach and Annie that night. They'd wanted to give the kids a special treat for Halloween but first needed to wait and see how things turned out. When I asked what kind of surprise, he just smiled.

'Don't be coy.'

'Oh, I'm nothing to you but your coy boy.

Hey, guess who was in here earlier.'

'A benefactor?'

'Ray Longobardi. He bought the butternut squash and apple soup. Made me promise not to tell his wife.'

'Guess he's going to have to mortgage his house.'

'Wait'll he tries these tarts. The poor man will have to claim bankruptcy too.'

'Now you're being a tarty coy boy.' He wiggled his ass and we both laughed. It felt good to laugh.

I looked over David's list on the counter and saw how much I hadn't been pulling my weight, as much as I'd been trying. Now with the custody issues behind us, I could focus on three things: Annie, Zach, and the store. I told David I'd take care of the ribollita soup and started gathering the ingredients. Chopping vegetables, pouring, chopping herbs, stirring, I counted my blessings, and kept counting as I shredded the pecorino and tore the day-old bread. I crossed off the soup while it simmered, and headed upstairs to work on the books. Through the window of the office, I looked down on the store that had survived the Depression, internment camps, fear, financial difficulties, and death, and now, at last, was renewed to be something nurturing and vibrant once more. I wrote checks, counted money that was still not quite enough, and counted more blessings. So many. Too many to count.

★　★　★

212

That night, David and Gil brought in a big crate with a huge sage ribbon tied around it. 'What the . . . ?' I asked.

'I know we should have asked you first,' David explained. 'But then you would have had the chance to say no.' He set down the crate and opened the front hatch, and out jumped two grey-and-white kittens.

'What the . . . ?' I said again, but Annie and Zach had already scooped them up. I stared at David and said, 'Totally, completely unfair.' The kids took the kittens down the hall, towards the bedrooms. Callie was beside herself, but I knew she wouldn't hurt them. She wouldn't even touch the chickens. But she was curious. Definitely.

'Look, you need something to help keep the mice down in the barn. Also, my dear, they'll help you with that rat problem.'

'Rat problem? You mean that little mouse?'

'Mice. They only come in multipacks, dear. But you do have one rat. And if I remember correctly, Paige is allergic to cats.'

'David. 'Rat' is awfully harsh. Be nice. It's over now. Cut her some slack.'

'Mohhhmy! We need your he-elp!' Annie called out from my room.

I shook my finger at David and Gil. 'You. *Kittens?*' We went to investigate. The kids' legs stuck out from under the bed, traces of mud lodged in the rubber tracking of their sneakers.

'They keep running under your bed so Callie can't play with them. But now we can't find them under there. We can hear them, though.'

We crouched down to take a look. Annie was right; we couldn't see them.

Gil said, 'I bet there's a rip in the box springs — they're probably up in the coils. My friend had a kitten who, uh' — he placed his hand around his neck in a choke sign — 'because it got caught up there. It happens frequently with kittens. We hear about it at the shelter too. The undersides of beds and sofas, they're kitty death traps.'

'We've got to get them out, then. And I believe it's your guys' duty to help me.'

Gil went for a can of tuna from the pantry and opened it, and both kittens jumped out like little rabbits.

'Okay, kiddos,' David said. 'Hold the kitties and stand over by the door. We've got to fix this bed.' Under his breath he said to me, 'The last thing you need around here are strangled kittens. Got a needle and thread?'

I nodded and went to the closet to get them. David and Gil removed the mattress and set it against the wall. Then they flipped over the box spring.

'The ship's capsized! Mayday! Mayday!' Annie shouted, while she and Zach jumped up and down with the poor kittens, who looked like they would die of dislocated necks anyway, despite our valiant efforts.

'Careful. You might hurt them,' I warned.

David and Gil were studying the underside of the box spring, which faced away from the kids and me.

'Well,' David said. 'Well. I'll be a monkey's uncle.'

214

'Uncle David, how many times do I have to tell you? We are *not*,' Annie insisted, '*monkeys*.'

But David ignored her. 'Um, Gil? Want to help the kids feed the cats in the *other room*?'

Gil nodded, led the kids out to the kitchen, closing the door behind them.

'Ella? Sweetheart? Don't look . . . ' He'd gone pale. I couldn't imagine — an old dead kitten skeleton?

I stepped over the bed frame and around the box spring to look. There was a rip — more like a slit — in the sheer fabric that covered the box springs. And up, tucked away in the coils, were several very thick packets of what looked to be letters.

21

We stood, staring, not speaking. Finally, David said, 'I feel a chill. Perhaps we should fire up the woodstove.'

'David . . . I . . . '

'No one has to know.'

We still hadn't moved, hadn't taken them out to look, to make sure they were what we knew them to be. I thought I might vomit. David put his arm around me.

'Ella. No one has to know.'

I shook my head. 'That's not possible.'

'Sure it is. I don't see anything.'

'David. *I* see. *I* know.' A roar howled in my ears, and my whole body pulsed in time with my heart.

'Well, don't read them, then. They're probably full of requests for him to keep the kids forever. That's what I perceive them to be.'

'No, you don't.'

'They could be.'

Through clenched teeth I let out, 'I could kill your brother right now if he weren't already dead.'

David whistled, let go of me. '*That's* harsh.'

'Anger is the easiest — of every fucking feeling I'm having right now. Anger is a breeze. Compared to the rest.'

'Listen, don't lose it. Listen to me. You have to think of Annie and Zach and what's best for them. And we both know that includes not being stolen away by her.'

'How do you know that? How do you know who she really is? We thought we knew *Joe*.'

'Joe had his reasons. I'm sure he thought he was doing what was best for the kids, and I'm sure it was best.'

'I cannot bear to hear excuses right now.'

'Don't open them. Don't read them. It doesn't matter, anyway . . . It's not going to change anything.'

'How can you say that? It changes *everything*.'

'You're the mom they know and love. You're the one who can provide a loving, stable home in the town where they'll grow up knowing everyone. If she takes them, we'll never see them.' He stopped and took a deep breath. 'Forget I said that. This wouldn't even begin to change a judge's viewpoint. I mean, we don't know what those things say. We can end this before it even starts.'

I cut back the fabric and removed the packets. I counted them, keeping them contained by their rubber bands. There were twenty-six, like a half deck of cards. The other half of the story. While I sewed up the fabric, I knelt on the letters, afraid that if I stuck them in a drawer, David might grab them and run. Instead, he leaned his back against the wall, crossed his arms, and in a rare silence, watched me.

I stuck the packets inside the waistband of my jeans, under my T-shirt, and we set the box spring back on the frame, the mattress on top of that. He shook out the down comforter; he

217

fluffed up the pillows.

Only when he left the room and closed the door did I stick the letters between the box spring and the mattress. Out in the not-so-great room, the kids seemed oblivious to the awkward silence between us three adults. Gil and David hugged the kids. Gil hugged me, but David left without even looking in my direction.

I had to keep moving. Put the litter box in the crate in the kids' room for the night. Crawl under both their beds to check for rips, to check, too, for more letters.

Both kids, revved up on kittens, screeched around corners from bathroom to kitchen to bedroom and back again until I yelled, 'Knock it off!' which set Annie on a round of knock-knock jokes, which she recited while jumping on her bed.

'Please! Just stop,' I said, my voice cracking.

'What's wrong, Mommy?' Annie asked, falling to her butt, still bouncing a bit on the mattress. 'Don't you like the kitties?'

'I do,' I said. 'I'm just tired.' Read them The Cat in the Hat, then hug and kiss them, sitting on the edges of Zach's bed, then Annie's. Smooth back their hair off their foreheads, a bit sweaty from all their racing around. Wonder if they'll want them cut again, or if they'll want to grow them out. Watch fluttering eyelashes, butterflies kissing dreams, until they finally fall asleep. Lift the kittens from their arms and place them into the crate, their soft mews reminding you that this was their first night away from their mother. Stick an old stuffed bear from the toy

218

box and a small clock behind it in the crate, a poor substitute for their mother's beating heart.

I lay in bed, but there may as well have been elephants tucked below my mattress. I turned on the light, retrieved the packets. They were sorted by postmark. Some were addressed to Joe, some were to Annie and Zach, all in a neat and angular script, though the first were shaky, then shakier, until gradually getting smoother through to the last. Only the five envelopes bearing the earlier postmarks had been opened.

I made a cup of tea, staring at the water until it boiled, dunking the bag in over and over until it turned the water almost black, then climbed back in, patting the bed for Callie to join me. I wanted to read every word, but I didn't want to know.

I did not want to know. My life, as I'd imagined it, depended on me not knowing.

I shoved the letters in my nightstand drawer, turned facedown the picture of Joe on the nightstand, and tried to turn down the high hum coursing through my veins, like the hum of an intercom that precedes the crackling announcement: Prepare for imminent disaster.

22

All day I picked up the phone, then set it back down. My mom? No. Lucy? No. David? Definitely no. Marcella? Heavens no. Gwen Alterman? Hell no.

They would all freak out about the letters. Like David, they might tell me to burn them. Or they might tell me to take them out to Bodega and throw them into the ocean.

Early the next morning I dropped Annie and Zach and the crate of kittens off at Marcella's, but instead of heading to the store, I drove out to Bodega Head. I took the letters with me. I wanted to think, to come to a decision on my own. I passed the cemetery, but I didn't stop.

Mine was the only car in the gravel parking lot. Like the Green Hornet had been when Frank and I left it, that first horrible day of summer. Now the fog bank lay thick, obscuring the view. A great egret stood in the ice plant, along the cliff, its white neck curved in a question mark. Joe had once pointed to one and said, 'I have but one great egret.' I'd smiled, and instead of asking him if he really did have one great regret, and if so, what it might be, I said, '*Casmerodius albus.*'

I held the packets of letters in my hand, snapping the rubber bands in a steady rhythm. I did not know what to do. I wanted to do the right thing, but mostly, to do the right thing for

Annie and Zach. Paige had cared more than I'd thought. Cared at least enough to write twenty-six times. I tried to push away the selfish fact that I couldn't imagine my life without Annie and Zach. But how do you push a fact like that away?

I got out of the Jeep and headed towards the cliff, letters in hand. I stood and watched the waves, steady, predictable, calming, even — but the locals knew better. And Joe had known better. 'Never turn your back on the ocean,' he'd told the kids and me over and over. Then he'd gone and done exactly that, focusing all his attention on the way the cliff stood against that morning's light, totally disregarding the way something could sneak up from behind and knock a person clear to kingdom come.

A black Ford Explorer pulled into the lot and parked; a man and a woman, their four children tucked into the backseat. The woman was screaming; I couldn't hear what she was saying through their closed windows but could see her contorted face, her hitting the dashboard.

The man got out of the driver's seat. He was trim, neatly dressed in khaki shorts and a polo shirt. He looked out towards the ocean and stretched, then walked around and opened the back of the Explorer. He took a six-pack of Pepsi from a cooler and methodically plucked each can out of the plastic holder, then placed them back in the cooler. He then ripped each plastic ring, in what I thought was an act of concern for the environment, until he dropped them on the ground.

221

One of the children, a girl of about eight or nine, turned in her seat and watched him. He looked back at her, but no one spoke. Carrying one of the Pepsis, he opened the passenger door and handed it to the woman. He took a brown prescription bottle out of the pocket of his windbreaker. He tapped out one pill and held it out for her in his open palm.

She took it and swallowed.

He returned to the back of the Explorer, and before he pulled the hatch down, the girl looked at me, speaking to me now with her eyes.

The man followed her gaze and said to me over his shoulder, 'Don't you have anything better to do?'

Until then, I hadn't realized that I'd stopped and was blatantly staring. I mumbled, 'Sorry,' and turned and walked back to the car, still carrying the packet of letters, which now felt as heavy and conspicuous as a body.

★ ★ ★

The only thing I saw on my ride back were those young girl's eyes. The knowing stare of a child. I drove straight home, took the phone out to the porch, and called my mom. But I didn't tell her about the letters.

I said, 'Tell me about Daddy.'

I expected the beat of silence before she said, 'Well, Jelly? What would you like to know? I mean, we've talked about Daddy over the years. I think I've told you — '

'You've told me what a great father he was. I

222

mean, tell me about your marriage.'

'Oh! Our marriage? Well? Let's see . . . '

'Was it a good marriage?'

'Yes . . . I mean, all marriages are hard, honey. Everyone goes through difficulties. But I loved your father very much . . . '

'Were you happy?'

'Were we happy? Yes. Sometimes . . . '

'But . . . ?'

She let out a long, loud sigh, like air escaping a balloon. 'There are certain things that are private. That you don't need to know. Your father was a good man. He died way, way too young. You were robbed and I always felt so sad for you.'

For me. But not for her. 'Were you with him when he died?'

'No. I wasn't.'

'Where was he? How did you find out?'

'Ella . . . I don't really remember . . . '

My voice shook. 'Now I know you're lying. Of course you remember. Because I remember. Something happened and no one would talk about it. But. I knew. I *knew*. And I said something . . . something to Grandma Beene. And she slapped me.'

'Grandma Beene slapped you?'

'Yes . . . and she told me, 'Never say that again' . . . '

'What did you say?'

'I knew something. That I wasn't supposed to know . . . '

'You did? You do?'

'Mom. Stop it. Just tell me what *you* know.'

223

There was a long silence. I watched Callie chase a covey of quail in vain, their black feathered hats bobbling in front of their plump bodies like middle-aged flappers. That spring, Joe and I sat out here in the evening, listening to the males' courting call: *Whereareyou? Where-areyou?*

My mom said, 'I never wanted you to know. His death was hard enough.' I waited. The quail lifted together like one wing and lit on the butterfly bush. Callie's attention turned to a gopher hole, and she started to dig. 'And to find out now? When you're in mourning? When you're in the heat of a custody battle?'

'Just say it. Please.' But in the corner of my soul, a lid lifted and the words floated, whole, up to my lips before they touched my brain, and I blurted them before she could make herself say them. 'He was having an affair, wasn't he . . . with my teacher. Miss McKenna . . . And he was with her when he died. At her house.'

'You knew that? How?'

'Mom. Of *course* I knew. The way kids always know.' The way that little girl's eyes could tell me she knew why her mother was screaming again, why her father chose controlled silence. And it all started coming back to me. 'I thought it was my fault, that if I'd had Mrs Grecke for third grade instead of Miss McKenna, and if I hadn't fallen and split my knee open on the blacktop, Daddy wouldn't have had the chance to fall in love with her. God, I think every one of us was in love with her. The boys *and* the girls.' More words that escaped the editor in my brain. 'I'm

224

sorry . . . God, I'm really sorry I just said that.' Then another memory that I had the decency to keep to myself: When I wasn't feeling guilty, I was fantasizing about Miss McKenna marrying my dad and becoming my mother — all light and perfume and pink lipstick and exclamation points in comparison to my own mother, who at the time, now understandably, was morose and prone to sitting alone out in our parked station wagon for extended periods at night.

'I'd filed papers for divorce three days before he died.' Her voice broke. 'I always felt responsible, like those papers must have prompted the heart attack.'

'No, Mom. It was me. It was my fault he died.'

And then I told her the story, the light and shadowed images, fully developed, always waiting for me to finally pluck them up and hang them out on the line between us.

★ ★ ★

Months before my father died, Leslie Penberthy had pointed out Miss McKenna's house to me, and one Saturday afternoon, when I was walking my dog, Barkley, I'd gathered up my courage to knock on her door. I was going to tell her that I just wanted to say hello but thought that perhaps she would invite Barkley and me inside, offer me blue Kool-Aid and Rice Krispies Treats, show me picture albums of her own childhood, the one in Iowa that she'd told our class about.

Miss McKenna answered the door in her robe, seemed very surprised to see me, blushed, and said she was just going to take a nap, that she felt a cold coming on and needed to get some rest but that it was so nice of me to stop by. I didn't notice my father's blue truck parked on the street, one house down, until I walked past it and Barkley jumped at the door. In the truck bed, I saw more pickets for the quaint front-yard fence he was erecting. I never asked him why his truck was parked on Miss McKenna's street that Saturday, or the next. Or why we never went camping anymore, just the two of us traipsing along the Olympic Peninsula, writing down the names of plants and birds and insects we'd see. Now on the weekends, whenever he said he was heading to the hardware store, I made it my habit to walk Barkley, carrying my Harriet the Spy notepad, his birding binoculars around my neck. And though my father always came home with hastily purchased supplies for a new fix-it project, I knew something besides our house was in need of repair.

And then one Saturday, his truck in its spot down the street from her house, I quietly opened the side gate to Miss McKenna's backyard and peeked in an open window, and then another, until I saw my father sitting up in bed, a sheet up to his waist, reading the paper and smoking a cigarette.

'Dolly?' my father called. 'Can you get a poor fellow another cup of your fabulous coffee?' And then Barkley did what dogs do, especially dogs named Barkley.

'What the hell? Barkley? Jelly Bean? *What the hell?*'

226

Our eyes caught each other, and I realized, as I was telling my mom the story, that my father's eyes, at that moment in time, had forever been locked on me; the panic, the terror, the sadness, the shame of that single moment had never left me.

'Jelly, wait . . . *wait* . . . ' But I was already fumbling with the gate that swam behind my tears. I ran, pulling Barkley instead of the other way around; I ran until I couldn't, then walked and walked and walked until dark, when I finally made my way up our porch steps, my mother waiting on the swing, her cigarette glowing and reflected in the front window, as if there were two cigarettes, hers and my father's, instead of just hers alone. She jumped up and asked me where I'd been, that she'd been so worried, that she'd called the police, and I shrugged and said, 'Nowhere.' She held me in her arms. She tucked my hair behind my ear. She told me my father had gone to heaven.

'So,' I said to my mother across the phone line, between sobs, 'it was *me*. Snooping around. That gave him a heart attack. That literally scared him, scared him to death.'

'Ella,' my mom said. I could almost see her herding her thoughts. 'I'm so sorry that's what you've thought. All these years. Honey, you're a scientist. Look at the evidence: The man smoked over two packs of cigarettes a day, worshipped butter and bacon and cream, and apparently was rigorously fucking a twenty-two-year-old. None of this was your fault. Or mine, for that matter.'

I understood that she was right, that by finally

speaking the truth about what I did know, I could see a more truthful version of what I as a child hadn't known, couldn't have known.

My mom said, 'Oh, I'm so sorry. I should have known that the change in you was more than . . . I . . . just . . . it was easier for me; *you* were easier. And I guess, all these years, bringing up your father felt like digging up his grave. You know, let the dead be perfect. It's all they have.'

'It's beginning to occur to me . . . perfection is a weight none of us can bear, alive or dead.'

My dead perfect father. My dead perfect husband. No longer perfect in my mind. I knew I'd somehow freed them both and was even starting to free myself. But I still had a long way to go.

'I wish you could have told me about this back then, Jelly. You kept this all to yourself?' I said I had to hang up, that the kids were walking in the door, even though they weren't. I stood on the back porch, taking big, deep breaths. Callie sprinted up towards me and rubbed her muddy nose on my leg, thwacked me hard with her tail. Back from her most recent excavation.

I went to get an old towel and wiped the fresh dirt off her nose and paws.

23

What was I doing? I had enough to figure out without unearthing old pain-laden memories. I needed to focus on the letters and try to unscrew all Joe's screwing up, instead of focusing on my father's just plain screwing my third-grade teacher almost thirty years before.

I called Lucy and told her about the letters. Lucy whistled. 'What do they say?'

I told her I hadn't read them yet, which she couldn't believe. 'They're not addressed to me. Plus, it's tampering with evidence. If — '

'If you submit them as evidence, which you won't.'

'But then I'm *withholding* evidence.'

'Look. I can come over. I'll open them if I have to. You have to know what, exactly, you're dealing with. I know the real reason you don't want to open those letters, and it has nothing to do with breaking the law. Ella, you know. It's about breaking your heart. And everyone else's in this town.'

'It's about a lot of things,' I said too quickly, too defensively. Lucy had my number. I told her I'd think about it.

★ ★ ★

Later, in my kitchen, while I washed dishes and Marcella dried, I told her about the letters. She held a glass up to the light, rubbed it with the towel again. She set the glass in the cupboard before turning to me. 'You,' she said, 'cannot believe that my Joey would have hidden those letters! Paige was in your house! She was there alone with the kids that day Aunt Sophia had one of her spells! That woman planted those letters there. It's as obvious as the empty tomb.'

'Marcella, they were postmarked.'

She threw her arms in the air, the fat shuddering like a long afterthought. 'They can do anything on the computer these days. That doesn't mean diddly-squat. Have you read them?'

I shook my head.

'She abandoned my grandbabies, Ella. Zach was only two months old. He was still taking the breast! Do you know how much he screamed and cried those first weeks, while we tried to get him used to the bottle? I will remember those screams for the rest of my days. She has no rights as their mother. You are their mother. Now, behave like it. And don't you go talking about your husband like he was some sort of lying criminal!'

She turned and walked out. Joe Sr, who'd been feeding the chickens with the kids, heard the last of it as he came in through the kitchen door. He said, 'Ella, I love you like you were my own. But I don't know how Marcella will get up in the morning if she loses our two *bambini* along with Joe. A person can only take so much in one life. A family can only take so much.' He ran his hand over his bald head and sighed. 'My big brother? Lost to the war.' He paused. 'Even my papa — we lost for a while.'

'But he came back.'

'Yeah, but not the same as he was. Different.' He reached out, held my shoulder. 'And it wasn't just Sergio, you know. Marcella's papa, Dante. They took him too. They were treated like criminals when they did nothing wrong. I love this country. But I don't trust the government when it comes to my family. Let 'em take all our money and call it taxes. But for Christ's sake, not our papas. And not our grandbabies.' He gripped my shoulder tighter. 'Please, honey. Don't let 'em take our grandbabies.'

⋆　⋆　⋆

Later that night, after I'd read stories and put Annie and Zach to bed, Callie barked. I walked down the hall and saw Marcella through the glass. I opened the door. We stood facing each other, not saying a word. Her face bore the ravages of those past months, and I wanted to say something — anything — to ease her pain, to ease mine too.

Her eyes held tears. Finally she spoke. 'I've loved you like a daughter . . . but you won't listen! That store you call Life's a Picnic? That store is for Annie and Zach. You remember that. We helped you because of *our grandchildren.* Because we trusted you with their future! Ella, those letters. Burn them. Don't read them.'

'I have to read them. I have to know.'

'*No.*' She kept her dark sad eyes on mine,

231

lifted her hand, and slapped me, hard, across the face. She covered her mouth, her eyes wide.

The sting spread like hot needle points. My eyes watered, in more of a physical reaction than an emotional one; I was too shocked to cry. She turned, walked, wringing her hands, down the steps, got into her car, and sped off.

24

I had felt the same sharp burn on my cheek only once before. The day of my father's funeral, my grandma Beene and I were in her dark, cool basement getting a few jars of homemade pickles for the company. I had been carrying around a question for days. I knew better than to ask my mother. Grandma Beene had always been easy to talk to, laughing when I made childish blunders that seemed to irritate other adults. My question was part of a puzzle I was piecing together in my head, based on fragments of conversations I'd heard and episodes of *As the World Turns* that Grandma secretly allowed me to watch with her, unbeknownst to my mother. I felt I was on the verge of understanding an important concept, and it seemed the quiet moment in the cellar pantry was right, and so I asked her, 'Grandma? Did God make Daddy die because he loved Miss McKenna and took naps with her?'

The slap came fast then too. My grandmother spoke to me in a voice I'd never heard. 'Don't you ever, *ever* say that again, or anything like it! Your father was a wonderful man. And don't you forget it, young lady. Shame on you! *Shame*. On. *You*.'

She turned and stomped up the stairs, her thick-heeled shoes clunking heavily on each wooden step.

I stood, staring at the jars of raspberry jam,

apricot preserves, green beans that bore the label BEENE's BEANS, the rows and rows of pickles for which she was locally famous. Bread-and-butters, sweets, hot dills, extra-hot-pepper dills, and mild dills. Grandma Beene was a hallmark of efficiency and productivity, yet she moved and spoke with a calm gentleness and patience that usually evaded the extremely pragmatic.

For her to have responded so out of character . . . I knew my question was horribly wrong. Or maybe, I thought, she was referring to my spying, the *Shame on you* was because she somehow knew I'd scared my dad so much his heart had stopped. My hands felt sweaty and I wiped them on my plaid skirt, over the large golden pin that held the overflap in place and sometimes snagged the lining of my winter coat. The piece about my daddy's heart stopping seemed to fit with the piece no one else knew about — that I had scared him and made him yell. I knew my own heart was pounding from my grandma's slap. Maybe my own heart would stop too. I prayed that it wouldn't and I prayed that my daddy wasn't scowling at me from his satin-lined box in the ground.

There was more. Grandma Beene wasn't done teaching me the lesson. But I had things to think about other than my own old sad stories, and I needed to focus on those letters.

25

Early the next morning as I swept crumbs out from under the deli counter, Frank walked in, started pouring himself a cup of coffee. 'This old-lady tweaker who lives just over the bridge, she's stoned out of her mind, nothing new. So she decides it's a nifty idea to take her kayak out on the river. Only problem is, she doesn't come home. So old-man tweaker calls us. We've gotta do the whole search and rescue, the helicopter, the whole bit, because grandma's so stoned she doesn't realize she's paddling in circles.' He held up his cup of coffee as if to toast me. 'And that, ladies and gentleman, is where your mighty tax dollars are going.'

'I wonder what happened to her.'

'Absolutely nothing. That's the point, El. We found her enjoying the moonlight out past Edwards' Mill, just after midnight. In la-la land.' He shook his head, took a swig of coffee.

I had meant that I wondered what happened to her before then, long ago, but I didn't feel like explaining that to Frank, explaining that I'd recently concluded that everyone had their reasons, whether they knew it or not. That even Paige had her reasons, and I intended to find them out.

'More coffee?'

He nodded. 'I'll get it. This one is to go. Gotta go save a meth addict or two, civil servant that I am.'

'Frank?'

'Yeah?'

I didn't want to tell him about the letters in case he had some sort of civic duty to report me.

'Do you think Lizzie would talk to me? About Paige?'

'Lizzie won't talk to *me* about Paige.' He stared at me, waiting, as if to say, *Why can't you talk to me?* Frank missed Joe too. I could always see it in his eyes; they didn't match up with his cocky stance. He shrugged. 'But what the hell? What have you got to lose?'

★　★　★

I knew Lizzie was home even before I opened the white picket gate. It was a sharp blue day, and wafts of spearmint, rosemary, lavender, lemon, and cocoa butter fragranced the air. She worked in their converted barn out back, after Molly left for school each morning. The old me would have been nervous to approach Lizzie, to walk around to the barn and lean my head through the Dutch door. But I was pretty sure nothing she could say to me would make things any worse. All I was after now was the truth so I could decide what to do about the letters. I stood there for almost a minute, blind, until my eyes adjusted and I saw Lizzie, long tables with pots, and walls of supplies.

Her blonde curly hair was clipped up away from her forehead, and she was humming while she poured olive oil into one of five huge saucepans. Two Mexican women weighed cups of palm and coconut oil. Lizzie looked up. 'Oh! Frank's not here.'

'I'd like to talk to you. If you have a minute. Actually, more than a minute.'

'Oh? Well, okay . . . I just . . . I can't really leave right now. Can we talk here?'

I looked over at the two women, who were both watching us.

'Very limited English, mostly having to do with soap. If you'd like to discuss another topic, your privacy is pretty much guaranteed.' She said something to them in Spanish, they both smiled and nodded as she introduced us, and then she said to me, 'Anyway, while this is melting, I do need to add the lye to the pots outside. Come on.'

We walked out to a table where three more pots were cooling. 'You need to step way back,' she explained. 'Lye is nasty stuff. You don't want to breathe it in.' She turned her head while she poured it into a measuring cup, instructing me to move back even farther. 'Now, this will bring the temperature way up, and then we need to let it cool to a hundred and ten degrees.' She pointed to yet another table. 'Those should be ready for us to start stirring. Grab a seat and a spoon. We need to stir those babies until they thicken. Think fondue.' I recognized her demonstration voice from the Elbow Christmas Bazaar — friendly, efficient, in charge.

We both took seats and spoons and began stirring. I said, 'Lizzie, I know you and Paige are friends . . .'

She looked at me for a long minute before she

said, 'Are is a strong word. Were isn't quite accurate, though, either. We don't talk anymore, but I still think of her as my friend. And I miss her. I miss the old Paige. I don't really know the new Paige.'

'No one in Joe's family has anything nice to say about either Paige — old or new . . . '

Lizzie directed her eyes to my pot of liquid. 'Keep stirring. You want to feel it starting to thicken.'

'But I have a strong feeling . . . there's more to the story.'

'Look, Ella. If you're trying to dig up dirt on Paige in order to build your custody case, you can take your shovel somewhere else.'

I knew I was one sentence away from being led out the front gate. 'I know it seems that way. But at this point, I want to understand Paige. To understand Joe. I'm beginning to believe . . . that Joe . . . he may not have treated her fairly.'

Lizzie's head jerked up. Her face reddened, her eyes and mouth opened wide, her fist hit the table. And then it was as if a cork blew. 'No shit! But try telling my husband that! Or anyone else in this town.'

'I live in this town. I want to know the truth.'

'Now you do . . . '

'Yes. I do.'

'To better serve your purposes . . . '

'No, believe me. My purposes — as far as custody — would be better served by not asking, not knowing, just as I have always done. I'm trying to do it differently now. But I could use your help.'

She stared at me, sizing me up as she stirred, stirred more. Finally, she said, 'Paige seemed like the perfect golden girl. When she started to struggle and show signs of slipping away, no one could deal.' She stuck her chest out, rocked her shoulders back and forth, pursed her lips. 'It wasn't *allowed* in the Family Capozzi.'

'What was she like before this happened?'

'She was always beautiful — but, you know, real. Her house was picked up, but there was no Paige the Stager. No feng shui, flung shit, or whatever. She was always guarded, or shy, but kind. I liked her a lot.'

I concentrated on my figure eights. It was hard to hear anything good about Paige.

Lizzie said, 'I've gotta say, I was shocked that Joe moved on so quickly.'

My face felt hot. I kept stirring.

'Joe and Paige were crazy about each other from day one. But then, right after Annie was born, Paige stopped being crazy for Joe and went just plain crazy.'

'What do you mean?'

'First she stopped returning my calls. Then, when I'd stop by, I'd see her hair was greasy. She wore her robe all day.'

The paisley robe.

'She had been excited during her pregnancy, but then she wasn't interested in Annie at all. It was weird. She started asking me to watch Annie. Joe was beside himself. Of course, Marcella to the rescue, and all that. Paige kept telling me what a terrible mother she was. That she should have never had a baby. She cried all

239

the time. She looked at Annie like she was nothing more than an odd-shaped lamp. To Joe's credit, he started coming home from the store every chance he got. He'd hold Annie and sing to her.'

While Lizzie prepared the moulds, she told me more. When Annie was about four months old, Paige seemed better. Now it seems obvious she had some kind of postpartum depression. But six years before — in 1993 — no one talked about it, much less understood it. Paige emerged, but somewhat changed. She was even more guarded. She was still a good friend to Lizzie, and a good mother to Annie. Paige and Joe seemed to regain their footing. But then she got pregnant with Zach. She told Lizzie it was a mistake and that she was terrified. She didn't want to go back to that dark place. She never mentioned abortion, but Lizzie said she had the feeling Paige was considering it — out of nothing but desperation. Paige talked to her doctor, but he wasn't adequately concerned. No one was. 'No one in the family, including Joe, wanted to talk about Paige's depression, as if talking about it would bring it back. But I could see in his eyes, Joe was terrified.'

I was listening so intently to Lizzie that I'd stopped stirring, and she pointed to the wooden spoon. 'Oh, sorry,' I said, resuming my figure eights. I didn't want to ask, but I forced myself to say, 'Is there more?'

Her eyes searched mine before she spoke again. 'I haven't talked about any of this with anyone. Ever. But maybe this will finally help

Paige. And you.' Lizzie sighed, kept her eyes on the liquid. 'But of course the depression came back anyway, and this time it was worse. The doctor finally prescribed an antidepressant, but Paige flushed them, which scared Joe even more. She was afraid they would be bad for Zach. The one thing she could do was breast-feed, but she did it with this . . . I don't know . . . detached determination. She had him on a strict schedule. But when he nursed, she barely looked at him or engaged him. One day I told Joe, 'She needs to be hospitalized.' He looked at me, shocked. He was so in the thick of it, he was no longer seeing clearly. And he said, 'No, she'll be fine — we just have to get through the first four months like with Annie.' And I said, 'This is *different*.' Soon after that she told me she shouldn't be near Annie or Zach. It was a Saturday, I remember, and I took the kids home with me and kept them until the store closed and Joe could pick them up. When he did, I told him what she'd said, and that time, he heard me. But the next day, she was gone.'

'Did you hear from her after she left?'

She shook her head. 'Just once. I sent her cards, tried to keep in touch after that, but she never replied.'

She took a deep breath. 'Wow, I guess I needed to talk about this.' She looked up to the rafters, started to say something else but hesitated. Finally she said, 'Frank did tell me, just since Joe died, that he'd told Frank that Paige had written letters he'd never opened. The mother of his children was trying to contact him, but he ignored her. Right before he died, Joe told Frank that Paige had called him. That Paige wanted a custody arrangement. That Joe was going to have to talk to you — and he was dreading it.'

I let go of the spoon, held my head in my hands. Remembering. We never had the conversation that night, because after we'd made love for the last time, I had waved off his request to talk, floating in my contentment, wanting to wait until the following day. 'Tomorrow, then,' he'd said, and touched my nose.

Tomorrow . . .

Lizzie touched my shoulder. 'I'm sorry.' She smiled. 'But I still need you to stir. You can't quit on me now.' The colour of the liquid had lightened from dark gold to cream, and the consistency did remind me of fondue. We lugged the pots back into the barn, my eyes trying to adjust again while Lizzie went ahead and set her pot down. 'Over here,' she called. I made my way to another workstation, where rows of small bottles and jars filled an old glass-doored cabinet. 'Now the fun begins.' We added oats and powdered milk and cocoa butter to one batch, pear essential oil and dried calendula to another. Rosemary essential oils and lavender petals went into my pot. We kept adding fragrance and sniffing, then adding more.

After we poured the liquid into the moulds, Lizzie turned to me. 'There's something else I want to say. Joe and I shared some harsh words. Me and my tough talk. But Joe was a good person. I think he was just scared. He got hurt.

242

He wanted to protect the kids and himself
. . . and you. But had he had more time — ' She
looked away, then back at me. 'I think he would
have made it right. With time.'

'Certainly you don't think he would have just
handed over the kids to Paige?'

'No. I don't. But I like to think he was on his
way to a more . . . I mean, as Joe was building a
life with you, he was getting over his anger at
Paige. If Joe had lived, I'm certain he would have
seen that shutting Paige out completely wasn't
good for Annie and Zach. You know? It was the
most convenient thing at first. Actually, it was his
only choice at first because that's what she told
him she wanted. I get that. And I feel for you,
Ella, left with all the fallout. I do not envy you.'

Before I left, Lizzie gave me a box of soap,
including two bars from her children's line, Milk
& Honey Bunny, and a bottle of bubble bath
called Here Comes Bubble, to take home for the
kids. 'This,' she said, 'is not your mother's soap.'

* * *

I walked home, waving at the cars that honked
hello without lifting my head to see who it was.
Someday Annie and Zach would have questions
about why Paige left. Because they were kids,
they would feel that somehow it was their fault.
Annie probably already felt it, a thorn of blame
she couldn't quite identify, like a tiny thistle
woven into her sock. Those letters might tell
them the real story. If I didn't give them to the
court, but let the kids read them when they were

243

older? They would know I'd withheld evidence in order to prevent Paige from having custody. But if I did hand the letters over to the court, if I did the right thing? The judge could very well still rule in my favour. In Annie and Zach's favour. I believed he would still think that staying with me was in their best interest . . . no matter what the letters said.

Still. I would be risking everything.

I held a bar of soap up to my nose and sniffed. Not my mother's soap. Not my grandmother's, either. There was yet another layer to the lesson she'd taught me that day.

★　★　★

I don't know how long I'd hid in my grandmother's basement after her slap, but eventually hunger overtook my disgrace, forcing me upstairs to her kitchen. Neighbours were putting out plates of ham sandwiches with bowls of potato and macaroni salad. Grandma walked in carrying a tray of peanut butter cookies. When she saw me, she set down the tray, took me by the arm, and marched me back down to the basement. She pulled me over to the utility sink, picked up an orange bar of Dial soap, and held it under the running water. 'I hate to do this, dear, but you have got to learn that certain things are inappropriate for a young lady to say. This is the only way I know of that will make you remember. It's unpleasant, but a valuable lesson, all the same. Now, open your mouth.' I pressed my lips tight, but she forced the soap through them. It scraped against my teeth while I gagged, eyes tearing, the waxy fire of it searing my throat and my mind too. The burning taste seemed to go on forever, but not nearly as long as the burning shame. Afterwards, she handed me an enamel cup of water and a pink towel from the dryer. 'Now. That's done. Do you understand why I needed to do that?'

I nodded, though I realized that I understood nothing about my life and the people I loved. She pulled an embroidered handkerchief from the sleeve of her white cardigan and wiped the tears from my cheeks. 'I will see you upstairs in a few minutes.' And she climbed heavily up the steps. When I reappeared in the kitchen, she said, 'Why, *there's* our Ella. Help yourself, dear.'

I took a peanut butter cookie and she bent down and kissed the top of my head, and that was it. She never mentioned the incident again. And I certainly didn't, either. Until the conversation with my mother just days before, I'd set it back in some far corner of my memory. There was now the undeniable fact that I'd lived much of my life according to that one lesson: Look the other way. Don't ask. Ever. And good God, don't say what you really think.

★   ★   ★

That night, the night before we were to sign the stipulation that would give me custody, Annie and Zach climbed into the tub while I poured in the milky bubble bath, unwrapped the bars and gave them each one. I sat on the floor and reached over and lathered them up — their pale, soft hair, their sweaty necks, their torsos and arms and legs, the bend of each elbow and each knee. I knew every freckle, every one of their scars and where each had come from, and what the weather had been like each fateful day. Rinsing their sudsy heads back in the water, I soaked in their giggles when I washed between their toes.

Zach held up his foot and asked me the question that he asked every bath: 'Mommy? Are you getting the stink out of my stinky dogs?'

'Yep.'

'Now they're sweetie dogs?'

'Kissable sweetie dogs!' I grabbed his foot and kissed his toes while he squealed and tried to pull free from my grasp.

While Annie and Zach shivered, I dried their heads and bodies with warm towels from the dryer, then held pj's out for them to step into, aligning their feet into the footsies, buttoning tops, snapping snaps, combing down squeaky-clean hair. They climbed up into my bed that night, and I held them, and I held them, and I held them.

Around 3.00 a.m., I slipped out of bed, stoked up the woodstove, retrieved the letters from the closet shelf, and tiptoed back out to the not-so-great room to discover exactly what it was that Paige Capozzi had written to my husband and children after she had left them on that rainy Sunday, more than three years before.

26

Dear Joe,

I have to leave. I can't keep pretending to be what I'm not. You know I love Annie and Zach. You know I love you. But there's this other part of me . . . I'm scared. It's like I'm my mother down deep inside. But you won't listen. Dr Blaine won't listen.

This is the hardest thing. It's not fair to you or to them for me to stay. I'm not coming back. I should not have become a mother in the first place. It was crazy to try. But I am crazy.

All the rain makes me feel even crazier. It's the sound of water sputtering, pressing me down, all day every day. Las Vegas is dry. It's warm and light here.

Please don't tell the kids I'll be back. You all need to start a new life without me. Your family will help you. Keep doing the things that come naturally to you, the things that seem to evade me. Play with them, kiss them, hug them, and please never let them go.

Remember that I tried to do better.

~Paige

This was the letter Joe had told me about. He hadn't lied. There was a card addressed to Annie and Zach that had a bear on the front with the words, *You know how much I love you?* And when I opened it the arms unfolded a foot on each side. *This much! And so I'm sending you this bear hug.* It was signed *Mama.*

April 11, 1996

Dear Joe,

Please stop calling. I know you're trying. This isn't what I wanted, either. I cancelled my Dr's appt. I can't get up today. Something's always pressing me down. Besides, it's not like the doctor can do an exorcism on me and get rid of my mother. It's not like he can go back and change my DNA.

What if something had happened to Annie or Zach? Think about that, Joe. Look that in the face. It changes everything. I think I can live with leaving. But not if I'd hurt them. What if I'd done something like my mother did?

~Paige

July 2, 1996

Dear Joe,

I know for certain I can never go back. Not to that dark, depressing kitchen that was getting smaller and darker. Soon I would be crouched in a corner on the floor.

Thank you for not calling again. I can't be with Annie and Zach . . . and hearing about them is too hard right now.

I have to say good-bye for good now. I'm sorry. I have an appointment with a doctor tomorrow. Aunt Bernie is taking good care of me. Someday, when Annie and Zach are old enough to understand, tell them their mama loves them.

~Paige

I wondered why Paige's lawyer would subpoena these letters. How could they help her case?

A card for Annie and Zach that said *Some Bunny Loves You*. There were more cards addressed to them, all unopened. But there were no letters to Joe for more than five months. The next one was still sealed, never opened. As were all the others that followed, even those addressed to the kids. I held the next one addressed to Joe, kept turning it over.

It was postmarked October 15, 1996. Joe and Annie and I — with 'help' from crawling Zach — had just decorated the house for Halloween, I remembered; we'd strung orange lights and filled baskets with maple leaves the colour of fire, with Indian corn and gourds. We cut the pumpkins we'd grown in the garden and lugged them up to the porch. Joe had honoured Paige's request. He had moved on. Even to the point of deciding not to open this letter that had come eight months after she had first left, insisting she wouldn't return, five months after she'd said — for the last time — she would not write again, four months after Joe and I had fallen in love. I took a breath. I was tampering with evidence if I opened it. But what I once refused to know, I had to know. I pressed my thumbnail down under the sealed seam.

October 15, 1996

Dear Joe,

Dr Zelwig says I need to start writing you again. I told him you haven't called or written. He thinks that it's more than you just abiding my requests. After this morning's session, he thinks you're probably afraid of me. That I wasn't just scaring myself. That you've probably always been afraid of me.

I told him about the big test I threw at you when we first met. He thought it might be good if I wrote you about what I was feeling, and what your reaction might have meant. I know how much you love psychobabble. But these days my life is nothing but, so bear with me.

Anyway. I'd spent 20 years hiding. People kept telling me, 'You should model.' If they only knew. But I kept seeing you on campus with your camera clicking away. There was something about you, the way you looked at things. Patiently, beneath the surface, even. I'd see your name on the photo credits of the school newspaper. I asked you if you did portfolio shots just so I could meet you. You lied and said yes. You even ran out and bought that pretty robe and other clothes to hang on the shower rod to try to make your bathroom look like a model's dressing room! So we both started with lies, even if they were just white ones.

I guess I was ready for someone else to know. Someone besides Aunt Bernie to love me. All of me. It was an act of desperation, if there ever was one. From the beginning, I

250

knew what I would do.

Remember, Joe? Your clicking away. Your surprise at me shedding my clothes.

And finally, for the first time in my adult life, I show someone the other side of my story. I turn around and the clicking stops. But there's no gasp of disgust, no fleeing your apartment. I feel your gaze. Later, you'll ask me how and why. But first you hold out the paisley robe, and I slip my arms through the sleeves. You turn me back around, tie the belt in front. And then you hug me.

I always loved that story, even though we never told anyone. You promised to keep my secret. But today, when I told Zelwig, he said, Joe covered up the part of you that was too difficult to look at.

I hadn't thought of it that way. I was so grateful that you looked at all and that you didn't flee. I thought it was about complete acceptance. But maybe not. Maybe Dr Zelwig is right. Can you see how he might be?

~Paige

I didn't want to read the rest of the letters, well aware that I was opening a Pandora's box and could never go back. But I knew I had to read them for Annie and Zach. It was 3:25 a.m., but I called Lucy. She answered on the second ring. When I asked if she could come over, she said, 'I'm there. Give me seven minutes.' She didn't even ask me why or point out what time it was. And when she got there, she let herself in and curled up on the couch with me and took

251

the letters and started reading them, all without a word. When she had caught up, we read the next one together.

October 21, 1996

Dear Joe,

Today was the best session so far. I actually think Dr Zelwig might be able to help me! He's found a medication that doesn't zone me out or make me want to drop dead. And there's a name for this. Not Baby Blues, like Dr Blaine kept insisting. Most women have those. This is called Post Partum Depression.

It's triggered by childbirth. It can be hereditary and it can go on for years. Mine is a very severe case . . . But here's the best news of all: I'm not my mother! Dr Zelwig doesn't think I would have hurt Annie and Zach. Because there's also a rarer form, a more elevated form, that is called Post Partum Psychosis. It only happens in a very small percentage of women.

He says my mother was one of those women. Joe, she wasn't a monster. She was just very, very sick. And medication and hospitalization could have helped even her. Had they known back then.

Even today a lot of doctors aren't aware of anything beyond the Baby Blues. Like Dr Blaine. But you know what? This has been around forever. Dr Zelwig gave me all this information I can send you if you want. But here's an amazing quote, from a gynaecologist from the 11th century: ' . . . if the womb is too moist, the brain is filled with water, and the moisture running over to the eyes, compels them to involuntarily shed tears.'

I've been crying non-stop. Relief. Despair for my mom, for what didn't need to happen to her or to me. And for the first time, Joe. HOPE!

~Paige

'Paige had hope? On October 21, 1996, Paige still had hope?' I said, 'I wonder what would have happened if Joe had opened the letters, if everything would be different now. If he would have sat me down and held both of my hands and told me Paige was coming back. To be with Annie and Zach. And Joe.'

'El, Joe adored you. You breathed life back into him when you showed up here. And Annie. And Zach. Don't bombard yourself with a bunch of what-ifs, my dear. That's not going to help anyone.'

We kept reading.

December 15, 1996

Joe,

Still haven't heard from you. Finally I called Lizzie. She says there's someone new. Really, Joe? Just like that?

Here is the photo of us we sent out last Christmas. Aunt Bernie brought it from her refrigerator. I've cut my face out. (The nurse had to watch me. We're not allowed to use scissors without supervision. Just like Annie's preschool.) Maybe you can glue in her face. Ella's. Ella Bean?

~Paige (your wife)

'Ouch.'

Lucy said, 'Look, I don't know what she expected of him. She told him to quit pining away and get on with his life. That's what he did. Thank God he did. Open the next one. Here, give it to me. I'll open the damn thing.'

April 8, 1997

Joe,

Well, I finally hear from you and it comes in the form of a manila envelope and divorce documents. And a note that says, I know this is what you want. What makes you think you know anything?

I know I signed and served you papers for a legal separation. I know I wrote and told you to move on. But I was confused. I'm sorry I said that. It's not what I wanted then, certainly not what I want now. Haven't you read any of my other letters?

I don't have it in me to fight right now. I'm concentrating all my efforts on getting well. I can't handle a court battle yet. But someday I will.

I can't believe you're doing this. Zelwig says it's lack of information and fear.

They're MY children, not HERS.

~Paige

Lucy said, 'You're wrong about that one, honey.'

'Not entirely . . . '

'Ella.'

'Well? What *happened* to Paige? Something must have scared the bejesus out of her when she was little. Something her mom did . . . She obviously did love Annie and Zach. It's not like she ran away with some Hells Angel to find herself.' I tore open the next envelope, no longer caring about evidence and tampering.

May 1, 1997

Joe,

The court order came today. You got custody only because I didn't fight it. Make the most of this time, because you know it's only temporary.

Maybe you don't think I'll ever have it in me to fight. But that's because you don't know the new me. The me that has forgiven my mom and myself. And maybe someday, even you.

~Paige

There were several more letters pleading with Joe to work things out, telling him about her new career, then threatening to call the kids, threatening a legal battle. And then this:

February 16, 1999

Joe,

I've been hesitant to see Annie and Zach without your cooperation. My attorney wants me to move forward with a custody action, but I keep hoping you'll return my calls or letters. For Annie and Zach's sake, if not for mine.

What have you told them about me? Did you tell them I died? Is that why you're not responding?

It's for their sake that I haven't just knocked

on the door or called them. Talk about temptation. I fight it every day. But I've tried to be patient and give you time and space to adjust to the idea of me being back in their lives as well as making absolutely sure I was ready emotionally and financially. I've tried, but every day without them tears away at me.

If we get in a full-blown legal battle, it won't be good for anyone. Please, Joe. You have a new life. You don't have a right to keep me away from my kids.

~Paige

I opened the last letter. Sent six days before Joe drowned. Five days before Joe said he had something he wanted to talk with me about.

June 15, 1999

Joe,

I'm going to call you today at the store and send this. After that, you'll hear directly from my attorney. Please work with me. I am literally begging you. I have to make things right with Annie and Zach. I'm ready and I'm done waiting for you to be ready.

~Paige

I folded the last letter and put it back in its envelope, as if it were an object I could simply put back in its place. The fire rifled a loud pop. 'What am I going to do?' was all I could think to say. 'What the hell should I do?'

'Ella.' Lucy took my hand in hers. 'That is a question I simply cannot answer.'

'What would *you* do?'

'I don't know.'

'Lucy, throw me a bone here.'

'No way. No. This is something only you can decide. Dig deep, El. You'll know what to do. In the meantime, and afterwards, I'll be here no matter what. Now try to get some sleep.'

'Yeah. Right.'

She hugged me and left. Somehow, when I climbed into bed, the mattress pulled me with a swift, relentless force into a maze of sweaty dreams.

27

I woke feeling damp and salty and disoriented, the sun already cresting the treetops. I jumped out of bed, not wanting the kids to think I was slipping away from them again.

Everything looked different, as if I had journeyed through another country and just returned. My bedroom, the bathroom, the hallway . . . all imprinted with new knowledge, a weary traveller's perspective. How had I not seen it before? This home had a history. Joe and I had made no major changes in the house since my arrival, except for the wall we'd torn down between the kitchen and living room. Maybe Joe was afraid walls could speak.

He had come home one afternoon that first summer and, instead of his usual roll around the floor with Callie and the kids, he paced in the narrow kitchen.

'Doesn't this kitchen bother you?' he asked.

I shrugged. 'No. Why?'

'It's dark, don't you think? And cramped. And the living room is too small. Don't you find the whole thing extremely *depressing*?'

'Not really.' *Depressing* didn't even sound like Joe.

'This wall — it could come down easily. It's not even a load-bearing wall. It's not a thick wall. It's just a wall. A wall that should have never gone up in the first place. I don't know why it wasn't kept open in the first goddamn place.'

'Joe?'

He left the house and headed for the barn. On the stove the beets from the garden simmered, bobbing in their ruby liquid. Joe walked in with an axe.

'Joe. What are you doing?'

'Take the kids outside to play. We all need light. We need space. We need *air*.'

'Are you okay?' He didn't look like a man who had simply decided to start a home-remodelling project. He smiled, but his lip was twitching. His eyes shone, daring me. For a second, a cold fear passed through my body — we had only been together a month or so, and I thought, *Okay, this is where my loving guy turns out to be an axe murderer*. But I saw a tear slip from his eye, a tender vulnerability cross his face. He took the axe to the wall like he was hitting a baseball. It tore through the plaster with a sullen crack.

'Daddy!' Annie called from the hallway.

'Take the kids outside. Please?' And then he swung again, breaking through to the other side, yellow swells of sun already seeping through.

When, two hours later, we returned from our walk to the school playground, Joe was sweeping up the debris in the new dappled light. He kissed me, kissed Zach in the backpack, picked up Annie, who exclaimed, '*Wowee!*'

'Welcome,' Joe said, 'to our official Not-So-Great Room.' I said, 'But it *is* great.'

'I don't know why I never thought to do this. I should have done it a long time ago.'

259

Now I understood why that particular day, he did think to do it. He'd received Paige's letter about the kitchen. The only letter he'd opened after I'd come into the picture. It was another letter instructing him to never call again. But was his motivation in tearing down the wall to bring Paige back? Or to make sure our life together never became what theirs had become?

Our walls were different, but we had them. Invisible walls. The illusion of light and space and even air. The kind you can't see, that are fragile as glass. They work great until an unseen force pushes you into one and the illusion shatters, so that every step you take cuts you, cuts those who walk alongside you.

I opened the door to Annie and Zach's room, and the kittens scrambled towards me. 'Close the door or you'll let them out,' Annie said.

'Him is mine,' Zach said, grabbing and holding up a kitten.

'No, Zachosaurus. Remember? They're both *both* of ours.' Even this sounded to me like a custody battle.

Annie explained that they had finally decided on names, Thing One and Thing Two. They just couldn't agree on which was which.

I made coffee in what had once been Paige's coffee maker. I stirred in milk with one of the spoons from her bridal-registry flatware and put the milk back in the same refrigerator on which she had once kept her family photos with magnets. I thought of that family photo she'd sent with her face cut out, and the words she wrote, *I've cut my face out. Maybe you can glue in her face*. I had walked in and slipped between their sheets. Hell, the very sheets she'd washed and folded and set in the linen closet before she walked out.

I didn't think she would be a better mother to them than I was. But probably not a worse one, either. She had been hurt by her mother, she had been ill, apparently something was horribly wrong with her back, but none of that meant she wouldn't be a good mother. And yet she hadn't been completely honest in the mediation, hadn't told Janice Conner that the first five letters she wrote to Joe told him she was never coming back, that he must never contact her. That's when I stepped in. And then she had got help. She had eventually even got well.

I checked on the kids, still playing hide-and-seek with the kittens. I walked out to the garden and admired its rows set in a quilt-like pattern, the abundant order of it. This was mine. This was what I brought to the picture. The only thing.

I looked back at the house. Joe and I had called its quirkiness Funk Factor. I loved it the first time I stepped inside it, and still did. The slightly sunken imperfection of it, the porch that wrapped around it like a hug. It was no longer Paige's house. In fact, it had never been the kind of home to her that it had been to me and was to me still. A set of flatware, some dishes and appliances, washed linens? So what. Joe and I and the kids had been happy here. Despite all the sadness she'd left in her wake.

How had it all fit me so perfectly? I had lived

in a house in San Diego for years, had picked out every dish, every rug, and never felt at home.

I had happened upon this town, a man and his children, this house, these trees. I'd stumbled upon someone's lost treasure. No, *abandoned* treasure, left behind.

I hadn't stolen it, but I didn't want to return it, either. What had been the reasoning of my subconscious at the time? Your loss, lady, my gain? How much did I know at some level, below the surface, what I'd refused to bring up with a simple question? Because I had my own fears. I'd feared honest but complex answers other than the convenient shrugged simplicity of 'She left and she's never coming back.'

No. I couldn't distract myself with who might be the rightful owner of discarded forks and spoons and land and trees, a building, a garden.

I could no longer simply claim my children as my own. They had another mother who loved them too. A woman who may not have been treated fairly. I looked at the house and tried to imagine it without Annie and Zach. The earth tilted sharply. I grabbed the garden gatepost and hung on for my dear sweet life.

28

Lizzie picked up the kids. I got dressed to go to court. I kept putting the packet of letters in my purse, then pulling it out. I had already taken out the unopened letters to Annie and Zach and put them in my dresser drawer. No matter what, those belonged to them, not the court. Paige had subpoenaed the letters from her to Joe. She had neglected to specify the cards to Annie and Zach.

I made one last call, this time to my mom, and told her what I'd read in Paige's letters. She said, 'You shouldn't have to deal with all this right now. You want to know my opinion? Like my own grandmother, every woman needs to have a trapdoor under her kitchen rug, Ella.'

'Are you saying I should have my own moonshine business?'

'I'm saying that you do what you have to do for your kids. Even if it means breaking the law.'

'Mom. I don't want Annie and Zach to grow up thinking their mother didn't want them. If I don't turn over those letters to the court, then what? I live a lie. Even if I do show them someday, they'll know that I withheld evidence that showed their mother wanted custody. If I turn over the letters, I don't think the judge will change his mind. Their life is here with me and the Capozzi family.'

'You *think* . . . but you don't *know*.'

'Here's what I do know. You want me to 'protect' them by lying, by keeping information from them that helps them understand that none of this was their *fault*? That they have no reason to feel blame or shame?'

'Who are we talking about here?' She paused. 'Jelly, I understand why you're upset.'

When I didn't reply she said, 'I'm going to catch a plane down.' I told her to wait, that I might need her more later.

I made it out to the Jeep without the packet, but then ran back up the porch steps and down the hall and grabbed it off the kitchen table, knocking over the pepper grinder. It rolled off the table and fell onto the floor with a thud. I picked it up and set it back on the table, watching it for a moment. Joe's favourite pepper grinder. Was he trying to tell me something? *Now* he was speaking up? I waited, but it stayed put. I shook my head, trying to shake at least a shred of logic into place.

I almost got out the door with the letters, but every step down the hallway echoed with the shouts and laughter and cries, the wondrous chaos of Annie and Zach, and I decided I wouldn't be able to do the honest thing, the right thing, after all. As much as I wanted to, I simply couldn't. I shoved the letters in the nightstand drawer, and this time Joe's picture flopped over. 'Stop it,' I said aloud. 'Don't do this,' and I rushed outside and to the car before I could change my mind again.

I passed the vineyard that had been all yellow light a few weeks before — now the leaves had

264

turned to blazing reds and oranges. A man stood with his back to the road, hands in pockets, staring out at the fields as if he himself had set it on fire and was simply watching it burn.

At the courthouse, when I saw the security X-ray machine, I was glad I'd left the letters at home. But they were letters, not a gun. Still, if I'd kept them in my bag, I would have been concealing a powerful weapon.

I sat at the end of a row of chairs outside of the courtroom, waiting. Gwen Alterman bustled down the hall towards me, seemingly impatient with her own short legs, thighs rubbing together in their maroon pant-suit casing. She said, 'I've already spoken to Paige's attorney. As I've told you, they'd like to work out a deal today with limited visitation with the possibility of increasing visitation as the children get older.'

'How much visitation?' I asked.

She slipped on her reading glasses and scanned the document. 'Four times a year for weekends. Two weeks in the summer. One week during Christmas vacation.' She shrugged. 'That's it. She does want them to go to her house, though. She's very adamant about that one — and is even willing to fly here to pick them up.'

Paige sat farther down along the wall, leaning towards her attorney, a tall, older man with a red bow tie and wire-framed glasses, who was talking to her.

Gwen went on. 'Read the stipulation over and go ahead and sign it. And then we'll go before the judge and tell him both parties have come to an agreement. We'll read it in court; you'll be asked if you consent. You'll say yes, and we'll be done and you'll go home to your children.' She added. 'Not to mention, save a boatload of money.'

Paige had already signed it. Her signature looped across the line; I recognized that handwriting now. I signed the paper. A few minutes later, Gwen Alterman stuck her head outside the door of Courtroom J and motioned me inside. Along the back row sat Joe Sr, Marcella, and David. I wanted to believe they were there to support me, but I knew they were making sure I behaved.

Paige entered, walking straight, as if she held a book on her head. I recognized now that the familiar stance of hers was a brave front. Her eyes, void of makeup, gave her grief away. I knew all about No-Mascara Days.

When we were called, we sat at the dark veneer tables in front of the judge's bench. Paige's attorney read the agreement in a soothing, kind voice that seemed out of place in the courtroom and softened the edges of words like *custody* and *petitioner* and *visitation* — as if he were reading a fairy tale with the foreshadowing of a happy ending — and if I just kept my mouth shut, everyone could live happily ever after. I focused my gaze on the bored-looking court reporter who was taking down what the attorney read. There was nowhere else safe I could look. Not to Paige and her own watery eyes. Not to the judge, who might read my face and instinctively sense guilt. Not behind me to the appointed guards of the Family Capozzi.

Paige stood first. She held up her hand to be sworn in and agreed to the stipulation. And then it was my turn. I stood, shaking, a drop of sweat rivuleting down my back.

I held up my hand. I saw Marcella's hand, raised, before it smacked across my face, trying to slap sense into me. I saw Grandma Beene's hand, raised, slapping shame into me. I would never slap Annie or Zach. And yet my raised hand was not any different; it was joining the ranks of the Silencers, hiding the whole truth, the most important truth, from Annie and Zach.

All I had to do was say 'Yes, I am,' and 'Yes, I do.' I said yes. I closed my mouth, waiting for the next cue. I opened my mouth. I said, 'Your Honour? Can I say something?' My heart hammered so loudly in my ears, I could barely hear my own voice.

The judge, who was almost bald but fairly young, probably in his late forties, smiled as if slightly amused. 'No, you should let your attorney do the talking.'

'But Your Honour?' I said. 'I have evidence that I need to submit.'

'And why, Ms. Beene, would you want to do that? Counsel, I think you better take your client out in the hallway before she — '

'Because it's the truth,' I said. Gwen gripped my arm. 'And I want the truth to be known. I found Paige's letters.'

Marcella's voice pierced the air. 'Jesus, Mary, and Joseph!' Paige's attorney stood. 'Excuse me, Your Honour, we asked for those letters and Ms.

Beene swore under penalty of perjury that they didn't exist.'

Gwen also stood up. The judge said to her, 'Counsel, is it correct that your client was asked to produce those letters?'

'Your Honour, I haven't seen them yet. I didn't know my client found anything.'

'Ms. Beene, where are these letters? And when did you find them?'

'They're at home. I found them Sunday night. Your Honour, I still think my home is the best place for Annie and Zach. But I don't want that decision to be based on a lie.'

The judge sighed. 'Ms. Beene. You've evidently been watching too many *Law and Order* episodes. Had you not thought to discuss this with your counsel? How far away do you live?'

I told him I lived a half hour away.

'I want you to get those letters to your counsel. I also want you to let her speak on your behalf. That's what you're paying her to do.' He turned his gaze on Gwen and ordered her to get copies to everyone.

The judge motioned the clerk towards the bench, and they spoke while she leafed through a book. He nodded and she sat back down.

'My clerk just told me,' he said, 'that a case that was being tried has been settled, so I have some time on my calendar this afternoon. I'm going to hear any objections there are to receiving those letters into evidence.' He spoke to Paige's attorney. 'I'll consider a continuance if you want it.' His gavel made one dull thud and he ordered us all back at two o'clock.

I sat, still not looking to the side or behind me. Gwen closed her briefcase and said under her breath, 'So. I'd say that just knocked the slam dunk out of this case.'

Paige and her attorney had already left, so we walked out of the courtroom. Marcella approached us. 'What's the matter, Ella? You think the government knows better, what's best for Annie and Zach? These people, they rip families apart. You be careful or they may put our babies behind some barbed-wire fence in the middle of nowhere.'

I wanted to reassure her, to tell her not to worry. To tell her that the judge will still rule in our favour. I wanted to say, I will raise my kids and not have to hide a shameful secret from them, that would somehow wedge itself into their subconscious and create a quiet, persistent havoc in their souls. A secret that might stifle them or blind them so they can only see what they want to see. And I wanted to tell her and the rest of the family all how much I still loved them and needed them, that I didn't do this to hurt them.

Instead, I mumbled that I was sorry and let Gwen guide me past them, through the door, and up to the cafeteria, where I called Lucy and asked her if she could run to the house and then bring me the letters.

'Are you sure?' she said. When I didn't answer, she told me she'd be at the courthouse within the hour.

Lucy brought the letters. She hugged me long and hard and said she'd be out in the hallway if I needed her. Gwen set a coffee down in front of me, which I didn't touch. She left to make copies of the letters and deliver them, then came back and started reading.

Finally, she looked at me over her reading glasses. 'Ella, where did you find these?'

I told her about the kittens, the box springs. I told her about how I had opened the sealed envelopes.

She shook her head, looking directly in my eyes before I could avert them. A chair scraped the linoleum from somewhere behind me.

'Gwen, tell me I did the right thing.'

She shook her head. 'You should have told me so we could have been better prepared. But I'm not sure I could have prepared for this.'

'Annie and Zach shouldn't grow up thinking their mother never wanted them. I want the truth out. But I still want the kids to be with me. Won't the judge still see that's best? I thought judges in California ruled in favour of what's best for the children.'

She stirred her coffee, kept stirring, then said, 'For me, this case goes beyond wanting to win. I agree that those kids should be with you. But you're their stepmother. Even though you may see it as a technicality, the court doesn't. The birth mother still has all the rights.'

'But you said — '

'Forget what I said. These letters change things. Right now we have to figure out, do we have any objections to these going in as evidence?'

'Well, no, that's the point, isn't it?'

She explained that we couldn't pick or choose between the early and later letters. 'It's got to be

270

all or nothing. So I say we don't object because I think the court will let them all in anyway.'

I nodded. She left to meet with Paige's attorney. I sat and tilted my head back to keep the tears in place, pulled out my cell phone, and dialled Lizzie's number. I wanted to hear Annie's and Zach's voices, but no one answered.

Gwen returned and said that Paige's attorney agreed and had notified the judge that the letters would be admitted, but Paige had also made a settlement offer.

'It's joint custody with physical custody going to Paige. Visitation for you . . . four times a year plus two weeks in the summer, one week after Christmas.'

I shook my head. 'Visitation for *me*? Absolutely not. Come on, Gwen. You yourself said that I'm their real mom.'

She pulled her sleeves down so they showed under her suit jacket, splayed her chubby fingers over the letters. 'Ella, our entire case was built on the abandonment issue. These letters make that go away. You, as a stepmother, have no rights when a loving, willing birth mother wants to have custody of her children. You weren't even made their legal guardian.' My throat tightened. 'Those letters prove that Paige should be in their lives. But we still have the issue of what's best for Annie and Zach on our side. Elbow, where they've grown up with their close extended family? Or Sin City?'

She pressed her fingers to her temples. 'Look, we don't have to decide on the offer right now. Let's hear what the judge has to say.'

271

Back in Courtroom J, Judge Stanton let out a long sigh. His gaze ping-ponged between Paige and me. He spoke with tired resignation. 'I have read the letters, and they do certainly shed a new light on this case. In fact, the mediator's recommendation was based on the fact that the petitioner had not communicated with her children for three years. The letters disprove that and reveal a loving but emotionally disturbed young mother, who by leaving was acting in what she believed was in the best interest of the children. It very well may have been. I have to say, I am dismayed that the now deceased father did not work with the mother to reunite her with the children. One cannot help but wonder what role the stepmother played in all of this. I'm going to order a custody investigation and set this over for a hearing once that can be completed. But I'll tell you right now my inclination is this: with respect to the youngest child, his mother figure is Ms. Beene. With respect to the older child, her mother figure is Ms. Capozzi. And maybe that's the way this custody situation should be handled.'

I grabbed Gwen's pen and wrote *NO!!* on her manila folder.

She stood. 'Your Honour, before we get into a drawn-out investigation, can we each talk to our clients?'

Gwen and I sat in an attorney conference room. I said through clenched teeth, 'They cannot be separated.'

'This judge is so over the top, it's ridiculous. He could be grandstanding. It doesn't happen often that a judge splits up the children.'

'You heard him. I cannot take that chance. How is this *happening*?'

'Look. It's not happening today; he's speculating. First there has to be an investigation. They'll look into everything. Everyone will be interviewed. It's going to be an intense six months. And expensive.'

'I don't care about the money. I'll *find* the money. It's just that this is taking its toll on everyone. Marcella . . . I don't think she and Joe Sr could live through much more of this. But it's going to be the hardest on Annie and Zach.'

'And we've barely scratched the surface, compared to what's coming with an investigation. Ella, right now Paige is offering you joint custody. We can also ask that the court retain jurisdiction for either party to seek a modification, which means it can be revisited in the future.'

'But she gets physical custody?'

Gwen nodded. 'We could let this go to a hearing, and the judge could rule that she has full custody and you have nothing. Not even visitation. And that's possible. Typically, stepparents have no rights when it comes to custody.' She leaned into the table. 'Except when you can prove abandonment. Ella, the best-case scenario is that you get Zach but not Annie. And you clearly don't want them separated.'

How did this happen?

The letters happened.

'Gwen, what would you do if they were your kids?'

She placed her hand on my arm. 'Joint custody. I would agree to their stipulation. This may be the best we can do right now. Okay?'

I nodded but couldn't say the word *yes*.

She left me in the room so I wouldn't have to talk to Joe Sr, Marcella, or David, and went to draw up the papers. I sat with my face in my hands, knowing without a doubt that I had tried to do the right thing and instead had failed everyone I loved.

29

Lizzie answered the front door and hugged me. 'Frank called. You did an amazing thing.'

My throat clenched. I shook my head, heard Zach's voice, 'Mommy's here! Mommymommy-mommy!' He ran to me, holding a stuffed T rex in a Hawaiian shirt, and I picked him up and did not cry. Lizzie looked away. Annie came out and slipped her hand through my belt loop. And I did not cry.

I thanked Lizzie, the kids thanked Lizzie. We drove the four blocks home. I didn't know how to tell them, because the reality still circled around, like the tip of a shark that would soon eat us alive.

I knew I didn't want Annie to piece together bits of whispered conversations on my end of late-night telephone calls. I also didn't want Paige to tell her first. Gwen had insisted that I be the one to tell the kids, and while the judge had agreed, he'd given me only two days.

I didn't wait that long. I sat them down on our back porch with the lemonade Popsicles we'd made together, Zach spilling a good portion of the lemonade onto the kitchen floor. I squeezed myself between the two of them and said, 'Something happened today that I need to talk with you about.'

Annie looked up at me. Her fringe was clipped back with a pink barrette — probably the work of Lizzie's daughter — and she looked more and more like Paige. 'What?'

'Well, you know your mama Paige?'

They both nodded, and Annie said, 'Of course, silly.'

I forced a smile. 'Of course you do. You see, when Daddy died, she and I had a . . . disagreement . . . about where the two of you should live. She thought you should live with her. I wanted you to stay here with me. So when two people can't agree, sometimes they go to a place called court and talk about it until a decision is made. And this morning? It was decided that both of you should live with Mama Paige right now.'

'Why?' Zach said. He'd been swinging his chubby legs, kicking the lattice beneath the porch, and he stopped, searching my face. His Popsicle dripped streaks down his wrist, his arm, and onto his big-boy jeans.

Because I blew it. Because I didn't fight hard enough for you. Maybe I didn't do what a real mother would have done.

'Because,' I said, 'since Mama Paige is your . . . birth mother, she wants to have more time with you than she's had.'

'Why? Because I was in her tummy?'

'Because. She loves you. And she really, really misses you.'

Annie finally spoke. 'What about you? *You* love us.'

'Yes.' I swallowed. 'I love you very, very much. And I will miss you.'

'Are you sad?'

I nodded. '*But*. You and Zach will have a

wonderful new adventure. You'll get to live in your mama's big, beautiful house with your own rooms and play with lots of new friends. And I will still get to visit you.'

'*Visit* us? Like Nana Beene visits us?' Zach asked.

'Yes. Sort of like that.'

His eyes went wide; his sticky chin crumpled up in a trembling mass of dimples. I pulled him to me and held him in the crook of my arm.

He said, 'No way, José.'

Annie said, 'You *promised*!' Her voice shook, and a tear traced down her cheek. 'You said you'd never leave us! You *lied*.'

'Annie, I never wanted this to happen. I love you. I promise. I — '

'Don't promise me *anything*!' She threw her Popsicle, scrambled up, and started to run into the house, but then she turned around at the door, hands hanging at her sides, tears streaming, eyes on me. 'You pinkie promised! You said never, ever!'

'Come here, Banannie.' She ran into me, and the three of us huddled on the porch, Zach wailing now too.

Annie said through her sobs, 'I don't wanna be brave anymore.' I stroked their hair. Two clouds drifted on the horizon, wispy white as baptism gowns. 'You can cry,' I told her. 'You can be angry. That doesn't mean you're not brave.'

★ ★ ★

Even to this day, when I play it over in my mind, our good-bye happens in the slowest of motion,

277

but in reality it happened quickly. I guess Judge Stanton believed in the fast-ripping-off-the-Band-Aid approach. But people aren't Band-Aids.

★ ★ ★

Two days later, the day before Annie's seventh birthday, the cold morning sky low and grey, Paige stood outside in a teal silk dress and heels, opening the car doors, opening the trunk. Inside, Annie led Zach through their circle of embraces and kisses: Marcella and Joe Sr, David and Gil, Lucy, Frank, Lizzie, Callie, Thing One and Thing Two, until the two of them stood in front of me, looking up, waiting. Marcella turned her wide back to us. Zach clenched his Bubby and picked up his Thomas the Tank Engine suitcase. He insisted on wearing his Thomas slippers that matched the suitcase, and I didn't have the heart to argue with him, feeling like that was the least I could give him.

But Marcella turned back around and came up to me, and said, 'You put shoes on him. Right. This. Minute.'

'Marcella. He wants to wear these. It's the one thing he asked for. Let's pick our battles.'

'What do you know about fighting a battle? You give in. That's what you do.' She turned back around.

Annie wore her Birkenstocks and jeans instead of the dress and patent leathers she'd insisted on wearing the first time she'd visited Paige. I toed her toe with my own Birkenstock, then opened the screen door for them. Taking their hands in mine, I led the three of us down the porch steps and across the gravel. Still, I hoped for some divinity or act of nature to intervene, to say, *Stop. This was a test. The old Abraham-and-Isaac routine, but forget it, turn around, take them back inside, it's over now.* I concentrated my energy on not feeling, not crying, not looking at Paige, not throwing the kids into the Jeep and racing towards Canada or Mexico.

Callie followed us, circling around Paige's rental car, while the rest of the family waited on the porch. Annie's shoulders shook in a silent attempt not to cry, but when Zach saw her clenched face, he began howling. Paige yelled over him, 'They'll be fine! We just need to go!' *You know nothing*, I wanted to say, but didn't. I buckled the kids into their car seats as I had always done, and I kissed them, hugged them, wiped their tears and snot with my sleeves. I told them I would see them very soon and that I would call them that night.

Paige and I both lifted our hands, barely, and she started the car, Zach screaming now, 'I . . . want . . . my . . . MOMMY,' over and over as we stood on the porch, silent, waving, listening to his screams get smaller and smaller until the screams, and Zach, and Annie, were gone.

Everyone else filed down the stairs. Frank and Lizzie and Lucy all offered to stay, but I only shook my head. Joe Sr turned to me, his lip trembling, and said, 'At least you could have put Zach's shoes on for him. No man should have to leave his family in his slippers.' I didn't know

279

why the shoes were so important to Marcella and Joe Sr, but that was the least of my worries at the moment. David hugged me, but the hug was weak armed and quick, with a pat on the back — nothing like the Italian embraces we usually shared. David told me, 'Take some time away from the store. We'll cover for you.' I knew they needed time away from me too. Marcella left without looking at me.

When they were gone, I walked directly to the kids' room. Callie followed. I closed the door behind us. I threw myself on Annie's bed, burrowed my face into her sweet-smelling pillow, and I howled just like Zach, his pain-filled screams that I could not comfort wracking through me. Callie yelped as if in pain too. Sobs came from my core; I could not stop them. I cried without ceasing. I tried Paige's cell phone three times, but she didn't pick up.

★   ★   ★

Callie's bark woke me, followed by a hard, persistent knock on the front door. Disoriented, I grabbed for my alarm clock that wasn't where it should be, remembered that I was in Annie's bed, still in my clothes, and then remembered why. The knocking continued, and I let myself think, for the instant I climbed out of bed, that it was Paige, back with Annie and Zach, to tell me she'd made a horrible mistake. Instead it was the UPS man with a delivery. It was a box addressed to the kids from Paige, sent a week before. Instead of signing for it, I scratched out the

280

address and wrote *Return to sender*.

Paige still didn't answer. I left a message. I left four messages in the next four hours. I got three calls that day; not one from the kids. They were from the three other people on the planet who were still speaking to me: my mom, Lizzie, and Lucy. I screened them and didn't pick up; I didn't want to tie up the line in case the kids were trying to call me. My mom and Lizzie said they were thinking of me, to call if I wanted to talk. Lucy said she was coming over after work the next day, no questions asked.

The only responsibilities I had were to feed Callie, the chickens, and Thing One and Thing Two, clean the coop and the litter box, and pull up weeds. I did these things. Callie kept trying to nudge me into a walk, bringing me her leash, cocking her head with the sad eyes I usually could not resist. But I didn't have the energy, and I didn't want to see anyone in town.

I walked through the house, holding the sleeping kittens like babies in the crooks of my arms, and everything I saw stabbed me. The pictures of the kids, their toys, their art projects. The clay vase I kept on the bookshelves. Annie had made it for me in preschool. It had said *Happy Mother's Day* in macaroni letters, and I'd always loved it. The *M* had fallen off and left an indent soon after she brought it home, but only then, on that day after they'd gone, did I notice that without the *M* it read, *Happy other's Day*.

The refrigerator kicked in humming, the clock ticked, a log fell in the woodstove. I sat on the couch and channel surfed for hours until I happened upon TV Land — solely devoted to old shows from the sixties and seventies. I watched *The Brady Bunch*, *The Partridge Family*, *Room 222*. These were the shows I'd watched religiously after my father had died, wondering why my mom couldn't be more like Shirley Partridge, why my parents hadn't had more children so that I'd have a group of siblings I could start a rock band with too.

I let out Callie and thought about calling the kids again, but it was nine o'clock. They were fast asleep in their new rooms, their first day without me, and we hadn't talked. I had to wait until morning. I let Callie back in and she lay on the floor next to the couch. I fell asleep with the TV on — *Mister Ed* — and woke in the morning to *I Dream of Jeannie*.

I repeated my short list of chores, thought about cleaning the house, but, really, why? The day stretched before me: *Room 222*, *Gilligan's Island*, *The Courtship of Eddie's Father*, *Green Acres*, *That Girl*, *Please Don't Eat the Daisies*. When Callie was a puppy, still chewing up everything in sight, Joe and I decided our life was less *Please Don't Eat the Daisies* and more *Please Don't Eat the Porch*.

I tried the kids again. Still no one answered. Finally Paige called, wanting to let me know they'd got home late last night, that their plane had been delayed.

'Can I talk to the kids?' I said.

'I know this is hard for you. It's also really hard for them.'

Zach was crying in the background, 'I . . . want

282

'. . . my . . . mommy! I . . . want . . . my . . . mommy!'

'Ella, I really don't think it would be a good idea to talk to them right now. Give us a little time to adjust. They miss you, and talking to them will just make it worse. We need to work through this, the three of us.'

'Are you fucking *kidding* me?' I said. 'Let me talk to him. I can help him feel *better*.'

'I don't think so,' Paige said. 'Look. What you did in that courtroom was noble. It took courage. But now I'm asking you to give us some space.'

'Who the hell do you think you are?'

'I know who I am . . . I'm their mother.' And she hung up.

'*Bitch!*' I screamed into the phone, to no one, and hurled it at the wall.

It wasn't enough. I felt as frantic as a cat on acid. What could I do? Zach was crying! Joe's tripod was still propped up in the corner of the not-so-great room as some kind of makeshift memorial. I grabbed it and headed outside, still in my pyjamas. I swung the tripod in the air like it was a bat and I was next up. I walked over to Joe's truck. His beloved Green Hornet. I planted my feet. I swung as hard as I could, smashing the windshield, smashing it into oblivion.

30

What had I expected from Paige? Overflowing gratitude? Forgiveness? A certain willingness to work things out? Yes, yes, and yes. I had told Gwen Alterman that I didn't believe Paige should be shut out of Annie's and Zach's lives. I thought Paige would believe the same about me. I had mistaken her for the Paige who wrote the letters three years ago — a desperate, vulnerable, hurting mother. But even Lizzie had noticed, there was an old Paige, and now this new Paige: who believed in the order of things and their placement, who seemed convinced that the placement of Annie and Zach should be in her home, with none of my personal chi flowing through the door, or even through the phone wires. She'd cleaned out the clutter of having me as their stepmother. *(Who needs two when one will do the job? Decide which box — Give Away or Throw Away, and then don't look back.)*

I called Gwen, who told me to let the dust settle. I doubted Paige *had* any dust. She reminded me that Paige still had to allow for visitation in a month. If she refused, she would be in contempt, and then we'd actually have grounds to do something.

'A month?' was all I could say. 'In one month I'll get to see them for two days? Today's Annie's seventh birthday and I haven't even got to talk with her.'

'There's nothing fair about this. But it sounds like she's off to a rocky start. So. Keep track of every conversation, but don't badger or harass. This could go completely in our direction. You just have to be patient.'

*　*　*

Lucy let herself in that night. She found me in the kids' room sitting on the floor amid neatly arranged stuffed animals and dolls, having a tea party. I'd packed presents in Annie's suitcase, but I couldn't stand not being able to see her open them, not making her favourite carrot cake.

I'd tied a bonnet on Callie, the way Annie sometimes did. I was pushing Buzz Lightyear's button over and over, so he kept repeating, 'To infinity, and beyond!' Without saying a word, Lucy walked into the kitchen, came back with an open bottle of petite sirah, from which she poured enough to fill two of the pink-and-white miniature china cups. 'Sorry, Elmo, you're underage,' she said. She turned to me. 'Hey, it's going to take a helluva long time to get drunk this way.' She held her cup out for me to toast. 'Ella, oh my God, honey, your eyes. You look like shit.'

I shook my head. She hugged me, rubbed my back, 'I know, El. I know.' It wasn't long before we moved out to the back porch, exchanging our teacups for big-girl glasses. She tried to get me to eat something, but I couldn't. I did bum cigarettes off her, though, and for the first time in my life, smoked them without guilt or regret.

Lucy gently suggested I start taking the

antidepressant that Dr Boyle had recommended. I told her no, and also said no to her offer of more wine. I knew I needed to feel this, no matter how much it hurt.

She offered to come over again the next day, but I told her I wanted some alone time and she grudgingly complied.

Knowing now that no one — absolutely no one — would stop by, I dragged out the boxes I'd moved to our garage from the storage closet at the store. The ones with all the photos of Annie, Zach, Joe, and Paige, the extended Capozzi family. I told myself I wanted to see pictures of the kids, but there was still a part of me that was trying to understand the story of Joe and Paige, what that meant to the story of Joe and me, the story of Annie and Zach and me . . . and Paige. And the question still, what had Paige revealed to Joe that day when she turned around?

I pulled a box in by one of its cardboard flaps, pulled it down the hallway until it sat in the middle of the not-so-great room. I took out stacks of photos, placing them in a mosaic-like pattern on the floor around me. At first Thing One and Thing Two kept batting at the pictures and sliding across them, but then they got bored and snuggled up with Callie on the couch.

Here were Paige and Joe at Marcella's for Christmas; Paige wore huge red ball Christmas ornaments in her ears and Joe had a bow stuck to his forehead. They were laughing. Another picture: Paige and Joe's wedding day. So different from ours, with my short halter sundress and sweet peas picked from the yard. But theirs was like Henry's and mine: the elaborate white gown, Paige's high necked and beaded, the regiment of bridesmaids and groomsmen, the ring bearer, the flower girl, the perfectly round bouquets, the exhausted and completely overwhelmed smiles.

I found cards too — anniversary, birthday, Valentine's Day — all declaring unfaltering love and adoration. *I'll love you forever*, as if they were trying to ward off any curses or uncertainty, the evil spell that loomed on the periphery.

I placed the cards down along with all the photos, even the nude ones, arranging and rearranging until I got the sequence right along with the order. *How feng shui of me*, I thought. When I got to the bottom of one box, I spotted a pink edge stuck between the cardboard flaps. I unfolded them and out popped what looked like a pink passport, maybe something of Annie's. But it was stamped with the words *Enemy Alien*. Inside, a picture of Grandpa Sergio in his forties, the typed words: *Sergio Giuseppe Capozzi*, his address in Elbow — the same as our address — along with his date of birth, August 1, 1901, his fingerprints.

Those words struck me harder than the tiny bits and pieces of the story I'd heard. The fear. The paranoia. Enemy? Alien? Grandpa Sergio? Who loved this country, owned a little market. Who built this cottage . . . had his family ripped apart, as Marcella had yelled. It struck me how easily paranoia sets in during times of war, and I knew that my own fear of Paige — the whole family's fear of Paige — wasn't exactly fair, either. Still, what we'd all feared most had now happened, and my attempt to be fair had landed us here.

I set the ID down too, along with pictures of Sergio and Rosemary standing in front of their new house, now our old house, and I felt connected to them in a way I hadn't before. Their family had filled this house with its noise too — its laughter and arguments. Rosemary had walked these very rooms, filled with the vacancy of Sergio's absence. She, too, knew the way an expanding emptiness pressed on the walls, the ceilings, the floors.

I pulled out another box; it turned out to be the box with Paige's robe. The robe Joe had covered her secret with, the robe she'd hidden in all those months of depression. I put it on, over my clothes. Embarrassing to admit now, but I guess I saw it as a necessary piece of the puzzle. I pulled out more boxes until I'd covered the floor in the living area, and started in the kitchen, then down the hall. I left curving paths that spiralled out from the centre of the room, reminiscent of the labyrinth Joe and I had once walked at Grace Cathedral in San Francisco the New Year's after we met. We'd walked in silence, each holding a question in our minds. When we finished, we stood at the centre and Joe asked me if I would marry him. It turned out we'd both come to the labyrinth with the same question and had received the same answer while we walked it: Yes.

I'd covered the not-so-great room and kitchen, part of the hallway, and half of Annie and Zach's room when I ran out of pictures. I pulled out our own photos, the ones taken after I came into the picture, so to speak. And my shoebox of pictures of my own childhood, my mom and me clam digging, my dad and me posing on a rock, arms folded, wearing our birding binoculars. I lined more photos along the floor in the kids' room and worked down the hallway and into our bedroom, finishing the path off on top of our bed because of the lack of floor space.

I worked with a welcomed detachment from my present life, or even the lives represented in the pictures — completely absorbed in the structure of my creation, the pieces of the puzzle. It was all a bit crazy, but craziness made perfect sense right then. By the time I finished, the room had dimmed dark.

I must have lain down then to sleep. The next morning I woke in a sea of pictures, staring at Annie holding up a salmon almost as big as she was. Pictures were stuck to my arms, my hands, my cheek.

I climbed out of the bed, took it all in. I know how strange this sounds now, but I was intrigued with what I'd done. There was order, purpose. I felt I was on to something. So I made coffee, careful not to disturb the layout on the floor, and attended to my life's current responsibilities: Callie, chickens, kittens, vegetables. I forced myself to eat some toast. I played with the kittens on the porch, then put them in their crate for a rest. And then I walked my labyrinth. And walked. And walked. Callie stared at me through the French doors, giving me her saddest face, and at one time, I swore she shook her head at me, *What? You can't even take me for a measly little walk and here you are walking in circles all pickin' day? You won't even let me in? Who is this person you've become?*

But I turned back to my task, took another step, studied another photo. See Paige and Annie in matching Easter dresses. See Joe sleeping. I wanted to crawl in next to him, but I wasn't the one who'd taken the picture. It was taken before I knew Joe existed. When he loved Paige and Paige loved him. She loved him enough to want to capture him sleeping peacefully, his lips parted, his hair flattened on one side; looking the same way he had on mornings when I had watched him sleeping and loved him too.

But see this: Annie, Zach, Joe, and me, in that very bed. It had been morning, the bed was messy, our hair was messy. Joe had set up the tripod and climbed in. Annie hit him with a pillow just as the camera clicked.

Outside, the clouds broke open all at once, and rain pounded the gravel, battered the porch. I was on my fourth round of the path and had left my third message to Paige when someone knocked on the front door. On the other side of the door's window, Clem Silver held up his hand. Clem Silver at my house. Clem Silver never visited people at their homes, even when he was invited. But now that the question of my emotional and mental health was displayed in paths of photographs winding from room to room, there he was, first in line to bear witness. I opened the door.

He had one of those seventies clear bubble

290

umbrellas, which he collapsed and set on the porch. 'I heard,' he said. 'And ... well, I'm sorry.'

'Thanks.'

'And I brought you this.' He waved a green garbage bag. I held the door open.

'Ignore the, ah, mess.'

He stepped inside, but there was nowhere to walk, so we stood close to each other in the hallway by the door. He smelled of his cigarettes and turpentine. He stared at his shoes. 'I had — have — two daughters.'

'Really?'

He nodded. 'When my wife left, I was so mad, and she was so mad. She went to Florida, and I can't think of a place I'd hate more to live, except, maybe ...' He looked up and gave me a little smile. 'Las Vegas. So I stayed put and she talked bad about me and those girls grew up without me. And I don't feel good about that. Tears me up just about every day. I love it here, you know that. But I acted like a barnacle and I wish I'd been a bird.'

I kept nodding, trying to picture shy Clem surrounded by a houseful of females.

'It's none of my business. I'm not trying to tell you what to do. Or maybe I am. But I thought, if you ever decide to — well, you'll have it. And if you don't need it, that's okay too.'

'Do you want me to open it?'

'I'm gonna go now. And then you can if you want. And then we'll just see.' He started to pat me on the shoulder but I hugged him, and then he was gone.

291

I looked in the bag and saw a roll of paper. I unrolled it. It was another map, hand painted, more tans and browns than greens, but still a work of art. It was a map of Las Vegas.

31

The phone finally rang. I made a run back along the path, *Hold on, kids,* to catch the phone just before the answering machine got it.

But it was David. 'Ella? Thank God you picked up. Listen. Remember when I told you *Real Simple* magazine wanted to do a story — a big spread — on you and the store?'

'Sort of . . . I thought it was *Sunset.*'

'Well, they might too. But this is more about *you* and the store. A human interest thing. Anyway. I can't believe this got by me, we'd confirmed last week, but with everything that's been going on, they called again yesterday, but I forgot to check the messages on the store — '

'What got by you?'

'They're here.'

'Here?'

'At the store. They love it. Totally gaga over every inch of it. We need you down here pronto. They want to interview and take pictures of you and the — Hey, can we get the kids back for a day or two?'

'What?'

'Listen, I need you to pull through for me. I can't tell you how important this is, what an op-por-tun-i-ty. We need this, Ella. You're the one who got me into this thing in the first place, remember. I can't hold them off any longer. They like the angle of a woman rising above her pain, the lemonade out of lemons, which fits with the whole grocery-store-into-picnic theme. Do that cool thing with your hair. See you in a few minutes.'

'*David!*' But he'd hung up. 'Shit,' I said. 'Shit, shit, shit.'

I don't think I'd ever felt worse. Or looked worse. I peered in the mirror. I still had Paige's robe on over my clothes. Eyes still swollen. Hair matted like some ridiculous new invention. Carrot-flavoured cotton candy. Not exactly the strong woman rising above her pain.

I wanted to curl up with my pictures and wait for my phone to ring, to hear, 'Hi, Mommy.' But David needed me. It was the least I could do after I'd screwed up everyone's life. I changed into my sage green flowered dress, the one Joe always loved; he'd called me 'flower child' when I wore it. I spritzed water on my carrot cotton candy and pulled it up into the pretty clip the kids gave me the previous Mother's Day. I washed my face and even put on makeup and silver and jade earrings.

As I stepped gingerly over the photos, cutting from path to path, Sergio's booklet caught my eye. I stuck it in my pocket.

The rain had stopped as quickly as it started, and the sun was already working on drying out the store's puddled parking lot, which swarmed with activity. A woman with short, dark hair, dressed in cream slacks and a crisp white blouse, a couple of guys with camera equipment, a younger woman in jeans carrying two oversize vases of flowers, all filed up the porch steps. I followed them in. David introduced me to the photographers, who reminded me of Joe, the way they carried their cameras and lights with such confidence.

David mentioned to the dark-haired woman, 'Ella, this is Blaire Markham. She's writing the article for *Real Simple*.'

Blaire smiled and extended her hand, which felt cool in my clammy one. 'You have quite an inspiring story. I am so sorry about the loss of your husband.'

'Thanks.' I felt sweat beads breaking on my upper lip.

'We like to feature women who defy odds, who carve out a unique life for themselves that truly reflects their personality. That's why we've chosen to write about you.'

I nodded, kept nodding, kept myself from letting out a big, fat *HA!* Joe Sr and Marcella walked in, wearing their church clothes. They stood back by the board games, Marcella's arms folded across her chest, her black patent leather purse hanging from the crook of her elbow.

David introduced them to Blaire.

'Great!' she said. 'I'd love to get a multigenerational shot in front of the store, so we could lay it out next to this one.' She walked over and tapped the frame of the photo of Joe and Joe Sr and Sergio that hung on the wall by Joe's apron. 'Where are your children? We like to include lots of pictures of the family in the spreads we do at *Real Simple*, since they're always a central part of the story.'

'It's not that simple,' I say. 'In fact, it's Real

Complicated.' I let out a nervous laugh. The room fell silent, and while Blaire waited for me to explain, Marcella said, 'Multigenerational, my foot. Ella's not my daughter. And she's not my grandchildren's mother.'

David said, 'Ma. That's not fair.'

'It may not be fair, but it's the truth. What is she even doing here? This store is for my grandchildren, who no longer belong to her. For a woman who's so bent on telling the truth all of a sudden, she forgot a few very important details. If you ask me.'

'Which, as I recall, no one did.' David was the one laughing nervously now. The timer went off, and he called out, 'Saved by the bell! Snickerdoodles for everyone,' and went to pull them from the oven. He set them down on a table, poured mugs of coffee, and said, 'Ma, Pop, sit. Ella, get busy in the kitchen.' He placed a basket of lemons and a pitcher on the counter. 'And we can even get a lemonade-out-of-lemons shot. Here, hold the knife.'

I took the knife from him. The lemon felt slippery in my grip. The photographers adjusted lights, changing positions, angles. Trying to make me look my best.

'I can't do this,' I said.

'Oh, my mistake.' David handed me another knife. 'Much sharper.'

'No, David, I mean *this*. I mean pretending like everything's lemonade and snickerdoodles when at this particular moment, it's horrible and rotten. I mean not talking about what's really going on, so people can see only what they want to see.' Blaire took her pen and notebook out, clicked her tape recorder on, like we were celebrities and she was writing for the *National Enquirer*, as if anyone would care about our little family's heartbreak.

'Ella? Now? Really?' David tilted his head.

'Yeah. Really.' I turned to Blaire. 'Marcella's right. I'm not Annie and Zach's mother. I'm their stepmother. Their real mother just won custody of them and moved them to Las Vegas. My husband drowned. And this store? It was drowning in debt. We took a huge risk and remodelled it, and we're trying to bring it back to life because we can't bring him back to life. And that sign out there? Life's a Picnic? Yeah, sometimes. Other times you've got to lay out your blanket in a barbed-wire internment camp.' I pulled out Sergio's ID and waved it. 'Because the man who built this store? The sweet, hardworking, America-loving Italian immigrant who moved here to start a new life? They called him an 'Enemy Alien' and he was sent away to an internment camp during World War II. Yep. Apparently, it wasn't just the Japanese who were victims of that disgraceful human rights violation. But no one knows about it because no one *talks* about it!'

Joe Sr got up. He shook a finger at Blaire Markham. 'You turn that thing off.' She nodded and obeyed. He came to me with his eyes filled and reached for the ID. 'Where did you find that?'

'In one of the boxes way in the back of the attic at the store.'

297

'I've never seen it before.' He took it, sat back down, and opened it, and in doing so, seemed to open doors that had been shut for both him and Marcella for almost sixty years. They both stared at the pages, tears running down their faces.

I said, 'He's gone now. His story . . . It should be told.'

'What do you care about this family?' Marcella asked.

'Marcella? This family *is* my family. You know that. You both do.'

They stared at me. David came up and tucked a strand of my hair behind my ear, then placed both of his hands on my shoulders. 'Ella's the best thing that's happened to this family. You've said it yourself, Ma.'

Marcella nodded while she held her hankie to her eyes. Finally she said, 'February 21, 1942. They took both our fathers. They took my papa in his slippers! They didn't even let him go inside to put on his shoes.' Now I understood their admonishment about Zach wearing his slippers.

Blaire held her pen to the paper but asked Marcella, 'May I?' Marcella looked at Joe Sr and said, 'Not today. Maybe later. But I want to say this. I still remember a sign at the post office. I had just learned to read at school. It said, DON'T SPEAK THE ENEMY LANGUAGE! SPEAK AMERICAN! That's when we all had to learn English. Even at home, we stopped speaking Italian. We felt guilty.'

Joe Sr told us that more than six hundred thousand Italian immigrants were under regulations. Many of their homes were raided. 'They

298

had to stay within five miles of their homes and had an eight p.m. curfew. Like they were children.' He said that thousands of Italian American coastal residents were relocated and had to find new places to live. The government said they couldn't be trusted along our coastline. Fishermen lost their livelihood. Some of them came to Elbow.

'Did both your fathers come home unharmed?' Blaire asked.

'Yes and no,' Joe Sr said. 'Papa returned after twenty-three months. But he had lost his bravado. He was quiet. He worked even harder than before. But he never wanted to talk about it.'

'My papa,' Marcella said, dabbing her already puffy eyes with her handkerchief again. 'He carried home a heavy shame. Our family was changed for ever. He had once been so proud. Proud of Italia, proud of America. And Joe Sr and I?' Marcella put her hand on his back and leaned towards us. 'When we were children, the first words I spoke to him at school were' — she lowered her voice to a whisper — ' 'Did they take your papa, too?' And he nodded. And that was it. We never talked about it, either. But it' — she linked her fingers together — 'it bound us together. Our secret. But now our secret is our curse.'

'My brother,' Joe Sr said, 'he died in that war. A man gives his son, but he's treated like the enemy. And you know what my father did? The Fourth of July, after he was released, he threw the biggest celebration this town had ever seen.

That's what started Elbow's tradition. He said, 'Let them try to call me an enemy. I'll be the best goddamn patriot this country has ever seen.''

David said, 'You've gotta love that. I always thought you and Grandpa decorated for the Fourth with more flourish than *any* gay man ever has.'

Marcella leaned against Joe Sr, the tears and sobs taking over. 'We're cursed.'

He stroked her shoulder. 'Joe Jr, and now Annie and Zach . . . ' Joe Sr's voice trailed off. His eyes went moist.

I said, 'Annie and Zach are not dead.'

He shook his head. 'I know, honey. But they're gone. Taken from us. They used the word *custody* with our fathers too, *taken into custody*. And now our government decides this too?'

We sat in silence. Blaire Markham stood. 'Clearly, this was bad timing. As far as I'm concerned, everything said here was off the record. Unless' — she looked directly at Joe Sr and Marcella — 'you change your minds. Here's my card if that's the case. It's an important story, and I hope you'll consider telling it.'

★ ★ ★

After she and the photographers left, the four of us sat around the table, nibbling on the cookies, tired from it all but becoming more and more easy with one another. There were hugs and apologies, and I knew I had to tell them what I wanted to do.

I'd been holding a question as I'd walked my crazy labyrinth. Did the kids need Paige? My answer had come. It was yes. But I'd held another question too. Did the kids still need me, now that they had Paige? I knew that answer too. And so I said to David, 'I don't want to bail on you. But do you think you could cover things for a few weeks? I want to fix this. I want to go to Las Vegas.'

'Of course I want you to bring Annie and Zach home. But Ella? Is there a chance in hell?'

'Look.' I turned to Marcella and Joe Sr. 'You didn't read her letters. She really did feel like she had to leave, that she had no choice. She didn't *want* to walk out on Annie and Zach . . . or Joe, either. She was very ill. Her thinking was muddled. But she did what she thought was best. And then she was shut out. Shunned from her home. She couldn't see her kids.' I took a deep breath. 'Not unlike your fathers.'

Joe Sr sat up. 'Don't you ever — '

'Joseph. Stop. She's right. This has all gone on long enough.' She touched his rough cheek. 'I just want my grandbabies back.'

★   ★   ★

I only packed a few large suitcases and two boxes of the kids' clothes and toys and the unopened letters to Annie and Zach. I stuck those in the glove compartment of the Jeep. I wasn't sure how long I'd be gone — I figured two weeks at the most. I had no plan other than to drive to Las Vegas and call Paige once I arrived. She couldn't turn me away once I got there.

Lizzie had agreed to keep the chickens in her coop, and David and Gil had promised they'd watch Thing One and Thing Two. As I was slipping the boxes into the backseat, David came walking up the road, carrying a bunch of cornflowers from the photo shoot that never happened and a picnic basket — my favourite picnic basket — from the store, and he handed it all to me. 'Look inside,' he said. It was full of the things I loved: a jar of Marcella's minestrone, her jam — made from blackberries the kids and Joe and I had picked last summer — one of her pesto and chicken salad sandwiches, and a lamb shank for Callie.

'Does she know you're giving me all this?'

'She helped me pack it. I'm so sorry about the interview thing. I should have never thrown that on you. And I'm sorry about not standing by you. I've been an idiot . . . so bent on trying to help turn the store around, be the saviour, keep the kids here. It took Gil to point out that I've had the sensitivity of a rhinoceros.'

I pulled out a list and handed it to David. 'I'm sorry,' I said. 'It's a helluva lot, I know.'

'The thing is, El, I love it. I love the store. I love everything about it. You were right. I *did* want to be the one who took it over. I was jealous of Joe. Of how he got handed this thing on a silver platter, something he hadn't really wanted, at least not since he was a little kid, while I was practically jumping up and down saying, 'Pick me, pick me!' If it weren't for you and your idea for Life's a Picnic, I'd be a very

302

bored person married to a very fat man.'

I laughed. 'Gil *was* starting to look a little plump when you were shovelling all that food down him.'

'For that reason, and many more, we are eternally grateful to you. And that's why we've decided to give you this.' He handed me an envelope. Inside was cash. A thick wedge of hundred-dollar bills.

'David. I can't take this. I'll get a temp job when I get there.'

'No. You need to focus on talking to Paige, not filling out job apps. This money was Gil's idea, and it's absolutely the right thing. We love you and we want to help. Do what you need to do to at least get her to talk to you. Take your time. I'll take care of the store.'

'I don't know what to say.'

Callie came running up then, carrying what looked like a small snaggled tree stump. But as she got closer I could see it wasn't a tree, but some kind of animal skull. I took it from her and stared into the hollow eyes, the remaining yellowed teeth, the empty, dusty dryness of it.

'Oh God,' David said after a minute. 'That could be Max.'

'Max . . . ?'

'Joe's dog when we were kids.' David nodded, then shook his head. 'Grandpa Sergio buried him in the redwood grove when I was about nine. You should have seen him in his glory days. A huge golden retriever. Max *owned* Elbow. He'd walk down the street from house to house. Everyone knew him. He was like the town mascot. I thought he'd live forever. Poor Max.' David fell silent, his mind turning over memories.

'What happened to him?'

'Oh, that's a sad story. Joe never told — ' He stopped himself.

'Nope. Add it to the list, I guess.'

He nodded. 'I'll tell you. But not right now. You've got some miles to cover.'

The breeze kicked up and we both stood there, staring at the skull, taking in the warm sun, the stirring air that carried the scent of the bay trees and rosemary bushes, the Douglas fir from the ridge.

'Come here.' He wrapped me in one of his real hugs. 'Things will be better again. Just hang in there. We'll be here waiting. I'll be here, you know, trying to figure out what *else* wasn't said at dinner all those years. How much of the stifling in that room was about me being gay, and how much was really about Grandpa Sergio and Grandpa Dante . . . *Internment* camps. Shit. I feel another identity crisis coming on . . . You better go, before I climb in with you.'

★　★　★

On my way out of Elbow, I turned and headed up to the cemetery. I reached back and pulled up the bunch of cornflowers and let Callie scramble out, though I kept an eye on her. I certainly didn't want her digging *there*. She circled around tombstones and started to squat by one, but I shooed her over to the trees. 'Callie! Have you no respect?' I laid the flowers along Joe's tombstone, and I whispered, 'Remember these? I had some just like them in my car when we met? *Centaurea cyanus*. I brought them into your kitchen and you filled a vase with water? Remember?' I knelt there, sitting back on my heels, waiting to feel him. Wherever he was, he wasn't hanging out there. 'The truth is, I still can't believe it,' I said. 'There's a part of me that keeps thinking you'll show up somewhere. Isn't that weird?

'There's so much I didn't know about you, honey. I'm sorry. I wish we could talk . . . I'm going to try to fix things. To fix the mess we made for Annie and Zach.' I traced the letters on the stone. *Joseph Anthony Capozzi Junior*. The same letters he said were spelled in freckles on my arm. 'I love you, honey. I was mad about some things. But I love you. And I'm going to bring them back.' I took two of the cornflowers back to the Jeep with me and stuck them in the visor. Callie sniffed them. 'Please Don't Eat the Cornflowers,' I said. And she didn't touch them again, not the whole way to Las Vegas.

★　★　★

I drove and I drove, and I thought about those cornflowers. After I'd had my fifth miscarriage, my doctor had suggested walking. It didn't help much. But I walked, anyway. Henry and I had agreed to divorce. I hadn't known what to do next, where to go, who to be. And so I walked.

One day, as I passed the massive flower fields

305

in Encinitas, I noticed a migrant worker who had stopped cutting. He was watching me. He ventured out to the edge, close to the sidewalk, ahead of me. When I approached, he said, 'Wait, miss,' and bent down, then stood back up, holding an armful of blue flowers. He pushed them towards me and smiled. 'For you, you take.' I stopped, my mouth gaping. 'No, I . . . '

'*Por favor*. Every day, you're sad. *Triste*. Beautiful flowers, *sí*? *Esperanza*. How you say in English? Hope? They mean this hope.'

I took the flowers. They filled my arms like a child. I couldn't help but smile. The next day all the migrant workers, including my friend, were gone. North, I imagined. And suddenly, I wanted to be with them, losing myself in fields of flowers by day, chatting around a camp-fire by night, always moving. A hard life, but one with camaraderie. That's when I started packing my Jeep. I wasn't really going to track down the sweet migrant worker, the only person who had instinctively known how to ease my sorrow. But I'd taken it as a sign, the way desperate people do, to do *something*. To head north, to find my true north. Maybe a job tracking juvenile salmon in Alaska. And that crazy impulse had led me to Elbow, to Joe, to Annie and Zach. Just as I'd hoped my crazy impulse to go to Las Vegas would somehow lead me to Annie and Zach once again.

32

I drove through dark desert and lonely straight roads, my eyes often drawn towards the brilliantly lit night sky; falling stars streaked across it, like the thoughts of Joe and the kids and the Capozzis and Paige that kept streaking across my mind.

David called me on my cell. 'Where are you?'

'Somewhere between a prickly pear cactus and a Joshua tree. With way too much time before the next cactus. So keep me awake. Tell me about Max.'

I could hear pans banging in the sink. 'I'd forgotten that whole thing until today. Joe loved that dog. Poor Joe . . . He and Max were walking on Jasper Williams' property. Jasper was the town asshole extraordinaire.'

'Do I know this guy?'

'Oh, he died years ago. Everyone avoided him. He was some retired military dude. But Joe was maybe eleven, had just got his first camera, and Jasper had the best view of the river. He yelled at Joe for trespassing. *Everyone* trespassed in Elbow. It was synonymous with being neighbourly. Apparently, Williams had lost some chickens and he blamed Max, which was ridiculous because Max wouldn't hurt a flea. He yelled, 'I told you all to stay away, you goddamn trespassing Wop. Should have locked you Kraut-lovin' Japs and Wops up forever!' and then he shot Max dead. What a fucking idiot. Joe wanted to call the police, but Grandpa Sergio and Dad said no.' David let out a long whistle and fell silent.

'David?'

'Oh my God. Now I get it. They said he *was* trespassing and they didn't want trouble and they didn't want to hurt the family name.'

'The only family name it would have hurt was Jasper whatever-his-face's.'

'Absolutely. Joe cried for a week solid I remember, even at Little League practice. At dinner one night my dad told him to quit being a sissy. Joe got up from the table and left, and I waited for all hell to break loose. But my dad sat chewing his food, looking across the table at Grandpa Sergio. My mother sat looking at her hands. And no one ever said another word about it.'

I could see them sitting around a table piled with comfort food, a vacant chair taking up the whole room, as all the unspoken secrets and anger and fears and humiliation passed back and forth between them. *Mangia, mangia!* Have another helping of silence.

★ ★ ★

As we approached Las Vegas, Callie woke and barked at all the lights upon lights upon lights — even though they were still far ahead. Soon they were like firework displays exploding too close; their heat on my face, flashing, running, strobing.

But those lights lost their bravado the next morning, when I got a clearer look at the Strip and realized they were mere compensation, meant to blind me to the fact there wasn't an ounce of natural beauty, or natural anything, anywhere. The only snippet of green lay in a row of planted palm trees in the centre of the strip. At a stoplight, I caught an older man and a much younger woman snorting cocaine in a black convertible. She took the rolled bill and mirror from him and went at it while he held back her long black hair. Is this what Annie and Zach saw on their way to school? How could Paige have moved herself, let alone the kids, from Elbow — with its lush, tree-crammed hills running all the way into the river, to *this*? I could not even begin to picture Annie and Zach being there, let alone calling it home.

But, I reminded myself, Elbow wasn't Utopia for everyone. The rainy winters had gotten to Paige and deepened her depression, she'd written. She wanted to be warm and dry. But the biggest reason, I knew from reading the other letters, was that she had nowhere else to go but to Aunt Bernie, who lived in a trailer on the outskirts, and who loved her. Loved all of her, Paige had written. I thought of this as I pulled onto the freeway, not really sure where to go or if I should call her. A billboard stood out against the legions of other billboards. Was it? It couldn't be. I leaned forward over the steering wheel and peered. Yes, by God, it was. There stood Paige, ten feet tall, in a power suit, with her arms folded, her tight white smile now the size of a turkey platter. WHEN IT'S TIME TO STAGE, CALL PAIGE. The same goofy slogan that was on her business card, the same phone number I'd been calling all week. Well, Aunt Bernie certainly *had a lot* to love. 'My, my, my,' I said to Callie, who rested her paws on the console between us and twitched her forehead nine different ways at me. It seemed that whenever I'd figured out something about Paige, or began to feel compassion for her, she'd show yet another side. Who was this woman who'd plastered herself on a billboard? Maybe pigeons would perch on it, leaving streaks of *Columba livia* shit all over her.

Still, how much more obvious of a sign did I need? I punched the number into my cell phone. As always, Paige didn't answer, so I left a message telling her I was in town. This time she called me right back.

'You're in Las Vegas?' she asked.

'Yep.' I was trying for casual, cheerful, even. 'Nice billboard.'

'Oh, that — I got a good deal on it. I actually get quite a lot of calls from it.'

I stifled an *I bet*.

'Why are you here?'

'Well, not to gamble. I want to see the kids.'

'Ella. You're not thinking about Annie and Zach. They're trying to make a huge adjustment. The judge knew what he was doing when he put the first visitation a month away. You don't live here. Why mislead them now?'

'Must I remind you that the judge was about to make a quite dif — '

'No. You don't need to remind me. Look, Ella.

310

I'm only asking for time. And I think you need time too. To rebuild your life without Annie and Zach.'

'But don't you see? You're cutting me out? Doing the same thing you say Joe did to you?'

'My number one concern is for the kids.'

'Then why did you take them away from me? We were happy . . . ' My voice broke, but I held it together. The last thing I needed to do was blubber at Paige. Besides, I was driving and a semi was on my tail.

'Go home, Ella. Wait a month. Then call us.'

'Who says I'm not home?' I blurted out.

She sighed. 'You mean you were lying about being here?'

'No, I mean maybe I *moved* here.' Did I really just say that? Silence.

'Paige? Can you hear me?'

'Yes.'

'So now will you let me see the kids?'

'You can see them in twenty-two days, as ordered by the court. Good-bye, Ella.' She hung up before I could respond.

That went well. I pulled off the freeway and found an ampm store and picked up the *Las Vegas Sun*. I grabbed a pint of ice cream too, knowing I didn't have a freezer back at the No-Tell Motel, knowing I'd have to eat it all in one sitting. My version of living life on the edge in Las Vegas.

Along one of the aisles, a yellow notebook caught my eye. It was bigger than the one I'd carried around before my dad died, but it looked similar, spiralled across the top like mine had been. Flipping through its blank pages, I thought about that little red-haired girl with her binoculars who'd been so curious, so full of *whys*? And *whos*? And *whats*? She'd finally woken up a few weeks ago after decades of sleep, had already been busy shaking things up, wreaking havoc, yes, but hell, I loved the kid. She was a good kid. She'd already taught me a thing or two. And she needed a notebook.

★   ★   ★

Even though I despised Las Vegas, I'd told Paige I'd moved. I'd left out the word *temporarily*. I couldn't stand the thought of Annie and Zach being raised in a town known for gambling, drugs, and prostitution, but more than that, I couldn't stand the thought of them being raised there without me. Nor could I stand the thought of returning to Elbow without them. And judging from our first phone conversation, things with Paige were not going to happen quickly. I had three options, and I hated all of them. A place was just a place. I could deal with missing Elbow. Temporarily. I opened the paper up to the classifieds and started looking for an apartment. I wrote addresses down in my notebook. I had time to kill, and I wanted to make Annie and Zach feel at home when they visited me, not sitting perched on a bed in a tacky motel room.

Each day, I walked Callie for hours, exploring different neighbourhoods where we might find an apartment, lingering in any slip of green offered up in the new and small manicured parks. The wind blew dust and debris, rolling tumbleweeds of Big Gulp cups, crushed cigarette boxes, plastic grocery bags. The sun beat down on us, forcing us to take frequent water breaks. I ached for Elbow, for the garden and the chickens, the cool river and the picnic store — but ached much more for Annie and Zach.

The court documents listed Paige's address, and I drove by. It was in a suburban neighbourhood in a new development with one tiny birch tree staked in each yard. The house was a new, huge stucco wedged into a minuscule lot, surrounded by similar houses in alternating A, B, C, and D models. As much as the red door — so feng shui — beckoned for me to knock on it, I didn't. Visitation was less than two weeks away, and I didn't want to sabotage the kids' visit to my place.

I wrote in my notebook: Who is Paige? How can I convince her to talk to me? I wrote: Why did Joe even agree to take on the store in the first place? Didn't he want to be a photographer? Since he was eleven? I wrote: Annie's laugh. Zach's toes. Us cutting lavender, hanging it in the barn. Annie's bee sting. Her crying and saying, 'At least that son of a gun makes honey too.'

★   ★   ★

I focused on finding a place, staying positive. I would show strength and tenacity, and if Paige didn't respond, perhaps a judge would acknowledge and reward my efforts.

I left more messages for Paige. 'I'll have an apartment soon. I'd like to talk with you. Please let the kids know I called and that I love them.' I also sent letters. I hoped she would not keep *those* from the kids.

★   ★   ★

Finally, I found an affordable apartment that allowed a dog and had a pool. Those were its three only features worth mentioning. Paige had a pool, and I wanted the kids to be able to cool off at my house too. Plus, Zach needed to get over his combined fear and fascination of water and just learn how to swim.

I sat on my sleeping bag in the empty apartment, the walls bare except for the map of Las Vegas that Clem had given me, tacked on one wall, and the Life's a Picnic map tacked on another.

★   ★   ★

David called one night and said the store was doing better than it had, but not quite good enough — yet. The rain hadn't let up in weeks. He needed to run an ad playing up the fireplace and the greenhouse in back. He was thinking about bringing in a musician, someone who would play just for tips. Gina was talking about moving away, and she might not be around long to fill in at the store. Still, his spirits were up.

'You are so in your element,' I said. I wasn't quite ready to tell him about the apartment,

314

especially since he was in a good mood.

'That I am. Let the man swim in Bolognese sauce and he's happy.'

'I don't understand this, David. Why did the store go to Joe? He didn't want it. He wanted to be a photographer. But you wanted it, didn't you? Since you were a little boy. Joe outgrew the whole Joey's store/Davy's store rivalry, but you never did, did you?'

He sighed. 'No. I never outgrew it. That was just a lie to cover up my utter disappointment and rampant feelings of total rejection. Oh God. We could do an entire *Oprah* show on this one, El, and I've got a little catering gig tonight.'

'You're catering now too?'

'This is the first try, but hey, whatever pays the bills . . . ' He promised me we'd finish the conversation later.

I sat outside on my balcony, remembering how Joe and I used to sit on the porch in Elbow. On mornings when the fog lay thick among the tops of redwoods, their trunks so tall that even the peaks of them looked like full-size trees growing out of a carpet of clouds, I'd imagine our house, warm as bread, was perched in heaven with the jubilant blue sky above us while those under the fog line were living that same moment in grey deprivation. And then a twinge of guilt rose up that our little place on the hill was anointed in light, blessed, lucky, *above* — it had felt that way sometimes.

Now I sat in the hot night, my skin going from green to blue under the flashing sign from the car lot across the street. I watched the herd of traffic one story below, snorting, fuming, waiting for the signal to change and set them free, until they reached the next stoplight a block away.

★   ★   ★

David called again a few days later to ask if I'd be home for Thanksgiving, and that meant telling him I had taken an apartment.

'You're *living* in Vegas?'

'Well, I'm not dying here. Not quite. They have me on a breathing machine. Which helps combat the effects of all the secondhand smoke.'

'You know what I mean.'

'It's not exactly home, no. But I'm staying longer than I thought. Paige isn't quite speaking to me . . . yet. I've got to figure out a way to get through to her, but she's still too angry. So I'm buying time. And it helps my psyche, just knowing I'm within fourteen minutes of Annie and Zach.'

David said to take my time, that he'd figured it would take a while. I asked about Marcella and Joe Sr, but he just said, 'Oh, you know . . . waiting.'

I missed them. I missed their oversize dinners and long hugs, Marcella's loud singing and Joe Sr's loud swearing, the way their faces opened when the kids walked into the room.

And I missed Elbow. The wild turkeys would be gobbling into town. It wasn't unusual to see one sitting on the rooftop of the car in the morning, or to see them flaunting themselves down the middle of the street, the males

316

spreading their huge fantails, prouder even than peacocks. I used to ask them, 'Guys? Isn't this the time of year when you should be, you know, *hiding?*'

I missed the kids most of all. On Thanksgiving, I called my mom, but she had a houseful of people, her 'homeless waif' dinners she always held, inviting all the people she knew that didn't have family living in the area. She'd offered to come down or for me to fly up, but I'd declined. Part of me, a ridiculously optimistic part of me, had hoped that somehow Paige would call, or at least would pick up when I called, that she'd see the light and invite me over.

Callie and I took a walk and ended up at the grocery store, where I bought a single serving of turkey in a plastic container, a single serving of mashed potatoes and gravy, single servings of stuffing and cranberries. I could not shake the feeling of despair. It was Thanksgiving and Paige hadn't answered her phone. I had not talked to Annie and Zach since they'd left Elbow.

At the apartment, I called David, and he'd had a bad day too, a fight with Gil, a depressingly quiet dinner, with too many empty chairs around the Capozzi table, too many leftovers.

'Basically,' he said, 'I'm lower than whale shit.'

'Oh dear. Then I guess we can pick up where we left off last time — you were saying something about your rampant feelings of rejection?'

'Wow. You've got a light touch.'

'I'm sorry, David. But would you . . . do you feel like talking about what happened?' I actually had my yellow notebook open, ready to take notes. I was getting rather obnoxious.

'No. But I will. If you think it will help your cause.'

I told him I had multiple causes at the moment, but one of them was to better understand his older brother, especially if it would help me communicate with his ex-wife so I could see Annie and Zach, which was my number one cause.

David said, 'Okay. It all happened at Grandpa Sergio's, so that would be in your house, in your bedroom. The curtains were drawn, they were heavy, and olive green, so it was dim and stuffy, and godawful warm. Grandpa Sergio was in bed, and I was sitting in a chair next to him, holding his hand. He and I? We were really close. I loved that man. I was nineteen.'

'Go on.'

'My dad was there too. But Grandpa kept asking for Joe Jr. Joe was hurrying back from the university, trying to get there, and Grandpa was trying to hang on. In my mind, I was always Grandpa's favourite, but he wasn't so interested in talking to me at the moment.'

'So what happened?'

'So Joe finally arrived. And Grandpa told us *everything*. All the stuff he'd never talked about came barrelling out, about how he was afraid he might never see his wife and kids again when they took him away. How he and Grandma Rosemary didn't have a stitch of savings, and the town pulled together to help Grandma and the store. He said, and I'll never forget this,

'The internment, it was based on fear. Fear of a person's origins. Fear of the mother country. They ask me, who do you love more? Italy or America? I say, ask me who I love more, my mother or my wife? I love them both, but differently. One is my past and one is my future. I say, I love this country, it is my future. But do I worry about my new country bombing my relatives? I do worry, I told them. But that, it didn't go over so well.'

'Grandpa told us how much he loved both of us. But he said he built his home and his store for his family and its future generations. He said we owed it to Elbow to keep it going. Capozzi's Market, he said, was this town's symbol of hope for withstanding the hardest of times.'

'But I still don't understand why he handed it down to Joe.'

'I'm getting there. That's when he turned to me. There was a lot of coughing and wheezing. But then he said, clear as a bell, 'Davy, I love you, my boy. I have some money I want to give you. But let's face it. You're not going to have any children.' Then he turned to Joe and said, 'You promise me one thing, Joe Jr, you promise me you'll take the store, and you'll do good by me, you'll do good by the Capozzi name so no one will ever question our family again. And one day, you'll hand that store down to your *bambinos*. Promise me.' That room fell absolutely quiet. Grandpa even stopped wheezing. I kept thinking, *Don't say you'll do it; all you've ever wanted was to be a photojournalist, travelling every corner of the planet. But Grandpa's*

319

eyes were filled with tears, begging him. And Joe finally told him, 'Yes, Nonno. I promise.'' David's voice broke, but he kept going. 'And Grandpa smiled. He'd never gone by that Italian name for *grandfather* and now we'd understood why. And he said 'Thank you, Joey,' and he closed his eyes, and when he did, the tears ran down his cheeks, towards his ears. I remember Joe wiping the streaks away with his thumbs. But Joe? He was crying too, so *his* tears were falling on Grandpa anyway. Within a few minutes Grandpa was gone.'

A full minute went by, maybe more. 'David. That must have been so hard.'

'We never talked about me being gay. I hadn't even come out to my parents. But Grandpa knew. He never said anything. He was never anything but kind to me. But he wanted that store to go down through the generations, and I wasn't his best bet for making that happen. The thing is? As hard as it was for me, it was harder for Joe. That promise was a chain around that poor guy's neck.'

'He never told me how it all came to be. He just said your grandpa wanted him to run the store, but he didn't say it went down quite like that.'

'Joe never complained; he just took it on as his duty. But that's why he couldn't ask for help, either.'

I hadn't taken a single note while David was talking, but after we hung up I wrote: Internment comes from fear. Fear of someone's origins. Fear of someone's mother country. Paige was afraid of her origins, of her mother. So she took herself away. She said in her letter Joe was afraid of her background too. But what were they afraid of, exactly? And how do I find out? David's told me so much about Joe. But who can tell me about Paige?

33

As the day approached when I'd have the kids with me, I bought the three of us beds. I thought about having our stuff shipped out but figured it would cost more to do that than buy replacements. Plus, I didn't know what I was doing, really. Was I staying? I couldn't quite fathom it, but I couldn't fathom leaving without them, either.

I hunted every thrift shop I could, passed over the same Crock-Pots and waffle makers, the sixties' teak hors d'oeuvres platters and Corning Ware bowls, and then stumbled across a find that actually made me smile. A Buzz Lightyear lamp for Zach. A little yellow desk for Annie. Shelves. At Target I found a dinosaur comforter and a green seersucker bedspread. Coordinating sheets and oversize pillows. I took my purchases back to the apartment, excited to set them up, and as soon as I stepped back to survey, I thought of their rooms at Paige's — bigger than our not-so-great room in Elbow, a *castle bed*, no less — and thick lead settled in my chest. We headed back out, and Callie waited, tied up in a strip of shade outside while I searched for that One Cool but Cheap Item that would thrill them. And then, right in the display window at the hospice store: a bright red trike for Zach. A shiny pink bike for Annie, complete with a white basket adorned with purple flowers. Together they cost me forty dollars. I couldn't believe my luck. Maybe the tide was changing, after all.

★ ★ ★

Just before the kids arrived, I set to work filling the apartment with delicious smells from the kitchen. Even though I'd blown my budget on all the little extras, the apartment would still not pass Paige's standards. But at least she'd know by the aromas coming from the kitchen that the kids would be well nourished.

At exactly five o'clock, they rang the doorbell. My heart blammed in my ears. I turned down the stove and opened the door and fell down on my knees to hug them. They knocked me over. Callie dove into our pile and we all laughed.

All except Paige. The corner of her mouth twitched as she held her smile.

'Would you like to come in?' I offered, still lying on my back. 'No. But thanks. I've got to run. Annie, Zach, can I have a hug?'

Zach looked at me, then, along with Annie, got up and hugged Paige.

She said, 'See you Sunday,' and she was gone.

'Look at you, look at you! Oh, I missed you guys so much!' I kept hugging them, kissing them, smelling their hair, their necks, their hands. They smelled different, like new carpeting and air-conditioning and the Macy's interpretation of jasmine and citrus. Their *terroir* had changed. 'Tell me how you're doing! Tell me everything!'

First, they wanted a tour of the apartment,

which took about seventy-five seconds. I opened the door to their room, and as soon as they saw the bike and trike, they whooped and hollered, jumping up and down so fiercely that I had to remind them about the neighbours living below us. Evidently, Paige hadn't bought them wheels yet. Good. I promised them they could ride after dinner.

While we were eating, I said, 'Tell me about your new home, your new friends.'

Annie said, 'As I've mentioned, our house is spectacular. It's very big. And very nice. But.' She threw her hands up in the air, out to the sides. 'There's no yard. No garden. No trees. Except for three very small ones.'

'No chickens or eggs!' Zach chimed in.

'But there is a lovely pool,' Annie reminded him.

'And stairs!' Zach said, who thought a second floor in a house was as noteworthy as a pool. I smiled, thinking of Zach writing a real estate listing: *Your dream home awaits you. Enjoy daily walks up your very own staircase!*

I laughed a lot that evening and the next day. How sullen I'd been since Joe's death, even before the kids left, but much more so since then. Now that they were there with me, I revelled in their every observation and gesture, their mispronunciations and new vocabulary, all the nuances of their evolving personalities. I wanted to film them and hit replay when they were away from me. But we were the only young family I knew without a video camera. Surprisingly, Joe hadn't wanted one. He said it was bad enough that he spent so much time behind his still camera.

'Well,' I'd said, 'I'll man the video camera.'

'Then we'll both be observing life. Who's going to *live* it?'

I thought about what he'd said and vowed to try to stay in the moment, safekeeping it all in my head and my heart. Remember this: Remember the way Annie keeps snapping her fingers. Remember Zach's quiet fascination with his boogers. Remember the way he dances with Callie, wiggling his hips like some kind of Chippendales dancer. And where in the hell did he learn to do that! Whenever my mind lurched forward, to when they'd be gone, I had to nudge it back to the here and now.

That night Zach wet the bed. Zach hadn't wet the bed since he was potty trained more than a year before. Annie said, 'He does it at Mama's house all the time. Even during the day! Pee-yew!'

Zach hung his head, sighed, and said, 'Oh, for Christ's sake.'

He was standing there in his Barney underwear; his torso looked longer and leaner than it had been just a month before. His haircut made him look older too. He *was* older. Joe's death, and now this huge change, had aged all of us. And yet there was Zach, embarrassed, feeling like a baby. I told him, 'Honey, it's just an accident. Sometimes lots of changes can cause accidents like this. Don't worry about it.'

Zach asked me, 'When are we going home?' At first I thought he meant to Paige's house, and that lead-in-the-chest feeling hit me again, but then he said, 'I miss Nonna and Nonno.'

I hugged him. 'I don't know, honey. Right now this is our home.' He looked around the room and sighed again, and again he said,

'Oh, for Christ's sake.'

★ ★ ★

We spent a lot of Saturday in the pool, with breaks for them to ride their bikes. Zach wanted to ride his trike around the pool patio, but I told him that would be breaking the rules, that the bikes were for outside the fenced area, not on the patio. Still, he swung his leg over the seat.

'Zach. We'll ride after our swim.'

'But I won't ride on the patio.'

'Where, then?'

'In the *POOL*. Like my very own *SUBMARINE*.' He laughed. 'I'm going to drive it all the way to Daddy!' I wanted to stop him right there, remind him, once again, that he couldn't ride his trike to his Daddy, that Daddy didn't live underwater. But Zach seemed so happy and carefree in the moment, I let it go. I figured, so some people swear heaven is above the clouds, but Zach has decided it's underwater. At least the kid can think for himself.

'Okay. Get off the trike, Captain. As in now.'

I knew Zach was just talking big. Annie told me he still wouldn't even go in the pool at Paige's, so I wanted to resume coaxing him back to his love of being in the water and work with him like I had those days at the river. I'd even bought him plastic water wings to wear on his arms to help him feel more secure. By the end of the day, he was jumping off the side, flapping his arms, then splashing into the water, where I would scoop him up in my embrace.

That afternoon, after they rode bikes, they wanted to do crafts, but all I'd brought from Elbow were crayons and colouring books, and they quickly tired of those. Annie suggested we make bookmarks from ironing crayon shavings in sheets of wax paper. But I didn't even have wax paper, so we went down to the store, them riding their bikes alongside me. When we got back, I plugged in my travel iron, while Annie carved the crayons with the scissors and Zach made a mess of the shavings. Annie said, 'We can't do this at Mama's.'

I asked, 'Oh? Too messy?'

'No. She doesn't have an iron.'

'Oh, I'm sure she does . . . '

'No. She doesn't.'

Paige could probably afford to send her laundry out. 'Do you have a washer and dryer?'

'Of course, silly.' Annie cracked up, like that was the funniest question she'd ever heard.

★   ★   ★

On Sunday afternoon, they asked if they could take their bikes back to Paige's. I hadn't planned to let them, wanted those bikes to be special perks at my place, our thing. But I knew I might not see them for a while and that the way they were growing, they'd hardly be able to ride them

327

before they outgrew them. Besides, playing that kind of game would punish only them, not Paige. I had to take the top off the Jeep in order to fit the bikes in the back. Zach asked if he could take his water wings too, and I told him sure, felt that jealous twinge, and let it pass.

I drove them back in a silent car. Then Annie said, 'This all feels like we're playing pretend.'

'What do you mean, Banannie?'

'You know. This place. Everything. It feels like playing makebelieve and we just keep playing it and playing it. I want *both* of you. And I want Uncle David and Gil and Nonna and Nonno and everyone.'

'I want *BOTH* of you too,' Zach said. 'And everyone!'

'I know it's hard. We've been through a lot of change.'

Annie said, 'Change sucks.'

'Um . . . ' She was right. I thought about pointing out her word choice but didn't. She couldn't have said it better.

When we pulled onto Paige's street and started up the hill, Zach started to whimper, saying, 'I don't wanna go without you to the mama lady,' and by the time we parked in the driveway, he was screaming, 'I wanna stay with my mommy!' Annie kept uncharacteristically quiet, then tried to smooth back Zach's hair.

'Zachosaurus. It's gonna be okay,' she said.

Paige came out, her arms open wide. I did not want to hand him back over to her. How 'bout we just get back in the car, guys? How 'bout we drive away and never come back?

328

She didn't try to take him, though. She rubbed his back and let him cry. Finally she said, 'I know you had a good time, and you'll have a good time with your mommy again, soon.'

Not soon enough.

As he laid his head on my shoulder, she kept stroking his back until he started to calm down, his stuttered breaths taking over for the sobs, until he was almost asleep, and he let her lift him from my arms. With his eyes closed, he pointed to the Jeep and said, 'Bike.'

'They wanted to keep their bikes with them. If that's okay.'

'Well, there's really nowhere to ride them here with the hill, except a little bit of patio out back, but of course, that's fine, that's really nice of you. We can ride at the park. I'll open the garage.'

I lifted the bikes out and watched the door slowly rise. Inside her immaculate garage was a Suburban — so soccer mom of her. I wheeled the bikes in and parked them along the back wall. The door to the house was closed. I wanted to walk in, to draw their baths, to wash their hair and have them tell me the story of their day, of our day.

I drove west towards the sunset, which looked like the gods had been throwing cantaloupes at each other, cracking them open across the sky. I pulled out my cell phone and called Paige.

'So, do you really think I can see them again soon? I mean, you told Zach 'soon'.'

'You'll have them after Christmas, which is just a few weeks away. And then in three months

329

after that. I'm comfortable with the court's decision.'

'Three months is a long time.'

'Try three years.' She hung up.

I needed to find a way to talk to Paige. Every time we spoke, hostility cut through the line — hers, and mine, too. I pulled into my parking stall at the apartment and reached over and opened the glove compartment. I'd stuck Paige's cards and letters to Annie and Zach in there.

How could I get through to her? I still had the cards she'd sent the kids. But she'd wonder why I hadn't given these to the court with the others in the first place, and she wouldn't believe I intended for the kids to someday open them themselves. She also knew I was desperate and would do anything to see the kids. And she still believed I'd known about all the letters from the beginning. This was clearly my one and only chance to make it better between us, and I did not want to blow it.

I had to figure out a way to make this stack of cards and letters work in the kids' favour.

It had been there all along, winking at me, saying, *Hello?* Paige's return address on Annie's and Zach's envelopes. Some were from a hospital. But some weren't. I had to guess they were from Aunt Bernie's, when Paige had been living there. That night I wrote: *Maybe, just maybe, Aunt Bernie can help?*

34

I knew it was rude to just show up at Aunt Bernie's, but I had no way of getting her phone number except to call Paige, which defeated the purpose. Following the map out to the edge of town — or I should say the last edge, because I could tell they kept adding as the place grew, edge after edge, like a beige braided rug that someone couldn't leave alone — I imagined that when Paige lived there as a child, it was out in the middle of nowhere. But now there was a Vons supermarket and a Rite Aid, some restaurants and a housing development. The trailer park had mature trees, and the trailers didn't look so much like trailers, but neat, boxy houses with tiny front porches and small multicoloured rock gardens. Much nicer than I'd imagined.

I knocked on the front door. No one answered. I was glad I'd left Callie back at the apartment, because even though it was morning, the sun already bore down relentlessly on the dry, dusty pavement. I waited, then knocked again. I was hoping to catch her before she left for work. But maybe she didn't work. Maybe she was still asleep. 'Aunt Bernie?' I called before I realized that was Paige's name for her, but certainly not mine.

Almost immediately, I heard her say, 'Paige?' and she opened the door. She was not what I expected, not at all. Midfifties, trim and tall, with a dark, stylish bob haircut and a lovely dove grey business suit. 'Oh! I thought you were my niece.'

'I know. I'm sorry. I didn't mean to call you 'aunt'.' I stuck out my hand. 'I'm Ella Beene.'

She stared.

I slipped my hand into my pocket. 'I was hoping we could talk . . .'

'Oh?'

'Could I come in?'

She stared another moment, then said, 'Oh, why not?' and turned and led me into her house. The front room was cluttered with boxes and magazines and gadgets and gizmos. 'The kitchen is this way,' she promised. 'Don't mind all this. I've been cleaning out the closets.'

Her kitchen wasn't dirty, just crowded with magazines and appliances and stacks of papers. I realized that her niece wasn't the only thing Aunt Bernie had saved. I also suddenly understood Paige's passion for feng shui and home staging.

'Here, have a seat.' She motioned to the table. She sat on the bar stool, stacks of *Redbooks*, *National Geographics*, and bills on the table. 'Excuse the mess. I don't have company much.' Her face coloured but she regained her composure. 'Coffee? Tea?'

'Tea, if you have it.'

'Dear, as you can see, I have everything.' She filled the pot with water.

'I'm sorry I didn't call,' I said. 'I didn't have your number. Paige doesn't know I'm here.'

'Yes, I figured as much. I don't have a lot of time. I'm on my way to work.'

'What do you do?' I was curious. She looked so professional, so out of place in her own home.

'Oh, I work for the IRS, if you really want to know.' She tilted her chin up in mock bravado. 'I am a tax auditor.'

'Good to know,' I said, attempting to hide my surprise.

She brought me the tea in a delicate cup and saucer. 'So you see' — she smiled as she set it down in front of me — 'I'm not used to people seeking me out. It's usually the other way around. Now, what would you like to talk about?'

'It's Paige.' I chose my words carefully. 'I'm sorry about everything she's been through, and I can understand why she's angry. But I love Annie and Zach too. I understand that I'm not, you know, their *birth* mother. But I love them that way. And I want to have a relationship with them. I want things to be more open.'

I talked about finding the letters, how I hadn't known Paige had been writing the kids and Joe, or that she had wanted to come back.

I said, 'I was nervous to come here. I figured you'd slam the door in my face too.'

Bernie nodded. She moved her watch around and around on her slim wrist. 'Actually, Ella, I am glad you came to talk to me. Yes, I am Paige's aunt, and I love her very, very much. But you and I' — she glanced up at me — 'we have something important in common.' She took a deep breath, readjusted herself on the bar stool. 'You see, I loved and cared for Paige since she was an infant. Her own mother had serious

333

problems; I won't go into that — that's Paige's private business. But I took her in and kept her under my wing as if she were my own. And although she called me her aunt, I felt every bit her mother, as I can see you feel towards Annie and Zach. She's my daughter, in my mind and in my heart.

'And so I do understand your position, Ella. My sister was never able to return. I haven't told Paige this: But if her mother had been able to return, if she had come back and taken Paige away from me, I would not have been able to forgive her.'

Her gaze shifted past me, and I followed it to a patch of sunlight, which seemed to have adhered to a crack along the wall like a bandage. Our eyes met as she continued. 'Paige is their mother; she deserves to be their mother. But I see myself in you, and I understand your pain — and your love.' She fished out her tea bag with a spoon. 'I'll try to talk to her. I'll tell her what I have never said to this day. I've kept my mouth shut when she says, 'But I'm their mother. No one can love them and take care of them like I can!' I haven't held her face in my hands and said, 'But, Paige, have *I* not loved *you* as a mother loves her child?' I have not said this, you see, because my sister was never a mother to her. Never a mother at all.'

'What . . . ' I picked up my teacup, then set it back down. 'What, exactly, did Paige's mother *do?*'

'That, my dear girl, is a question for Paige.'

As I was leaving, I passed the refrigerator. It was covered with pictures of Paige at different ages. When she was little, she looked exactly like Annie. And then I saw a paper cut-out purple heart. It said *Happy Valenites DaY Mama, from Annie, age 3.* Aunt Bernie saw me looking at it. 'That's the one thing Paige brought with her when she left Joe and the kids and showed up here. I told her it was her purple heart. For a long time, it was her talisman. It helped keep her alive. When she moved out, she said I could keep it. That she knew someday Annie would make her another Valentine's Day card.' She smiled. 'Paige understands how hard it is for me to let go of things.'

* * *

I got on the freeway, and I should have gone straight back to the apartment. I shouldn't have been so pushy, so determined to finally make a breakthrough with Paige. But I couldn't wait. My God! Aunt Bernie! Why hadn't I thought to talk to her from the beginning, or when I found the letters, at the very least, with her address right there in Paige's own handwriting? As if this whole mess I was in had come with simple, easy-to-follow directions on how to get out of it.

I turned up Paige's street. She and Aunt Bernie were probably just hanging up. With Bernie's endorsement and the letters from Paige to the kids — all unopened — she'd have to trust

335

me, to see that I was a good person and that we could work out something so we could both be a part of Zach's and Annie's lives. 'I want *both* of you,' they had said. Hell, if we had to live in this awful place, so be it. It's not what I wanted, not what Annie and Zach wanted, but I was willing to do anything to see them, to be in their lives.

35

I drove up the hill to Paige's house and parked. The sun spread itself like a big white sheet over the neighbourhood, which was treeless, except for the straight line of new birch saplings, staked one to a yard. I pulled the packet of the kids' unopened cards and letters out of my glove compartment and tucked them in my bag. Her grass had just been watered. I saw Bubby lying bedraggled in a puddle and picked him up. I breathed deep, knocked on the door, stuck one hand in my pocket, then pulled it out again and grabbed the strap of my shoulder bag. Paige answered the door wearing a white terry robe. Her bra strap, pink, peeked out from the collar. Her hair was wet, like she'd just stepped out of the shower. She looked tanned and healthy and strong. I crossed my sunburned skinny arms. She stepped outside onto the front step and closed the door behind her.

'What are you doing here?'

'I just want to talk to you.' *Stay calm. Don't blow this.* 'Have you talked to your aunt Bernie lately?'

'What? What do you mean? Did *you* talk to her? Unbelievable.'

'Paige,' I said. 'Please? I just want to talk.' Our eyes locked.

'Come on. Remember when you just wanted to talk to Joe?'

'This is different.'

337

'In some ways yes, in some ways no.'

She looked down. 'This is so hard,' she said.

'I know. But we're making it harder than it has to be.'

'I want you to leave us alone. They can learn to love me, but not when you keep showing up.' She looked down at Bubby. 'Where did you get that?' She reached out to take it from me. I held on. She pulled the slightest bit.

'They can love both of us.'

'But I wonder if you would say that, Ella, if the judge had ruled in your favour. I don't have time for this. I have to get the kids ready for school.' She pulled harder, and I pulled back. Bubby started to rip. I was horrified and let go, and she stumbled slightly, looked embarrassed.

We stood there, quiet, staring at the ground. As long as she didn't turn and go back inside, it wasn't over. I wanted to bring up my conversation with Bernie, but I knew that could make Paige mad again. I had to hand her the letters.

'I have something for you.'

She looked up. 'What?'

'Some of the cards and letters you sent Annie and Zach. The ones they never opened.'

'You mean, were never allowed to open?'

'It was wrong of him.'

Her shoulders fell slightly; her weight shifted to the other foot. She searched my eyes. 'Ella? I can't ever undo the fact that I left them. I can never get that time back.' The door behind her bolted open and there was Annie, screaming something indecipherable, her red face twisted, pulling on our arms, screaming, the words finally registering, 'Zach! Zach! He's hurt in the pool!'

'No!' Paige took off, with me right behind her. 'No!' She ran through the house and out the French doors and jumped into the pool, where Zach floated, his bright red tricycle lying overturned at the bottom.

She was tangled in her robe, pushing him over to me, so I could lift him, lift him out as she pushed him up, and I pulled him out, so heavy, so full of water, the water flowing out of him, and then I turned him over and breathed into his blue lips while Paige freed herself from her heavy wet robe in the pool, got out, called 911, and said, 'My little boy fell into the pool he's blue, he's not breathing, 1020 Hillside Way, I'll leave the front door open, hurry, hurry, he's not breathing, I thought I locked the gate, I thought I did I always lock the gate,' while I tried to remember CPR, tried to count to fifteen while I breathed into his mouth, was it fifteen, and how many had I done? And then two pushes on the sternum, I remembered something, what was it? One hand for a child, my child, and then Paige was there, taking over while I stood up to go flag down the paramedics, whose siren I heard, and I saw Annie standing by herself, wailing, 'Daddy-DaddyDaddy,' holding the little water wings I'd bought for Zach, one in each hand, and I saw Paige bent over my little boy, her little boy, and I saw then that her entire back was a terrain of hideous scars, a raised map of unbearable pain, as her back expanded and deflated with her breath, trying to push life back into Zach, back into our little boy.

36

The firefighters and paramedics worked on Zach, and I held Annie, who sobbed uncontrollably, still clutching the water wings. Someone had thrown a blanket over Paige, who slumped on the end of a lounge, staring at the dark blue uniformed arms and legs and torsos that attached themselves to Zach and started an IV, intubated him, put him on a stretcher, moved with him across the patio in synchronization. A man approached me and said, 'I'm the medical services officer. How long was he in the water before you started CPR?'

Paige looked up and said in a high, tight voice, 'Three minutes. I saw him inside right before I answered the door.' She asked me, 'How long were we talking?'

'Maybe three minutes, maybe even less.'

'And you started CPR right away?'

We both nodded. Paige's robe now lay like a blanket over Zach's trike in the bottom of the pool.

'Okay. That's good. That's a good thing. They're going to try to get him breathing on his own while we get him to the hospital. Luckily, we're minutes away from Children's.'

'Is he going to be okay?' Paige asked the question I was afraid to. He looked at Annie. He said, 'We'll have to wait and see.'

Only one of us could ride in the ambulance,

and Paige said, 'You, you go. I'll get dressed and take Annie.' I nodded, hugging Annie, and sat in the front. They wouldn't let me ride in the back with Zach. They were still working on him.

The hospital was only five or six blocks away, and they made me stay in a waiting room while they sped him down the hallway. I sat, staring at a television, not seeing anything but Zach's blue, bloated face. How long? They'd asked us. Minutes, we'd both said. Only minutes. I prayed the only prayer I could remember, which was *Please*. I prayed it over and over and over. *Please. Please, God. Please let him be okay. Please don't take him. Please, please, God. Please.*

I felt a hand on my head and I looked up to see Annie. I held her while she wailed, 'I wasn't watching him!'

I held her face in my hands. 'Annie. This is not your fault. Do you understand me?' Paige stood by the door in jeans and a sweatshirt, her hair dripping, her eyes frantic. In her right hand she loosely held a clipboard with registration papers; in her other hand she clutched Bubby, still wet from the puddle. I said, 'They took him. I don't know anything.'

She slumped down in a chair and said, 'I thought . . . I locked . . . the gate.'

I said, 'I know, I know. I shouldn't have come over. I shouldn't have bought him those stupid water wings. God. Or that stupid trike. He kept *telling* me he wanted to ride it in the water, to go see Joe . . . ' A doctor appeared. She was young, with short dark hair and stylish black glasses. She said, 'Who's the mother?' We both stood up

341

and mumbled words that came out, 'I am, we are.'

She shook our hands, said, 'I'm Dr Markowitz.' She looked at Paige, then at me. She said, 'It's going to be a long night for you and for Zach. But he has a lot going for him. Early CPR, early EMS support. We call this first hour the Golden Hour, and his has been good. They got him in here fast. But his breathing rate is very low, even for a child's. The ventilator will help. We're checking blood gases, pupil response. We'll be doing a CT scan to check his brain activity . . . '

'He is going to make it . . . He is going to be okay?' Only Paige's last word rose in a question.

'The next twenty-four to forty-eight hours will tell us a lot. We'll finish up our tests, and then you can see him.'

★   ★   ★

Bernie came. She took Annie away from the hospital for a while, to get something to eat, and even offered to go to the apartment and take Callie for a walk. I thanked her and handed her the key. Annie went along willingly, burying her head in Aunt Bernie's side as they slowly walked down the corridor.

When they let us in Zach's room, we stopped before going up to him, trying to get our minds around the fact that the blue-tinged swollen little boy was really Zach; the fury of arms and legs of the paramedics working to keep him alive had been replaced by blue tubes that ran every which

342

way from his nose and throat and arm and chest, and instead of the paramedics' knowledgeable chants of numbers and letters, Zach's vital signs now blipped and beeped on connected digital screens. Paige took hold of one of his hands and I took hold of the other. It occurred to me then, as we each gripped one of his hands, that we had both loved and lost the same man. We had both loved and lost the same children. We had both lost our footing, lost our way, lost ourselves. We had both touched down at the bottom, only to discover that the bottom was sinking sand. Hours before, we were heavy weights tied to Zach, dragging him under. He needed us to be his buoys.

*   *   *

I saw every action I had taken, every choice I had made, lined up like squares on a board game, as if I had led us all to this moment, this tragedy, as if I alone had rolled the dice that would move us to this day, with my decision to stop in Elbow for a sandwich. I could have kept going, could have ended up in Oregon, or Seattle, maybe in a cabin on one of the San Juan Islands, alone on a driftwood-strewn beach, making my life's work the study of tide pools, or working in a fish hatchery in Alaska, far, far away from these people whose lives were now destroyed. Everything would have been set in a different motion: Joe would have welcomed Paige back with open arms, they would have stayed a family, she would have known about the

343

store and helped him turn it around long ago, and he wouldn't have gone out to Bodega Head to take pictures that morning because they would have been on a family vacation to Disneyland or a second home in Tahoe. I would not have made my feeble, stupid attempt to try to make Zach feel better about Batman and Robin, confusing him about the permanence of drowning. Zach would not have ridden his red trike into a pool in Las Vegas; he would still be playing with his action figures under the butterfly bush. I promised God I would do everything and anything, even leave Zach and Annie in Paige's care for good, if it only meant that Zach could live.

Paige and I said little, just held on and willed Zach's eyes to flutter open, to say *Mama* or *Mommy*, it didn't matter which. It didn't matter at all. Sometimes I would look up and she would look up, our gaze full of regret and fear and sadness and pain and good intentions and hope and mother love — all the things we shared, that had been there all along, that we hadn't been able to see because we had seen each other only as a threat.

I called David from my cell phone in the waiting room, and he showed up late that afternoon, with Marcella and Joe Sr. My mom was on her way down from Seattle. There was no room in the small dedicated space for feuds or awkwardness, and we took turns embracing, not merely as if our lives depended on it, but because Zach's truly did. Marcella held me, her tears raining on my neck while Joe Sr hugged Paige, and then I was hugging David, Joe Sr. We stood in a circle around Zach, and I once again thought of the redwoods, how they formed their family circles, how they reached for the sun together and cast their long shadows together. A nurse named Lester came in and looked at Zach, looked at the blips on the screens, wrote something down on the chart, and when Joe Sr asked him what the prognosis was he said, 'We really don't know. We'll see how he is in the morning.' He kept nodding his head, even after he spoke, looking at each of us. 'Only family members are allowed in the ICU. You all family?' We nodded. 'Lucky kid.' Then he said, 'If you haven't eaten yet, now's a good time. He's stabilized.' Eating was the last thing I felt like doing, but Marcella and Joe Sr and David went to get coffees.

They opened the door to the rushing and crashing of carts and gurneys and doctors and nurses, of pages over the intercom and bright lights and the smell of distant Jell-O and macaroni and cheese. The door closed and the room fell quiet again, except for the hum and blip of the machines.

'Paige.' I looked across Zach. 'I'm so sorry.'

'No.' She shook her head. She didn't speak. I closed my eyes and continued my silent pleading with God to save Zach. Finally she said, 'I went about this the wrong way. It was *wrong* of me. I should have never done this right now, not right when Joe died. I had started talking to the lawyer before, and he said it was time to move, but I knew better. I'd already waited so long — for lots of reasons.'

She pulled a tissue out of her purse with her free hand, still holding Zach's. We stood in more silence before she went on. 'Joe didn't respond, but let's face it, I'd also needed that time. But then, when I was finally really truly ready, I got the call from Lizzie that Joe had drowned. I wanted Annie and Zach above all else — even above what was best for them. They always say kids are the ones hurt in custody battles. And now Zach is paying the biggest price.'

'And Annie . . . '

'Yes. But you've got what you need now. Zach's hurt, and you have proof I'm a bad mother.'

'Paige. Both of us were there. Both of us played a part in this.' She tilted her head, raised her eyebrow, as if to size me up, to see if I meant it. An orderly opened the door, letting in the echoes from the hallway, then let it shut without coming in. I thought about keeping quiet, keeping her secret under cover. But I was done with secrets.

I forced myself to say, 'When you were giving him CPR? I saw your back. I saw the scars.' More silence. 'Your mother . . . she was psychotic?'

Paige let out a long sigh. 'Only after she had me. I was her first and only.' She fell quiet while we listened to the machines; then she said, 'My mother had a horrible labour that lasted days, and then they ended up doing a C-section. This is all from Aunt Bernie. She pieced it together for me. I was colic.' She looked at her hands. 'My father was a salesman and gone a lot, according to Bernie. When I was about three months old,

346

my father . . . he told this all to Aunt Bernie. That he'd asked my mother to iron his shirts. He said she had been acting strange and he thought it would help her to have something to do. Besides, he explained, he really did need his shirts ironed.' She stopped and looked at me. 'Do you really want to hear this? It isn't pretty.'

I told her yes, I did. I wanted to know.

She continued, 'When he came home that night, every single one of his shirts was ironed and hanging in the closet.' She stopped, looked up at me again, looked at Zach.

'It's okay, Paige.'

Her voice quivered in a whisper. I leaned in to hear. 'My mother was also hanging in the closet. I was lying on my stomach in my bassinet, next to the ironing board, not able to scream or move. The iron was on the floor, still hot.' Her eyes locked on mine for a moment before redirecting them back to studying her hands, which now lay flat on Zach. 'The police report said, 'The iron was covered in a black substance that was later found to be the victim's skin.' The man who was my father took me to the hospital in the bassinet, afraid that if he touched me or held me, the pain would kill me. Then he left. He called Aunt Bernie. He told her everything. He cried. He said he was sorry. We never heard from him again.'

Tears were running again, down both our faces, snot running from our noses, and we each let out a little laugh — embarrassed, a bit shy — as Paige reached into her purse for more Kleenex and handed me several. 'So you see. Joe did have a lot to be scared of.'

'And you were scared.'

She nodded, and when she spoke, her voice squeaked, high and tight. 'It wasn't the same as my mother, but I was afraid it was . . . when I got sick. And then when he didn't respond to my letters? I didn't know how much he told the kids. I thought that maybe it was easier just to tell them I was dead. So I was afraid that I would scare them also.'

I nodded. 'But still . . . '

'Still, both he and I could have done better.'

'And me. I could have done better.' I reached into my bag and felt for the letters, then pressed them into her hand.

She saw what they were, then held them up to cover her face. And then we leaned over the bed, over Zach, and hugged, not tentatively or suspiciously, as we had that first night after the funeral, but leaning into each other, holding each other up, heaving out sobs, clinging to each other and Zach like we were clinging to a rock.

We finally pulled away to blow our noses. We each took long, stammering breaths. As I slipped my hand around his swollen fingers, I remembered him back on that morning when he and Annie and I were playing Ship, how he jumped onto the bed and pulled the sheet up, how he laughed so loudly, not knowing yet that his daddy had died. Now I imagined he was sitting on Joe's lap somewhere in a parallel universe, and I silently asked Joe to please tell Zach it was time to come back to us, that I needed him, and that Paige needed him too.

37

In the earliest hours of the morning, we watched in wonder as Zach's heart rate and oxygen levels rose steadily, his skin turned pink with the dawn, his eyes opened. He flung his arms, trying to remove the ventilator tube, but Paige and I reassured him while the doctors removed the tube from his throat. He smiled. He spoke; he complained that his throat hurt. He said, 'Mommy.' He said, 'Mama.'

Dr Markowitz said, 'I want to keep him here for another day or two, keep monitoring him. He seems like he's made a full recovery. But there are some things we won't know for years, as far as a diagnosis of brain damage. There may not be any. He's a tough little guy, and he's already shown great resilience. In the meantime' — she smiled, stuck her hands in her lab coat — 'celebrate.'

My mom, Gil, Lucy, Lizzie and Frank, Aunt Bernie — everyone came to welcome back Zach, an ongoing parade of balloons and teddy bears and dinosaurs and action figures in tow. Clem Silver sent a beautiful illustration of our cottage, with our garden billowing over the foreground and the redwood grove stoic in the background. Zach pointed to it and said, 'Let's go home.'

The room fell quiet. Paige and I shared a look. I said, 'Let's concentrate on getting better.'

Joe Sr, Marcella, Bernie, Paige, and I ended

up going together to the cafeteria. I took a bite of a tuna fish sandwich, thinking about how strange this all was, sitting with 'our' in-laws, actually *chatting*, actually laughing. Bernie excused herself, said she needed to get back to her office, offered to walk Callie later. She was so polished and efficient; you'd never guess that back at home she lived among piles of silly things she couldn't part with.

Paige looked at me, then took a deep breath. 'So when I said I suppose you have everything you need now that this happened . . . to Zach. To persuade a judge to change the court order in your favour . . . ' I kept my eyes steady on hers. 'I told you and I meant it. We are both responsible in our own ways. But Paige, Annie and Zach, they said they want *both* of us.'

Her eyes filled. 'They really said that? They told you that?'

I nodded.

She covered her eyes with her hand. 'You didn't have to tell me.' And then, 'Thank you for telling me.'

I leaned over and said, 'Paige? Would you ever consider coming back to Elbow?'

Marcella shook out her white embroidered handkerchief and blew her nose.

We waited. I took another bite of sandwich and chewed long after I could have swallowed it, afraid to move my hands again or change expression or do anything that might negatively affect the outcome of that moment threaded between the four of us, connecting us, tugging at our souls. All the hurtful things that had passed between us all hung there too, hooks we'd need to untie, one by one, with time.

Paige didn't answer, just kept her hand locked over her eyes while her shoulders shuddered. Joe Sr reached out and put his hand on Paige's other hand. I covered his with mine, and then Marcella extended her own hand, and we sat there, quiet, while the lunch crowd cleared, until all that was left was the circle of us.

★　★　★

The next afternoon, Dr Markowitz told us, 'Go home. And don't come back.' She went over things to look for, but she said she had high hopes that Zach was going to be fine. 'I've never seen a kid put away that much macaroni and cheese.'

When we left the hospital that day, Annie, Paige, and I packed up Zach's things. David and Gil took armfuls of toys down to their car. A mural of Noah's Ark adorned the wall leading to the lobby. Annie said, as she walked along, patting the picture, 'Two giraffes, two monkeys, two lions.' And then she stopped, letting us walk ahead of her, me pushing Zach in the regulation wheelchair, Paige carrying his balloons and suitcase. Annie gave us each a pat on our butts. When we turned, she grinned at us. She said, 'Two moms.'

Epilogue

The magazine did end up running a four-page story, and while there was a line about lemons and lemonade, the article focused on the internment of Grandpa Sergio and Marcella's father, Grandpa Dante, and wove in the family history and perseverance with the store's transformations. Other magazine features have followed over the past five years. *Time* even did a short article. The story of the Italian internment during World War II caught the public's attention, and many descendants of the interned — Italian, but also Japanese and German — have found their way to Elbow, and to the store, to enter the name of their relative in the book we keep open, to see the display Marcella and Joe Sr helped us arrange on the back wall — of Sergio's and others' Enemy Alien IDs and photos, the popular posters of the time with specific directions not to speak the enemy language, along with other memorabilia people have contributed.

There are also the hordes of foodies and wine connoisseurs that flock here because of the other, purely decadent write-ups in *Bon Appétit*, *Travel + Leisure*, *Gourmet*. David is making quite a name for himself as a chef, and I am making a name for myself as the person who does all the other stuff. Which is just fine with me.

As a way of singing the praises of the natural

beauty of the area without having to actually sing, I work as a guide for Fish and Wild-life a few times a month. The other day, as I led a hike along the river, someone complained about the squawking crows. I gave my spiel about how smart they are, how adaptable. I told the story about how they drop nuts at a busy intersection in China, then wait for the cars to run over and crack them, then stand patiently on the corner, until the light changes, so they can eat the cracked nuts without getting crushed by traffic. Usually, that gets people smiling. But this one woman was an exceptionally tough nut to crack, so to speak. 'I still don't like them,' she huffed. 'They remind me of death.'

'The *Corvus brachyrhynchos* are *so* smart and adaptable,' I went on, 'that they partake in cooperative breeding. In other words, they share in mothering, in all aspects of raising each other's babies. *They* didn't need anyone to tell them that it takes a village.'

Paige and I have found our own way to share in raising Annie and Zach, and though it's not perfect, it is what you might call cooperative. She lives in the next town, and we brag to each other about everything from Zach's soccer game to his reading abilities and his latest math-test grade. We know that other people don't want to hear it. We know not to bombard the kid with our relief that he is okay. (He is eight now, and starting to roll his eyes sometimes when I cover his forehead with kisses. But only sometimes.) Depending on whose turn it is to have them spend the night, one of us will call the other, unable to wait another day to report, 'Well, the guy aced his project. He seems to know his stuff.' It is our way of saying, *Yes, we have made mistakes, mistakes that have hurt our children, but there is grace in this life of ours. Sometimes we still disagree. Sometimes we have misunderstandings. We are still finding our way. But I am bound to you by Annie and Zach; there is no one else on this planet who cares about them as much as you and I do.*

Annie is eleven now, and the other day she told me that she is *seriously* considering medical school. 'What kind of doctor do you want to be?' I asked her.

'The kind that saves people,' she said. Annie still talks about when her daddy died and Zach almost died. 'Or, perhaps, a trombonist.'

'You could be a trombonist that saves people.'

'Exactly.'

What I want to tell her, but what she will have to discover on her own, is that no matter what she chooses to do for her profession, she will save people, and she will also do people grave harm — and they will be the same people, the ones she loves.

Sometimes when she and Zach are with Paige, and I have the day off, after I've played for hours in the garden, the knees of my jeans damp with that wondrous soil, I follow Callie down to the redwood grove, our sacred arboreal cathedral. Often, my arms and hair are still warm from the sun, but the air under the trees is always cool and dim. I lie on my back and look up through heavy branches, up at unknown particles drifting in the shadowed light. I whisper, 'My man of the *Sequoia sempervirens*. Peace be with you.' I whisper, 'I love you.' I whisper, 'I miss you.'

And so it has been for me in this place called Elbow, where the river bends and gives before it leads out to the Pacific, where years ago I stumbled upon a certain kind of happiness. I know now that the most genuine happiness is kept afloat by an underlying sorrow. We all break the surface into this life already howling the cries of our ancestors, bearing their DNA, their eye colours and their scars, their glory and their shame. It is theirs; it is ours. It is the underside of joy.

THE WHORES' ASYLUM

Katy Darby

Oxford, 1887. Even as Victoria celebrates the fiftieth year of her reign, a stone's throw from the calm cloisters and college spires lies Jericho, a maze of seedy streets and ill-lit taverns, haunted by drunkards, thieves and the lowest sort of brazen female as ever lifted her petticoats. When Stephen Chapman, a brilliant young medical student, is persuaded to volunteer at a shelter devoted to reforming the fallen women of Oxford, his closest friend Edward feels a strange sense of dread. But even Edward — who already knows the devastating effect of falling in love with the wrong woman — cannot foresee the macabre and violent events that will unfold around them, or stop Diana, the woman who seems destined to drive them apart.

THE BOOK OF SUMMERS

Emylia Hall

Beth Lowe is given a package. It contains a letter informing her that her long-estranged mother has died . . . and something she's never seen before — her mother's scrapbook. The Book of Summers, stuffed with photographs and mementos, records the seven glorious childhood summers Beth spent in rural Hungary. Then, she trod the tightrope between separated parents and two very different countries; her bewitching but imperfect Hungarian mother and her gentle English father; the dazzling house of a Hungarian artist and an empty-feeling cottage in deepest Devon. It was a time which brutally ended the year Beth turned sixteen. Beth never again allowed herself to think about those childhood days. But The Book of Summers will bring the past tumbling back; as vivid, painful and vital as ever.